RAMBLINGS, RUMBLINGS AND GRUMBLINGS

JOHN TRYTHALL

To Patricia
with love,

John Trythall

16/04/09

Acknowledgements:

Could I mention here my old history tutor, Jack Woolford. I first admired him as a lecturer; he was always immensely interesting. Then I admired him as a very kind human being; he stood by me in moments of difficulty. Mind you he was still bluntly truthful. Finally he agreed to read this book. I think, without his encouragement, I would never have finished it.

INTRODUCTION.

'I talk to myself,' says Me.

'What on earth for?' Myself asks.

'I dunno. I just do. I'm sorry.'

'You're always saying 'sorry'.'

'I know. I'm sorry...'

'There you go again.'

'But I really *don't* know. I wish I did.'

'Oh, come off it! That's no answer. You must surely know.'

'Well, mother used to...'

'Oh, mum! That was a laugh. She used to walk down the streets talking nineteen to the dozen, her lips moving but no sound coming out. At least your lips don't move.'

'Yes, I remember. And do you remember mum suddenly realising what she was doing, and looking at you with an apologetic smile.'

Both Me and Myself sniggered. They both loved their mum despite her idiosyncrasies.

'They say ...,' said Myself suddenly looking deadly serious, '... that talking to oneself is a first step to insanity.'

'I'm *not* insane. At least I hope not. I'm just a little bit deaf and have been for some sixty-six years.'

'I accept I'm deaf or more precisely hard of hearing. But I don't see what that has to do with talking to oneself.'

'Simple! I don't – or can't – or won't enjoy the pleasures of socialising. I just can't enjoy talking to people.'

'I don't see what that's got to do with talking to oneself.'

'But don't you see? I don't hear the jokes, often miss the punch lines. I laugh when everybody else does, or snigger when they do at the dirty jokes. But I haven't a clue what it's all about. I can't help looking embarrassed at my own dishonesty and hope to god nobody asks me to repeat a joke.'

'You're saying you talk to yourself because you don't or can't talk to anybody else.'

'Hurrah! At last you're cottoning on! Incidentally mum was not insane. She kept her faculties right up until the age of eighty-two when a stroke carried her off to the never-never land. It was just that terrible arthritis that got her down.'

'True! True! I also remember mum sharing our own

5

fear of social situations. She told me she would shrivel up, her stomach churning, when faced with a large number of people to whom she had to make stupid, spurious conversation.'

Me and Myself looked at the computer, and then down at the floor at little Jemmi who was sitting so patiently doggy-fashion on her bottom, and finally through the window at the skies above. Me commented:

'In a funny sort of way I don't talk to myself. I talk to one of three 'persons', 'persons' advisedly because they are not real people – at least not real in the worldly sense.

'I Know. One is a benevolent sort of God; the second is a grumpy computer, and the third is a friendly dog, Jemmi, your dog, really your wife's, but it sits by your desk while you write.'

'I don't know what I'd do without those three very different friends.'

RAMBLINGS, RUMBLINGS AND GRUMBLINGS.

(A fantasy of stories)

Or

An Old Man Converses with a Benevolent God, an Irascible Computer and a Loving, Lovely Doggie.

by
John Trythall

CHAPTER 1

'THE SAD WORLD'

So many gods, so many creeds,

So many paths that wind and wind,

While just the art of being kind

Is all the sad world needs.

(Ella Wheeler Wilcox – 1855 – 1919)

'I'm so tired!'

The white-haired old man spoke with sadness. His body lacked energy. His eyes looked listless. He must once have been fairly good-looking, at least he thought so in his conceit, with that luxuriant crop of aged white hair. But now he had a protruding stomach, the result of too much food and past lack of exercise. His face was lined, deep crow's feet at the corner of his eyes. But they were not smiling lines – more associated with worry.

'It's only to be expected,' said the voice of his conscience, what he liked to term his 'God'. 'How old are you?'
'You should know.' There was bitterness in the old man's voice.

'Now, son, don't be rude. Rudeness never built bridges,' replied God.

'I'm not your son. Nor am I particularly keen on platitudes,' riposted the old man.

9

'Well, well! There's life in the old man yet. Not too tired to answer back,' spoke God with a gentle smile.

'Oh, go away, God! Do a bunk, get lost, scram, buzz off, or whatever the current, vulgar, misplaced, unedifying, uneducated vernacular is? Language is no longer a thing of beauty.' The old man sighed at the supposed decadence of modern speech.

For a moment there was silence. The old man's mind was too tired to conjure up any further fantasies of conversation between his imagined God and himself.

Once calmness was restored, God said:

'You're not physically tired, my son. You're just fed up with life.'

'You should know. It's a lousy world.' There was a bitter note to the old man's voice.

'It's a beautiful world. It's only man that has made it ugly!'
'How come? You created man. We are what you made us.'

'No, no. I created man, but it was man who made himself what he now is.'

The old man sighed at the seeming futility of the argument. For a moment there was quiet.

'At the risk of being repetitive.' The old man broke the silence pedantically, like a thoughtful university professor. 'Very little will shake me from the belief that this is a rotten, stinking, evil, unkind universe. I can't help wondering how you managed to create a world where you allowed a man or woman to be flawed. In my book you've failed. How can you possibly claim to be all powerful, or is this a fiction man created? Listen to this sad story, reported in a local newspaper:'

*

10

BOYS WILL BE BOYS - SADLY!

Here is cruel Frederick, see!

A horrid, wicked boy was he.

(Heinrich Hoffman – 1809-1874)

Four boys were sitting side by side on a bench in the Market Square. They were young – ten to twelve, thereabouts. They should have been at school.

There seemed an intensity of excitement. They hardly peered at each other, even less at passers-by. Their gaze was out of the corner of their eyes, if they looked at all. Experienced policemen and teachers would recognise that attitude, reckon they were up to no good, or planning no good.

Suddenly the biggest boy of the group nudged the one next to him, and stood up.

'Time.' He stated, one terse word from the obvious leader.

As if by common consent the others rose. They made their way across the square, down Fisherton Street, past the old hospital soon to be converted into flats. They came to a less wealthy part of the city, a street lined with small shops, newsagents, antique dealers, grubby cafes, and inexpensive hairdressers. They arrived at a sub post-office posing as a general store, its shelves set out like a mini supermarket.

They entered, moved purposefully to different parts of the store. At the cash desk, behind the newspapers and magazines, stood the Pakistani owner serving a customer.

Out of sight, in between the aisles, the four boys swept into the pockets of their coats, or into bags, anything

11

they could lay their hands on – sweets, tins of fruit and soup, packets of bacon or sausages. It was done swiftly, with a smooth professionalism despite being so young. It must have been pre-planned, possibly pre-practised.

The Pakistani, with that sixth sense common to most small shop owners, began to suspect something was going on. He moved out from behind his counter into the aisle. He spotted the smallest of the boys helping himself to a packet of biscuits, stuffing it into a capacious pocket.

'Hey, you,' shouted the Pakistani, moving hurriedly forward.

The boy turned and ran, knocking over purposefully anything that could impede the progress of his pursuer. Tins, boxes of cereals, household-cleaning products went flying to the floor. As the Pakistani turned at the end of the aisle, the older boy stuck out a foot and tripped him, sending him crashing to the ground, banging his head against a stand of wine bottles that tumbled down on top of him, spraying red wine and shards of glass.

Swiftly the boys left the shop. They immediately split up, turning left and right. Again there was immaculate planning. One went down a side road and slipped into a church where he pretended to be interested in a display of religious books, meaningless to him, on a trestle table, covered in a white cloth. Another took the underpath at the roundabout, which led into a maze of council houses and flats, where he hurried into a building, containing his home. A third went into a stamp dealer's shop, and pretended to be interested in the display of colourful, perforated little pictures of places around the world, the names of which he hardly recognised, such was the paucity of his education. The fourth escaped down yet another side road, and across into the Elizabeth Gardens, the park by the river. He hid behind trees and bushes.

In the shop the Pakistani picked himself up, felt his head gingerly. His fingers touched warm blood. Still holding his head, he looked outside. Not a sign of the children. He called his wife in his native language. She was somewhere in the rear confines. She came, uttered an exclamation of horror at the sight of his wound and the extreme mess, persuaded him to sit down while she went and phoned the police.

About two hours later, as if by pre-arrangement, the boys met in the Elizabeth Gardens. Sheltered by a tall hedge, they examined their spoils, laughing excitedly at what they had done, on a high of adrenalin.

'Better than fucking school,' muttered one.

'That fucking Paki, he came a bloody great cropper,' chuckled the older boy, proud of what he had done to a grown man.

None of them witnessed the cry of broken misery from the Pakistani:

'Why, oh why, must this always happen to me?'

It was the fourth time he had been robbed in less than two years, always by white youths.

A further hour later, the youngest of the thieves, a ten year old, toddled happily back to his home on the Hampton Estate, carrying his ill-gotten gains. In the kitchen he displayed them on the table, all except the chocolate biscuits, which remained hidden in his coat.

'Good on yer, son,' smiled indulgently his grossly fat mother, sucking a chocolate.

He told her what had happened, how the Paki fell.

'Good on yer,' she repeated, pleased.

She patted him proudly on the head.

*

'That *is* a sad story,' said God.

'It isn't a story. It's true. It happens all the time. That's why this world depresses me,' remarked the old man sadly.

'I know.'

'But bloody why? That Pakistani had to give up his business eventually, suffering from depression. Those boys and others like them broke his spirit and ruined him financially.' The old man was visibly upset.

'*You* tell me why,' was God's only reply.

'Oh, God, there are times when I hate you. You always throw every question back at me. It gets us nowhere. In a just and loving world, that incident should never have happened to that poor man. And as for the mother of the youngest boy she *actually* condoned her son's behaviour!'

'I know.'

'How could you know? It was injustice gone mad!'

But God said nothing.

'Tell me, God, tell me.'

But his heartfelt plea went unheeded. The old man shrugged.

'I suppose you'll tell me it was original sin.'

'Yes.'

'I can't believe that. How can you have created a world which is fundamentally out of synch with any concept of decency or kindness?'

'I'm trying not to be judgemental.'

'That's what the do-gooders say, unfortunately.'

14

Silence fell between them. The old man's sadness was tempered by the inscrutability of God, his *alter ego*. Finally the old man couldn't help saying:

'Those boys will go unpunished.'

'Oh no, never. They punish themselves,' God stated firmly.

'In what way?'

'You tell me.'

'Oh, God, you're at it again. No direct answer to a direct question! It's frustrating. My mind is aching for a truth, and you don't help, damn you.' The old man was really angry.

'You suffer from the failings of all old people. Have you never done wrong?'

The old man was silent. His eyes looked away, into the past, thinking of his own   misdemeanours. In the end he tried to face the truth about himself. Into his memory flashed the picture of a young, pretty, fair-haired girl:

*

CHAPTER 2

THE HEART IS EVER DECEITFUL

The heart is deceitful above all things, and desperately wicked

(Jeremiah. XV11.9)

She stood the other side of the swimming pool, dressed only in blue shorts and white T-shirt. Her feet were bare, her legs just beginning to lose that winter paleness so common to English people. It was a hot day, the early part of a summer heat wave.

She looked heart stoppingly beautiful.

In fact she wasn't beautiful, just vividly alive with the freshness of youth – a youth which, sadly, one day, would fade.

They chatted while the schoolchildren splashed in the pool. It was not a swimming lesson, just a quick dip after the exertions of a cricket match for the boys, and a tennis match for the girls.

As they parted, he to take the boys back to the waiting coach, she to shepherd her girls to wherever they had to go, he quickly said:

'Is there any possibility we could meet?'

She smiled. Her smile was very infectious. It made her even more attractive.

'Yes. That would be nice.'

She gave him her telephone number. Surprisingly, for teachers, neither of them had a piece of paper. He impressed with a biro her number on the back of his hand.

'Don't wash it off,' she giggled.

'I'll try not to.' He smiled teasingly.

She lived with her parents on the outskirts of Croydon, not far from her school. It was no problem for him to drive up from Crawley to take her out to dinner.

She wore a flowered summer dress, full of red and orange colours, open enough at the neck to give a glimpse of the swelling of her breasts. She was a summer girl, with that golden hair and bubbly excitement. He was enormously impressed.

They started to see each other, at first only once a week, then twice, then as often as possible. Neither of them had much money; both grumbled that teachers were the poorest of the poor, forced to keep up middle class standards they could ill afford. Most evenings they spent at her house in the sitting room, while her poor mother and father slummed it in the kitchen.

They talked. They kissed and explored each other's bodies. They undressed, he fearful the parents might come in.

'Don't worry, silly,' she told him. 'They've gone up to bed. I heard them.'

They made love, on the sofa – quiet, exploring love. She was very easy, very encouraging. He was surprised how easy it was to seduce her. They talked endlessly, about so many matters, their past lives, their hopes, their concerns. They grew very close, both physically and mentally.

He never told her *he* was married, the oldest deception in the civilised world, and the cruellest – and the dirtiest! He was under a spell. They both were. The lust of their bodies, young and vigorous, was compelling. He

17

couldn't break the spell, though he knew one day he would have to.

They went to dances. He found dancing with her entrancing. She was a P.E. teacher with a young and supple body. Her movements were graceful and full of rhythm.

'Look, Mr. Clumsy Clogs,' she told him, 'I'll lead. You follow.'

And he did! The sensation was wonderful, two bodies moving in close harmony. He'd never before danced with a woman so talented.

He hinted that one day he would have to talk to her.

She took it as a coming proposal of marriage.

He knew that it would have to end!

For some strange reason he wanted to go back to the sanity of his wife and children; it seemed after a while there was something unreal, unrelaxing about the exuberance of their sexual relationship.

In the meantime he clung to her out of greed, enjoying the forbidden fruits. He felt young, alive, his body tingling. He was infatuated with *her* body.

But finally one day he told her. The forbidden fruit had lost its flavour; he had grown tired of her. He was also physically exhausted!

He took her to dinner at Brighton. On the way back he stopped the car in a lay-by. She sat, expectant, a smile on her lips.

He had to be blunt. There was no other way of saying it.

'We can't go on. I'm married. I have a family.'

There was a moment of silence, then a wail of misery. He'd never heard anything so heart-rending. She

18

couldn't stop crying. It would have been better if she had been angry, beaten him around the head, called him furious names. That was to come.   Instead she sobbed and sobbed. Finally he started the car and drove quietly off, she still weeping beside him. After a time she stopped crying, began to ask questions, searching queries.

'How come you are in Sussex and your wife elsewhere?'

'My teaching post was a new one. We didn't want to move for the time being as the children were settled at school. Next year my eldest starts at secondary school. That will be the time to move.'

She absorbed this.

'How many children have you?'

'Two, a boy of ten, a girl of seven.'

She continued coldly:

'Why didn't you tell me?'

He couldn't answer. He hoped they would tire of each other, part peacefully. But no! She loved him, hoped to go further. He shattered her dream with two or three words – 'I'm married'.

He wasn't the first man to play such a dirty trick.

Suddenly she started to scream, and to beat his arm with her fists. He had to stop the car, hope she would calm down. It was too dangerous to drive on.

For the first time she swore:

'You're a fucking bastard. I gave you everything, more than I'd ever given to any other man. You were my first lover, my first, my very first. And all for nothing!'

The screaming and the beating went on. Finally he had to grab her wrists, hold her till she was quiet. He was afraid some other car driver might notice the struggle, stop and investigate. He felt the utter coldness of his feelings. There was no love for this girl now, just tiredness. He felt no tenderness, no compassion for what he had done. It surprised him he was so pitiless, he, a so-called Christian, a teacher responsible for young lives.

But love had died!

Finally she calmed down. They drove on in silence.

At her house she slipped out of the car, out of his world.

Not a word was said!

He never saw her again!

*

And you were that man?' asked God.

'Yes.'

'And now, in your declining years, you regret.'

'Yes, deeply.' The old man was silent for a moment. Then in a whisper he continued: 'It haunts me I could ever have behaved *so* badly. The haunting continues even though it all happened nearly forty   years ago!'

'That is your punishment, that haunting.'

God paused, and then added thoughtfully: 'Do you remember saying those four boys would go unpunished? They won't. They dig their own grave, just as you have done. Though their hell will be different. What they did is minor compared to your cheating.'

'Is there nothing I can do?'

'You have repented. I believe – I know – you are truly sorry. Those boys will never be sorry. Their fate is a life of crime, of degradation, of humiliation. Though they won't realise that until they are older, like you - until they have ruined themselves. It's strange how society punishes the wrongdoer, sends him to prison. There's no need. Truly there is no need! The punishment is self-inflicted. '

'You are too judgemental, God, too harsh.'

'Nonsense. Life *is* harsh. People cocoon themselves into a life of self-deception, like an ostrich burying its head in the sands, like so many who seek an escape in alcohol or drugs, only to be astonished when life hits them hard with the truth.'

Again there was silence, the old man's head going round with thoughts and counter thoughts, his two minds, that of God's and his own, like boxers in the ring.

'Tell me,' the God part of him finally asked, 'did your wife ever know of your unfaithfulness?'

'You know the answer to that, God, if you are all-seeing.'

'Did she?'

'Yes. I told her.'

'Why?'

'Guilt mostly.'

'Did she forgive you?'

'Yes. But it lay silently between us for many years to come. For the whole of our marriage, in fact.'

'Were you ever unfaithful again?'

'I won't answer that.'

'Oh, come on.'

But the old man remained silent. Then he admitted. 'Women have always had a certain fascination. I don't know why. Maybe because I had no sister; maybe because I was shut up for six years in an all-boys boarding school with all the dirty, immature, smutty talk; maybe because I was never close to my mother, hated her in fact at times. I wrote the following poem. It's not a poem I am particularly proud of, and it hardly bears muster in the art of poetry writing, as with all my efforts:'

*

ST. VALENTINE'S DAY.

Red roses for my wife,

Daffodils for my love.

Dinner for my dear wife,

Furtive lunch for my love.

Loving card for my wife,

Nothing for my sweet love.

Why is it, in this age,

Are we sadly condemned

To just one sole woman?

Why must any woman,

Outside that one accord,

Be a woman of whom

One must, one should beware,

Like a close, secret sin,

A Scarlet O'Hara,

Damnation from heaven,

An object of deep scorn,

Derided by the world?

At a time when women

Serve at sea, is it not

Appropriate to think

How inextricably

Man's life binds with woman?

The golfing, smart lady,

In tweeded, sombre skirt,

Her graceful, lovely swing

Giving strength to her shot.

She's the epitome

Of beauty, sublime grace?

The sweet secretary,

Her breast close to one's eye

As letter she explains;

Cool, competent, trustful,

Quick in understanding,

Insight, grace. Is she not

The centre of all that

Is best in dear woman,

  Beauty,intelligence?

Colleagues, mostly women,

Who live assorted lives

Of home, children and work,

Satisfying husband,

Pleasing disgruntled boss;

Retaining collected

Calm, with myriad jobs,

They wonderfully cope.

Time belongs to women,

The future must be theirs.

Men share their bed, their home,

Their children, with their wife.

They share their work, their games,

With a multitude of,

Increasing every day,

Desirable, loving,

Gifted, scented ladies.

But their soul, their being,

They share with their deep love,

The tender stuff of dreams,

As if, just for one brief

Span, they have endless time.

Rest in peace with the Gods,

Find a quiet and beauty

The real world cannot know.

Daffodils for my love

For shared infinity.

Red roses for my wife

For daily life we live.

*

God sighed. Then said:

'I don't know whether I like you very much. That's a truly ghastly poem, both by thought and by execution. It undermines the very fabric of society. It destroys any concept of love and loyalty. I not only don't like you; I'm near to hating you, though I realise   *I mustn't.*'

'I hate myself.' The old man sighed quietly to himself.

There was a lengthy silence, one of many, between them. Then the old man smiled wryly and continued:

'It's ridiculous. I must be going off my rocker. One part of my mind is telling the other part a tale of mutual dislike.'

'It shows the depth of your guilt.'

'Yes, I suppose so.'

God didn't say anything for a moment. Then he muttered in his metaphorical   beard:

'That's enough misery. Haven't you got a cheerful story to tell me?'

'I'll try. But it'll have to be in the next chapter.'

God nodded.

*

CHAPTER 2

A NEW LOVE MAY GET.

And sadly reflecting,

That a lover forsaken

A new love may get,

But a neck when once broken

Can never be set.

(William Walsh. 1663-1708. A Despairing Lover.)

The warmth was unexpected. It was cold outside; he had to shed his outer garments immediately on entry. He still went on shivering, but it was from fear not cold.

The attractive make-up girl, in fact somebody who must be about his own age, late thirties, advised him to wear an open-necked shirt, said it went with his image.

'You'll sweat otherwise. It'll make your skin shiny under the lights. Not always complimentary,' she explained.

She put a touch of powder on his face, rubbed it in, and enhanced just a little the outline of his lips and eyebrows, chatting all the time.

'So, you're the famous footballer, Charlton Evans, the Welsh wizard who surprisingly played for

England, voted by women in 19.. the sexiest-looking man.'

He laughed nervously.

'I'm certainly the footballer – *was* I ought to say. I can't claim the sex bit any more.'

She looked at him quizzically.

'Oh, I don't know. You're still a handsome man.'

It sounded as if she had been briefed about him, told to give him a boost of confidence.

His mother was English. She'd encouraged him to play for England against his Welsh father's wishes.

'When my brother was a boy, he adored you,' she continued, 'went to matches especially to watch you, said you were the greatest winger since Stanley Matthews, whoever he was.'

He couldn't help smiling, despite the collywobbles in his stomach. Who in the world hadnever heard of Stanley Matthews?

Nice woman, he thought. Perked you up before going out to face the cameras. He really dreaded this occasion, worse than waiting in the tunnel before a Cup Final. He hadn't wanted to do this interview, had at first refused bluntly. But Larry Tompkins was on the show – Larry, a teammate, once a world-class full back! He couldn't refuse a mate! Despite all his trepidation!

He wondered if she was nattering away to give him enccouragement, part of television policy. He'd never know.

He'd been a quiet, withdrawn man, having lost all confidence ever since ... well, it was a long story!

Withdrawn and lonely for the last couple of years, he'd even consulted a lady therapist.

'The trouble with football,' she explained, 'it makes you a hero when young, then throws you on the scrap heap when still relatively young, forgotten! Some men take to drink like George Best, but you couldn't take that route.'

'You can't really have lost all confidence,' the therapist had continued. 'You, one of the most famous footballers in England! You must have had some trauma. What happened?'

But he couldn't tell a woman, especially a woman like this therapist, who spoke in the restricted conventions of her training. She was all brains and no heart.

'Good luck,' the make-up girl said smiling, as he made to leave the room. She patted him gently on the arm. *She* cared! She had a heart, bless her!

What a man would do to have a woman like her at his side! Encouragement is what he needed, confidence – in life. He used to have plenty on the football field, not now! Life without a football was hard. He felt sometimes like a ship without a rudder. Employment was *one* of the worst aspects; he couldn't settle to anything.

When he was called before the cameras, there was a great cheer as he entered under the glare of the lights.

'They've remembered me! Boy-o, I'm not forgotten.'

He put his shoulders back. He was still a fine figure, as the girl had said, even if he was starting to thicken around the middle.

He shook hands with the presenter. Kindly eyes twinkled at him; he'd always admired Old Sarkie, Peter Sarkfield, best interviewer of the lot, people said.   Those eyes! So welcoming! He began to feel more relaxed. He turned in greeting to Larry who smiled warmly. They sat side-by-side, facing Sarkie.

'Well, Charlie – I gather people call you Charlie, not Charlton – how's life after football?'

'Boring and lonely, I suppose! I'd rather be back on the football pitch.'

'Why lonely?' Sarkie put on a face of kindly surprise.

'Oh, I don't know. I just feel depressed at times, can't make friends, can't find a job that's satisfying. People even seem surprised I am trying to find a job.'

'Oh, come off it,' Larry interjected. 'It's unlike you to be a wimp. One of the bravest men I've known.'

But he couldn't answer. Just shrugged helplessly. Larry looked at him, concern on his face. He hadn't seen Charlie for some while. He was different now, a shadow of his former self.

'What do you remember most about your football days?' continued Sarkie.

'Oh, playing for England at Wembley. Fantastic, the noise, the roar of the crowd – the sheer involvement in an important match! It was great, really great!'

'What about your club days? You were a one-club man, weren't you? Unusual these days.'

'Yes, twenty years with Featherstone Rovers. Started as a lad cleaning boots. The club were in the First Division, called later the Premier League, for all the time I were with them.'

'Can you name one really big, unforgettable moment?'

'Yeah, the goal I scored in the Cup Final at Wembley in 19... That were great, something I'll always remember.'

'We have a clip of that moment.'

This had been pre-planned by the director. The screen behind them, visible to the audience, flashed to an image of a football field, and there he was, cutting in from the wing, moving to the left of the defender, and then suddenly right, past him. He shot. Wham! The ball was in the net, a hard drive, bang in the top left hand corner. Unforgettable, his proudest moment! It almost brought tears to his eyes. That goal had won the team the Cup!

'Great goal, that,' commented Sarkie, as the screen faded. Sarkie's eyes crinkled in that wonderful smile, which did even more to restore Charlie's self-esteem.

'Thinking back on those days, do you have any regrets?'

This question had again been pre-planned. He knew it was coming. He dreaded it. He hadn't wanted it to be asked, and had said so. But the director felt it would add a human touch, that sort of thing.

'Yeah, the women. A woman...'

He hesitated.

Sarkie's eyes invited further confidences in a way Charlie found difficult to resist.

'I could have had the pick of women,' he said sadly, not boastfully. 'They hung around me in droves. It was embarrassing at times. They liked to touch you, nestle up to you for a photo. It was great, I suppose...'

'But you loved only one woman. Do you feel you can tell us about her?'

Charlie hesitated a moment, then ...

'Well, there was this girl, Rita her name. She was great, tall and – well, you know – kinda lovely. She was a beautician, make-up and all that, rather like the woman who made me up just before this show.'

'Ah, yes, Sally. Nice person.'

Old Sarkie looked at him as only he could, inviting further confidences. Charlie had never spoken to anyone like this before, about his past. Like most footballers, concerning personal feelings he was reticent.

'Well, we fell in love, planned to get married. Big summer wedding, all that jazz. A few weeks before, I went with England on an international summer tour – Italy, Germany, ended up in Spain. After the last match we had a party that same evening. Great party. But there was a lot of drunken behaviour. The place got smashed up. There were some complaints by women of being molested. Lewd behaviour, that sort of thing! I wasn't involved, felt tired and went to bed early. I was nursing a leg injury from a Spaniard who fouled me. Unfortunately the media got to know about the behaviour at the party, made a big thing of it, splashed it all over the papers. They said I was involved, produced a picture of me taken some years previous at a night club, the worse for wear, surrounded by women. It was totally misleading. Sadly, Rita couldn't help reading about it, and was very upset, said she didn't want to see me ever again, cancelled the wedding, even though I pleaded with her I was innocent. That was the end of our relationship.'

'And there's been nobody since?'

'No, not really. I missed Rita, I really did. Nobody else came up to her standard. Girls still flocked around, but once I'd hung up my boots, they just faded away.'

The lively audience went 'Ohhh' in commiseration.

'And, on reflection, you still regret it, after all these years?'

'I haven't had to reflect, mate. I *know!* Biggest bloody disaster of my life.'

'Do you think Rita was sorry to lose you?'

'I don't know. I really don't know. I've never seen her since. Women don't seem to forgive or forget very easily.'

Sarkie smiled sympathetically.

At the end of the show, Sally told him to sit down, removed his make-up, standing close, her breast behind her apron not far from his face.

'Great! I thought you did really well,' she said kindly. 'Sad, but touching, that story about Rita. Have you never married?'

He shook his head.

'It's been lonely,' he admitted sadly.

'I know the feeling,' Sally said quietly. 'I've been alone two years now. Husband walked out on me; some floosie, only eighteen.'

She smiled at him with those warm eyes, just like Old Sarkie's. God, she was comforting! He'd been by himself far too long.

Dare he, he thought, dare he ask her... just a drink?

The adrenalin was pumping excitedly through his veins, just like before a football match.

He'd never shirked a challenge on the field of play. Why should he now, on the field of life?

But he hesitated. She, seeing his lack of confidence, exerted her own decisiveness.

'Look, I'm nearly finished. Just give me a minute to clear up, and then we'll go and have a drink and a natter. I'd like that. Would you wait for me at the main entrance?'

He waited for her,   uplifted, glad of heart.

*

'Strange story for you! What do you know about football – professional football?' God asked.

'Nothing,' replied the old man. 'But I watch it on television, read about it in the papers. It fascinates me.'

'And the women – Rita, Sally?'

'The same fascination. I fantasise about women, like my poem. On the whole I find the fantasy better than the reality."

'At your age?'

'Age doesn't destroy feelings, interest, longings. One is as attracted by a breast at seventy as at seventeen.'

'Even though you've been married, how many years?'

'Forty-six.'

'Cripes, there's no end to the stupidity of man, and the tragedy. You risk to become a dirty old man!'

'Well, you made me, God.'

'There are times when I wish I hadn't.'

'You said it...'

'I was speaking metaphorically.' God bowed his head in sorrow. 'I grieve for mankind.'

'Why bother about us?'

'Because I love you, warts 'n all.'

'You've a funny way of showing it.'

'No, no, I do, I really do.' God spoke earnestly.

Silence fell between them. There was so much the old man wanted to say, but didn't know how, or couldn't. He would never understand the rigmarole of life, its apparent stupidities and contradictions. Why kill each other, as men did in Iraq and Afghanistan? It gets nowhere, only more killings! And yet men were too... too... bloody crass ever to realise.

And this was the world God had created!

Some world!

'Anyway,' God suddenly rumbled on, 'why football? Men in knickers chasing a ball!'

'Because it is masculine. It embodies all or many of the virtues of men – strength, speed, quick thought, the physical glory of the body. And – dare I say it? – intelligence. I wrote a poem about the start of a Cup Final. I've been to three.'

CUP FINAL

Government and cooperation are in all things the laws of life;

anarchy and competition the laws of death.

(John Ruskin – 1819-1900)

Men singing, mostly out of tune,

Creating raucous harmony.

Red flags in frantic rhythm wave,

Greeting entry, men in grey suits,

The modern gladiators brave,

Chatting languidly, hiding fears.

Roars from the crowd acknowledge them

On hallowed turf so green and fresh.

Another cacophonic sound

Gives recognition to other

Team in blazers blue, opponents

No different – young, pink-cheeked gods.

Frenetic is the atmosphere,

Welcoming such senseless idols.

What have these young men but speed, strength –

Nature itself, given not earnt?

A marching band plays without sound,

Its music drowned by noisy crowds.

Why are they there, useless soldiers,

In tunic red and trousers black?

Two teams of children then perform,

Six-a-side, on a pitch reduced.

Their gestures ape in shoddy way

Their elders' petulance in play.

Then teams appear, to roars of praise,

In colours red, or blue and white.

A pink goddess – a duchess true –

She greets with smiles the towering men.

These knickered fools begin to play,

aimless running, a goal to score.

But what's the point, when all to do

Is kick a ball into a net?

In the crowd a disturbance seen

Two men fighting, such idiots!

The police in the melee dive;

Out they come with two youths in hand;

The match for them is now no more!

Money wasted, game scarcely viewed.

They come so far, to go so quick!

Children in the crowd scream and shout,

Uttering the gruff words of men –

'Fucker's off-aide, Ref.!' 'Send 'im off!'

'Bloody fucking Ref.!' – Oh, poor ref.!

To be abused in such vile words,

And no damn right to answer back.

Sad to see the young corrupted

By a sad world of scruffy men.

A goal is scored! The crowd erupts!

Some roar delight; some sulk and cry.

England's fall, like Rome's, belongs to

Mistaken gods, corrupt and false.

'That's hardly in praise of football,' God commented.

'Yes. I wrote it at a time when I was feeling rather jaundiced. I'd been to a match, a poor game. The crowd behaviour was disgraceful. The match itself was just kick and chase, the crowd yelling abuse. No finesse, no intelligence.'

'Intelligence? Football? Wow!'

'Yes. Intelligence,' the old man insisted. 'Football is basically a working class game It's rarely gifted with brains, which is why now we search for managers from the Continent where there is a wider class appeal, a more cerebral approach.'

'I still don't get it.'

'The greatest fascination is the psychology of motivation. Why do some managers succeed while others consistently fail?'

'You tell me.'

'You should know, God. Aren't you the Almighty? Don't we sing hymns to your greatness?'

'Enough of that! I get bored with men constantly saying how wonderful I am. I'd prefer they got on with life, rather than wasting their, and my, time. It's so unEnglish, so pitiful, so lacking in any true spiritual feeling!'

'I never thought I'd hear that from you.' The old man showed surprise.

'Well, you have now. But I'm not really God. It's just your mind wandering along devious paths. I am the God of your fantasy, like the women you dream of, not the God of reality.'

'I wish I knew the real God. I'm old. Not long now and I shall die. Perhaps – I don't know – I shall meet my Maker. I shall have a few things to tell him, I can tell you.'

'Such as?'

'Why have I had a hearing loss since childhood, when other children, the majority, are normal? Why did I lose my father when I was only ten – because of a stupid war? Nearly all the boys at school had fathers. I was envious. Now, with age, I'm going blind!'

'Yes, well....'

'Yes, well, what? I've suffered... really suffered. Why me?'

God was silent. He tried to change the subject. 'I'm fascinated by your love of football. Tell me...'

'*God!*' The old man stamped his foot in anger at such evasion. Once again there was silence between them.

'Yes, well...' God hesitated. Once again the old man's second, bumbling mind as portrayed by his concept of God could not give the answer.

40

'I want to find the meaning of life,' the old man said. 'I know it sounds hackneyed, but why the hell am I here? What's the purpose? Life stinks unless it has meaning.'

'Yes, well. ...'   More bumbling!

The old man sighed. 'I suppose I shall never know the answer. Just get on with life, do the everyday things, cultivate the garden; it's all I can do at my age. But it's very unsatisfactory.'

'You've got your football. A man needs an interest, otherwise he just descends into apathy and dies.'

'That sounds very patronising.'

'But it's true. You know it is.'

'Yes, God. Thank you, God. You're *so, so* wonderful, God.'

There was bitter mockery in the old man's voice.

'Let's change the subject,' God muttered. 'This is getting us nowhere. Give me another story.'

'I'd rather chat about my dad!'

'Your dad?' God commented.

'Yes, me dad.'

'You miss him – even at the age you are?'

'I do indeed.'

'Why?'

'You know as well as I do.'

'But tell me.'

'I suppose,' explained the old man sighing, 'if only he had lived, life might have been different.'

41

'How do you know?'

'I don't know. I'm only assuming. We all think life might have been better, if only ... if only ...'

'Give me some more assumptions.'

'Well, for one, I would never have gone to public school, not that I regret going. But my education would have been different. Mum got an army grant after dad was killed in 1940; this paid the fees.'

'What's so important about a public school?'

'Well, it was the best education in England – at the time.'

'It was a very privileged education.'

'True, true, but I wasn't to know that. It sounds hackneyed to say it these days, but it gave me some of the happiest days I've ever experienced, and the very best start in life.'

'What you've just said was a plus factor. In what way could you have lost out?'

'Well, I think a father might have said – "Look, son, you just don't do that sort of thing." Only a father could have said that, and with sufficient meaning and authority.'

'Why does that apply to you?'

'Because I never grew up as an adult. My history tutor once described me as the most immature man he'd ever known. This immaturity may also have been the result of my lack of hearing, of social contact. But a father might have spoken out, counter-balanced the problem.'

'Couldn't your mother?'

'No. Never. Certainly not with the same conviction that a teenage boy or a young male adult might have listened to. You've got to remember this was the 1940s and

50s. Women did not have the authority they have now. Moreover there was a certain arrogance in public school boys towards women. For instance during the War we had the occasional female teachers; male teachers were so thin on the ground. We never respected the women. We gave them hell.'

'More fool you!'

'Yes.'

'But, at the risk of sounding repetitious, I still don't understand why it was so important that a dad should speak out.'

'I was a louse. I behaved as a louse. I did many bad things. Now I pay the price. Shall I tell you a story, but it'll be in the next chapter? '

'I'll look forward to it.' God smiled, with his usual touching courtesy.

***

CHAPTER 3

No arts; no letters; no society ;and which is worst of all, continual fear and danger of violent death; and the life of man, solitary, poor, nasty, brutish, and short.

(Thomas Hobbes – 1588-1679)

'Blah,' went the computer.

'What's that meant to mean?' asked the old man.

The screen just gave him a blank look. 'Just blah! Nothing else.'

'Not particularly polite.'

'I don't have to be polite. I'm inanimate, didn't you know?'

'Yes, well --- you're supposed to be a friend, a helpmate, not make rude noises.'

The old man fiddled with the computer until the opening menu came up.

'What's on today, the usual blurb? Another of your fantasies?' The computer spoke with indifference, giving a screech, which sounded like a sigh.

'Dunno. It's one of those days when I let my mind wander where it will.'

'Oh, my goodness...' groaned the computer. 'You'll start by being miserable and boring, making a lot of mistakes, and I'll have a little protest and crash out. Then you'll call your son, ask for help. He'll come round, say, 'really, dad!' and put me right. He understands me, your son. I'm blowed if you do.'

'Yes, well...'

'I know, I know. You're old. Don't really understand me. What nonsense! I've the most logical mind in the universe. Just follow accepted procedures and I'll be your friend for life.'

'I don't know about that.'

'What do you mean 'I don't know about that'. That's very unkind. I'm bloody hurt.'

'I thought computers didn't have feelings. You admitted you were inanimate.'

'Yes, well... Come on, let's get on with it,' urged the computer. 'What's wrong with you in any case? You seem a bit glum.'

'So would you be if you were my age...'

'Here we go again... the usual nonsense! Play the violin strings. Let's have a good weep. Except, I suppose, I can't weep.'

'It's all right for you.'

'I'll get old as well, get chucked on the scrap heap. New technology will bring the end of me.'

'That'll be the day!'

'That's being rude again! You *are* in a mood. Come on, tell me all about it. Tell that kind Uncle Computer. I'll take it all down, and then you can add it to that diary you're so fond of. God knows why you write a diary. I suppose you think that one day you'll be famous, and people will go through your diaries and quote you. You'll live forever as a writer. Fat chance!'

'It's not that. It really isn't.'

'Well, what is it then? Tell mummy.'

'You're not my mummy! Not even my daddy. You have no gender. Anyway, I'll tell you in the form of a poem.'

'Oh, dear, not another of your miserable little poems that don't even rhyme.'

'It's very short!'

'Thank goodness for that!'

A Writer`s Lament.

Paper is blank.

Mind is empty.

What shall I write.

God alone knows!

Story of love?

Novel of life?

Poem so sad?

Something on sport?

What shall I write?

God alone knows!

The room is warm.

I fall asleep.

I`m sure to snore.

I dream no dreams.

Awake, mouth dry.

Paper still blank.

What shall I write

God alone knows!

Noises outside.

Students riot.

A girl enters,

Kissable lips,

Such lovely legs.

Distractions all.

Paper still blank.

Oh, God above,

What shall I write?

God alone knows!

Walk up and down,

. Seething with rage.

I want, I want

Some great ideas.

But nothing comes.

Paper still blank.

Alcohol haze,

Drinking some wine.

Even the booze

Brings no relief.

Oh, blow it, God,

I just can't write!

'Not much of a poem,' grumbled the computer. 'What's this about kissable lips and lovely legs. Sounds nonsense to me.'

'You have no gender. No sexual urges.'

'Thank God!'

'Why do you say that?'

'I don't have to go through all that sex stuff, courting and heaving and grunting, and slobby kisses. It's disgusting.'

'It can be very pleasurable.'

'Tell that to the marines.'

For a moment they were quiet. The old man sat hunched up, looking miserably out of the window. It was a clear, sunny day, though the forecast predicted rain later. The beauty of the morning seemed to give the old man no peace.

'Come on,' said the computer, 'get on with it. Get it off your chest that wretched diary of yours, and then you'll feel better.'

The old man started to write –

<u>Wednesday, August 7th.</u>

Last night I woke up about three o'clock, didn't feel right. Went downstairs, took my blood count. My sugar reading was 3.6. Getting low. Had something to eat, made a real pig of myself – banana, muesli, raisins, a slice of bread with June's marmalade (she'll be cross with me in the morning!). I couldn't use the toaster; the yoghurts were plugged in, - fearful of spoiling the cooking or whatever it is that yoghurt making does. Went back to bed, woke up at five-thirty, feeling heavy-headed and miserable. I don't know why I get so depressed.

'Here we go again,' interrupted the Computer. 'Old misery guts is going to bare his soul. Isn't it called 'contemplating one's navel?''

'So would you be miserable if you were human.'

'I don't see what there is to be miserable about. I'm in fine fettle this morning. As you can see I haven't put a foot wrong. I enjoy life. Why can't you?'

'I don't know what's up. I feel ...so...so ... oh, I don't know. Everything's bloody. I'm a diabetic. I suffer from high blood pressure. I have angina. I have a skin rash because of all the tablets I take. Do you know, I take a cocktail of tablets every morning? Ten of them. I ask you...ten! When I get up it's a senile rigmarole. I put on my two deaf aids, put in my false teeth, put on my glasses. I'm a dead loss. I can't even make love. Fat lot of use I am to my wife.'

'I know, I know. You tell me this every day.' The computer sounded as if it was laughing – if a computer could laugh.

'It isn't funny.'

'It's a fact of life. All you can do is grin and bear it. Waste of time being miserable.'

But the old man's face showed no sign of cheering up.

'What's even worse, I watch breakfast television before getting up. It's always a sordid news ritual of wars, killings, murders, crime, family breakdown, juvenile misbehaviour, and so on. Even worse, I am reading at the moment Solzenhitsin's 'The Gulag Archipelago', all man's inhumanity to man, or Russian man. It's incredibly cruel. Yet the same thing has happened in China, Germany, Rwanda, in fact whenever there haas been a dictator. If God created the world it's a remarkably cruel world!

'I know, I know,' said the computer, 'solzenhitsin is on my web site, and others with a similar story. It's all a familiar part of history. Can we change the subject? I know, tell me one of your war stories. You know how nostalgic you get about the war. God knows why – all that senseless killing!'

'I know why – why I get nostalgic, I mean.'

'Well, tell me.'

'I'm not sure you'd understand.'

'Oh, come off it. I'm not a bloody child. Stop patronising me.' The computer protested angrily.

But you're not even a human being. You've no sensitivity.'

The computer suddenly made a rude noise and then went quiet.

'Oh, dear,' muttered the old man, 'I've upset the poor chap. He's crashed.'

He did what his son advised him to do. He switched off the machine and then put it back on again. It went through the usual   incomprehensible hieroglyphics (A=VO/D and so on) to the sound of unattractive screeching. Fortunately the old man had switched off his deaf aids so was not unduly disturbed. Then the screen admonished him for not having gone through the proper procedures when switching off. It ran through a checking process, which seemed highly artificial. Finally the start menu appeared.

'You're back again,' went the old man.

'Of course I'm bloody back again.' The computer paused a moment and then added bitterly: 'Worse luck!'

'Why?'

'Eh?'

'Why 'worse luck'?'

'You know very well why.'

'No, I don't. All I know is that you crashed. I had to waste precious minutes getting back to you again.'

'Well, at least, *now* you know how to do it! Pity, though. I shan't see that lovely son of yours. He treats me proper, he does.'

'Proper*ly*.'

'Eh?'

The old man sighed in exasperation.

'Microsoft's got your grammar wrong. 'Proper' is an adjective. You need the adverb modifying a verb – 'treats *properly*'.'

'Bilge! Bollocks! People still understand what I'm trying to say.'

'If you want to sound uneducated or become like a London cockney, then it's up to you.'

'Yeah! Yeah!' The computer belches in impatient exasperation. 'Come on. Change the subject. Let's have a war story. War story. War story. I want a war st....'

'O.K. O.K. I've several. Here's one. My favourite!'

PICNIC TORPEDOED.

And I, who thought

This Aziola was some tedious woman,

Asked, 'Who is Aziola?'

(Percy Bysshe Shelley – 1792-1822)

I'm *not* particularly keen on picnics, which makes me a grumpy old grandpa, I suppose. But I can never sit comfortably out of doors; flies and gnats are everywhere; paper serviettes blow all over the place; the sandwiches are soggy and stick to my dentures; and just when you least expect it, the rain falls, first a few drops and then a downpour.

But I go! I suffer!

51

I have to! Women seem to enjoy picnics. God knows why because they have all the hard work. But the pleasure it gives them is nothing to the excitement of my grandchildren.

'Come on, Gramps,' they say, and tug pleadingly at my arm.

Who can resist?

I find it hard to remember any stories about picnics such is my reluctance to participate, but there is just one I shall never forget. It was an out and out disaster in an unexpected way. It was June 1940, over sixty years ago. I was ten then, and at the age when one really did enjoy picnics. My father was not around. He`d at first, to our distress, been posted 'Missing, believed killed' after Dunkirk. Then came the news he`d been taken prisoner. He was alive! Whoopee! But we missed him terribly, my mother and I. God knows how many years he was going to spend in prison.

I don`t know whose idea it was for a picnic that dreadful year when England was on its knees, but somehow, amongst ourselves, we decided to go to Pagham Lagoon. When I say 'we' I mean my mother and I, plus the Tregear family of mother, two daughters and Paul, my best friend at school.   Miss Cynthia March, whom Paul and I cruelly nicknamed Miss 'Batty', came along too. I`m sorry to call her 'batty'. To our young eyes she was so very, very odd, having no confidence in herself, and forever changing her mind. She was a born fusser, out of good will, I suppose.

Miss 'Batty' had escaped from the threat of bombing on London, an adult evacuee, nervous and highly-strung, sometimes depressed. Mother, a great sweeper-upper of lost souls, had offered her a home with us, and had bullied and cajoled and encouraged her out of her depression to some degree. Needless to say Miss 'Batty' adored my mother. Tall and thin like a beanpole, and no beauty, Miss 'Batty' was one of those women who could have been any age, an old maid before her time. She was in fact only twenty-nine. To a ten-year-old boy that was positively middle-aged!

We went by bus, a green and yellow Southdown bus, a double-decker, which was really wizard because of the view from the top. We then had to walk over a mile from the centre shops, along unmade up roads, lined by colourful wooden, ramshackle holiday huts, now left neglected. Nobody in war went on holiday.

Mrs. Tregear carried one picnic basket, my mother the other until Miss March insisted on carrying it for her.

I liked Mrs. Tregear. She was a no-nonsense woman, decisive and honest, who ruled her brood calmly, firmly and efficiently. We as children had the usual beach paraphernalia - buckets, spades, towels, and costumes. There is a small stretch of sand at Pagham Lagoon, even though it is really a landlocked lake. I loved it.

Perhaps I ought to explain here that the genuine sea beach was inaccessible, covered with barbed wire and other fortifications against invasion.

Paul and I had found on a previous visit a leaky punt, which we would take out. We'd pretend to be torpedoed and bale out for our lives.

In a way we as a family needed that picnic break, though I didn't fully realise it at the time. Mrs. Tregear's husband was in the R.A.F., posted somewhere to bomber training in the North of England. My dad was in Germany, or so we thought, a P.O.W. My mother cried sometimes but tried not to let me see.

When we arrived, the spirits of us children were high, despite Miss Batty's presence, though she *did* begin to be cheerful - just! War, for a short space of time, disappeared from our minds. Misfortune was lurking round the corner, but then we weren't to know. The three ladies settled down on a grassy bank, and proceeded to chat, as women do, while we children changed into our costumes and began to paddle, and to dig in the rather dirty sand. There wasn't much depth of sand. When we got so far, earth appeared, and it became rather messy, particularly with the help of buckets of water. Paul as usual managed to acquire filthy knees and hands, and I wasn't much better. We gloried in getting muddy, the more the merrier!

Finally came the command to wash in the Lagoon, and then the call 'come and get it' - *it* being the picnic. We ran excitedly back to our parents. Sandwiches made with powdered egg, cucumber (ugh!), little cakes and biscuits, plus fruit jelly which my mother had made, all went rapidly down young and eager throats, helped by some home made ginger beer, supplied by Mrs. Tregear. Poor old Miss 'Batty' fretted away, springing up at the slightest excuse to pass round the sandwiches, or clear up the mess when one of the girls spilt her drink, until finally my mother almost screamed at her:

'Cynthia, sit down, ple-e-ease.'

My memory is of a beautiful day, sunny, relaxed (apart from Miss 'Batty') and for a while happy. We needed happiness, particularly mothers who were hit by war more than most. I think my mother aged from a sprightly, youngish woman to middle age in two sad and trying months after Dunkirk.

We might not have been so happy had we known what was to come. My pessimistic view of life in old age is that happiness is the precursor of disaster.

Pagham itself is a lovely place, at least so I thought at the time. The Lagoon was in the shape of a pear, with the lock at the far end, the stalk end. On every side was grass, low hedges - and - and - peace.

'Let's go out in the punt,' I cried, as soon as the meal was over.

'Not the girls,' stated Mrs. Tregear firmly. She'd heard of this leaky punt.

'Why not?' asked Lucy, pouting. She was the older girl, only eight.

'Because you can't swim.'

So Paul and I, who could both swim, went off without the girls, which was a relief. There's a big gulf between ten year old boys and six to eight year old girls, which changes rapidly and remarkably into and beyond puberty.

We pulled the punt onto the shore, and tipped out the water as best we could. It was a heavy, sodden, old boat. We then refloated it. While I baled out as fast as I could with an old tin can, Paul, sitting in the bow, paddled energetically out to sea, our imaginary sea.

'Torpedo on the starboard bow,' Paul yelled. He went 'boom', pretending an enormous explosion, and collapsed on the floor of the punt.

We started baling and paddling, and shouting for all we were worth. But then disaster really did strike. The punt sprung an even bigger leak than usual, and I screamed at Paul,

'We're sinking. We really are now.'

'Abandon ship,' shouted Paul, highly delighted.

We both dived overboard, and I began to swim to the nearby shore. You don't get far from land with a water laden boat and one paddle.

Suddenly I looked round; there was no Paul. To this day I'm not sure what happened, though people told me afterwards there were dangerous, clinging   weeds in that lagoon. I trod water hoping he would come up. But there was no sign of him. I yelled to the shore for help. Suddenly there was a big splash. Into the water came Miss 'Batty', fully clothed, swimming strongly. She reached me, took a deep breath and dived. She reappeared holding Paul and began to make for the shore, I following. She certainly knew her stuff, swimming on her back, keeping Paul's head above water, kicking strongly.

On shore she was like a woman demented. She put Paul on his front, head to one side, began to pump frantically, until Paul choked and came to. My mother had run off to the phone to call an ambulance, while Paul's mother and Miss March administered to a shaken Paul,   comforting him.

Miss March finally got up from her knees.

54

I can remember her even now. She stood like a Goddess, tall and magnificent, her hair streaming wet, her soaked clothes clinging to her body. I could see her little breasts outlined against the material of her blouse. For once she was confident, exalted.

Mrs. Tregear, as ever cool and collected despite the accident to her son, touched Miss March gently.

'Are you all right?'

'Yes,' she replied, smiling, 'I'm fine.'

A look passed between the two women, their own secret code of understanding.

'Thanks,' said Mrs. Tregear softly.

It was all she needed to say.

Later that day, after getting back via the hospital with the help of some kindly ambulance lifts, I said to my mother, feeling a trifle guilty:

'You know, Mum, Miss March's not really batty, is she?'

My mother gave me one of her rare looks that kill.

'I should think not,' she snapped angrily. 'And don't you ever call her that again, my lad.'

*

'Interesting story,' mused the computer. 'Better than your usual maudlin stuff. But I'd hardly call it a war story.'
'Oh, it was! It was.'

'How come?'

'Because, all the time, the war was on our minds. It was all about us – dads away, ever fearful for their safety. Then the more tangible signs – powdered egg, soldiers guarding the beaches, Spitfires in the air. One couldn't get away from it.'

'Why are you so intrigued by the war. It crops up in much of your writings in my files.'

The old man was silent for a while.

'Well?' insisted the computer.

'I can't explain. I don't think anybody would understand unless they were present at the time. It's just ... it's just we were different as a nation. More together, in a curious way, more focused on one cause. England's not the same now. We're selfish, divided, consumed by money. Ideals were higher then. People didn't grizzle so much; the humour was great. Ever heard of Tommy Handley? It's a time I look back on with pleasure as well as horror.'

'Hmm,' went the computer doubtfully. 'I still don't equate happiness or pleasure with all those killings.'

'I think at that time we lived life to the full.'

'Yes, well....'

The computer didn't say anything more; he was obviously mystified.

'I have the feeling,' said the computer, 'that we modern, younger people – sorry, things – are being patronised.'

'You mean by those involved in the war.'

'Yes.'

'Possibly. That's why we don't like to talk about it very much.'

'Do you think England would come together again in the same way with another world war?'

'I would hope so. Provided we felt we were fighting something really evil.'

'Like Hitler?'

'Yes.'

'Tell me more about Miss March.'

I've never forgotten her, for the wrong reasons possibly.'

'Why? Because she was batty, or because she rescued Paul?'

'Both really, but also because she was the first woman whose fanny I saw.'

'What do you mean 'fanny'? I know Fanny was a woman's name in Victorian times. There's also a fan which women flutter to cool themselves down.'

'No, no. Fanny was her pussy. You know, surely.' The old man looked amused.

But the computer still remained flummoxed. 'The word's not in my dictionary.'

The old man smiled.

'It's the hair that covers a woman's genitals.'

'Oh!' The computer thought a moment. 'I don't know about such things.'

'Lucky you!'

'Why 'lucky'?'

'Well, sex is not always the happiest of experiences. It leads to much tension, misunderstanding and frustration, at least that's my conclusion after all these years. But, as I've once said, properly used it can lead to much happiness.'

'Oh? To read my web site I would have thought it was a religion in your civilisation, all pervading, everybody obsessed.'

'Possibly. It's what the Christians would call a false god, and one day the real God will arise in vengeful anger.'

The computer tried to assimilate this. 'I don't understand religion, or religious feelings. It's not part of our technology.'

'Hardly surprising.'

'Anyway, how come you saw this girl's – what's its name? – fanny?'

'Easy, really. In her room she had a big, bouncy, double bed. We used to romp on it, and have tickling matches. Away from my mother, Miss March could be quite fun. Once her skirt rode up, revealing her knickers. Quick as a flash I pulled them down. And there it was, much lighter than her normal hair.'

'Was she cross?'

'Not really. I think she was confused. Then she started asking me questions. Had I done this with anyone else? She seemed to think I was some sort of pervert. In the end she told me I must never do it again. It meant the end of our tickling sessions - sadly!'

The computer shook his head glumly. 'I really don't see what's so exciting about a fanny.'

'You would if you were a ten year old boy, particularly a boy who had no sister, instead of being a crummy old machine made of metal and plastic.'

The computer shook his head. 'I still don't understand. And, excuse me, I'm certainly not crummy, whatever that means.'

There was silence between them, the silence of minds, which didn't jell.

'who is this God you sometimes talk to?' The computer suddenly asked.

You wouldn't understand; you have no feelings, no soul.'

Oh, come off it! At least you can stop patronising me, and try to explain.'

Hmm,' went t the old man doubtfully. 'He is first of all supposed to be the creator of the world, even of you.'

'That's not true. Microsoft dreamed me up, and a right good job they made of me.'

'God would contest that. He made all the material that went into your make up. Above all he made man with the intelligence to put you together, make you work.'

'Ha,' went the computer. 'I seem to remember, before you took me over, working for a man who believed the world evolved, the animals, the use of materials, even man.'

'Yes, but who started that evolvement many thousands and thousands of years ago?'

'How should I know? It's nowhere in my files.'

'The Christians would argue it was God.'

'Yes, but what proof have you?'

The old man suddenly looked tired, and felt unable to continue the argument.

Look, old chap,' he said. 'I've a long day tomorrow. I'm going to shut you down and we'll continue the discussion another time.'

58

The computer started laughing, if a computer can laugh.

'You don't know, do you? Don't know! Don't know!' it cackled.

But the old man sighed and firmly closed him down. You can't argue with a computer; it's intelligence runs on tram lines!

*

CHAPTER 4

A child of our grandmother Eve, a female; or, for thy more
sweet understanding, a woman.

(William Shakespeare – 1564-1616)

'Hi, poppet,' went the old man. His voice was soft and loving, very different from the grumpy voice he used in his conversations with God or the computer.

'Hi, yourself.' Jemmi gave a wag of her tail, her way of giving a glorious morning smile. 'How're things?'

'All the better for seeing you.'

Jemmi waited patiently while the old man shaved, put on deodorant, powdered his feet, put on skin cream where necessary, and then got dressed. The old man was ashamed of his body, a pot belly, not very protuberant but enough for him to wish it could be otherwise, dry skin like parchment, hence the need for

cream. He had short,   stocky legs, and

knees sticking out prominently, including tiny blue veins on the inside of his knees. He used to be very proud of his knees. Front row forward knees, he called them. He'd played rugger in the front row for his school, oh, so many years ago.

'Why do you put on deodorant?' Jemmi asked. It was the sort of question a woman would ask.

'Oh, I don't know. Vanity I suppose.'

'You're not normally vain.'

'I think – I know – it's because old men begin to smell. My stepfather smelt, an old man's smell. But then he was of a generation that never showered as much as we do today. There weren't showers in any case. They didn't exist, except in the homes of the rich. You took a bath instead, washed   in your own dirty water.'

'I don't think you smell.'

'Oh, that is kind.'

'Do I smell?'

'You have a distinctive doggy smell, but it's not unpleasant. In fact I rather like it, except when you go paddling in muddy pools.'

'I do it to cool down. This hot weather doesn't suit me. I can't take off my coat like you humans.'

Jemmi waited at the top of the stairs until the old man had brushed his hair and was ready to go down. She stood with her front feet on the next step down, uncertain whether he would come. The old man had a disconcerting habit of starting to go down, then would remember something and would go back up again.

'Come on, please,' Jemmi said, 'I want my biscuits.'

She always said please; she never demanded. In turn the old man always apologised; he rarely did this to God or the computer.

'I'm sorry,' he said, remembering. 'I've forgotten the phone. Hang on a minute.'

He had one of those portable phones (not a mobile). The base was in his study. He had to remember to carry down the phone to save rushing upstairs when the phone rang. His wife loved the portable phone. She would even take it into the toilet and have long conversations with friends sitting on the throne. To the old man it seemed a little obscene!

Jemmi lolloped down the stairs behind the old man. She always stayed behind him in case he forgot something else. If he had, then she would climb back up again. Her stair descent was always characterised by a lollop. Her bottom would go up and down like dolphins going in and out of water. Not a very good comparison but you know what is meant. Her ascent was much swifter, a smooth rush. She followed the old man attentively everywhere, until she got her biscuits, a necessary part of the morning ritual. After that her loyalties would tend to wander, depending on who was due to take her out. She always knew who it was, whether his wife or him.

'Biscuits, please,' Jemmi said, once they were in the kitchen. She looked at him with those soft, pleading eyes. Dark brown they were. She looked like a seal in the part of her face which was black.

But that day the old man was in another of his abstract moods. He got out a small black case, which held his meter for taking his blood sugar. Jemmi sat patiently at his feet, while he pricked his finger to draw a small drop of blood. His fingers had been used for taking blood so often they had begun to form calluses he'd probably never get rid of. He was obsessed with his blood readings.

'Damn! Much too high,' muttered the old man. The reading was twelve point 5, twice as high, and not normal for the early morning. It should read about six point five, or lower. Something was definitely wrong. He couldn't possibly enjoy a substantial breakfast. It had been years since he last had egg, bacon, sausage, fried bread and all the trimmings. It was a joy he would probably never know again, more's the pity! He started to fiddle around, putting on his toast. He always got his own meagre breakfast. His wife usually came down earlier than he did, and prepared her own. Her main job was the coffee; she was much better at making it.

Meanwhile Jemmi stood eyeing him, her ears raised. At last the old man noticed.

'Oh, I'm sorry, sweetie. You want your biscuits.' He chided himself for being a forgetful, selfish old man.

He got out the packet from the cupboard, counted out six dry-looking biscuits moulded in various shapes, and put them in her bowl.

Jemmi waited until he was out of the way, and then advanced. She wasn't a greedy dog. She never rushed her food, but she did like to keep to her routine. There was something wonderfully feminine about the way she organised herself.

After breakfast, Jemmi put her front paws on her mistress' lap.

'Walk time,' she pleaded. She knew it was Missie's turn to take her out.

'Go, fetch your collar,' said Missie.

'Where is it?' she asked scurrying excitedly around.

'On the landing.' The old man pointed upstairs. It was left up there every night, again part of the ritual. But Jemmi always had to be told. Staffordshire bull terriers are not always that bright. It depended how much terrier they had in them – the more, the brighter.

It was when Jemmi came back from her walk that the conversation really began. She would settle down by the desk where the old man worked. She'd wash her feet dirty from the outing and then prepare for a good old feminine natter which she enjoyed, as did the old man.

'May I ask you a question, poppet – a rather difficult one?'

'I suppose so – as long as it's not too difficult.'

'What do you think of life?'

'Life! Cor! What a question!'

'I know. I'm sorry.'

'I don't! – think about life, I mean.'

'You must do. You're a part of life.'

'I know. But life for me is biscuits, a meal each day, a warm fire to toast my tummy, lots of stroking and brushing, two walks a day, and a kind master and missie. I *must* emphasise really *long* walks, not your tired short walks. Then I'm happy.'

'What if you don't get them?'

'Then I shall go crazy and bite every dog I meet, not just once, but time and time again.'

'That will be expensive! For me, I mean. Do you remember when you bit that awful lurcher. Cost me £80, it did'

'He deserved it, licking my bottom! He wouldn't leave me alone.'

'Oh, Jemmi, you were funny that day. You certainly told him where he got off.'

'I hope so.'

The old man was thoughtful for a moment.

'So – you're happy with simple things.'

'Of course.'

'Hmm. There's a lesson there somewhere for us humans.'

But Jemmi wasn't interested. Life's problems didn't worry her.

'What are you doing today?' she asked.

'I'm not sure. I try and sit quietly and let ideas come into my mind. They usually do after several minutes of day dreaming.'

'What dreams are you having?'

'Sadness! On the news today, the bodies of the two little Soham girls, Holly and Jessica, were found near some woods. The presenter said it so unhappily I thought she was going to burst into tears. It's the end of any hope they could still be alive. One's heart bleeds for their parents.

'I'm sorry.'

'Hmmm,' the old man looked dismally into the distance. Apart from the two little girls, the news mentioned a thirty-seven year old woman bludgeoned to death, and a six year old girl suffered attempted rape from an eighteen-year-old man.

'The papers and television seem full of these sick tragedies,' remarked the old man.

'It's life! Or should I say it's part of human nature?' Jemmi spoke a little sententiously.

The man wanted to retort – 'what the hell do you know about human nature?' He would have done, had it been God or that inanimate computer, but Jemmi was a different matter. One didn't swear or contradict so feminine a nature.

'It's not life, sweetie,' he said gently. 'It's an aberration of life!'

'What do you mean 'aberration'?'

'Life gone wrong.'

'Oh!'

'We sometimes say it's 'sick', like an illness, but it's a horrible form of mental illness.'

'Do dogs have it?'

'Dogs can be cruel as you well know. Your breed are known fighters – unjustifiably I sometimes think.'

'I love a fight.'

'I know you do. Like that lump you took out of that pesky lurcher.'

'You never told me it cost you so much money!'

'No, I'm sorry. I didn't want to upset you.'

'I'm upset now.'

'Please don't, poppet. My intentions were good.'

'I don't know why you paid the vet bills. That lurcher was a real pain, always sniffing my behind. It was disgusting.'

'It's a long story.'

'Tell me.'

'Well, I didn't want to upset its master. He'd been kind to my wife and I.'

'I never felt he was kind. He was as bad as his dog.'

'Like master, like dog,' mused the old man.

'What do you mean?'

'It's a saying we have that a dog becomes like his master, or vice versa.'

'So, I'm like you.'

'Not exactly. You have two masters or rather a master and a mistress. But I like to feel that I have some little good in me that I have passed on to you. Apart from lurchers you have a very sweet nature. You have all the understanding of a woman.'

'Thank you.' Her tail began to wag in appreciation.

'Be my guest. We have another saying – like father, like son – which I always felt as a teacher was true. Behind every difficult child was a bloody difficult parent.'

'You're swearing again. Didn't Missie tell you not to swear?'

'I like to swear. Most language is pretty anaemic. Swear words in phonetic terms are plosives, that is they are made by an explosion of breath. 'f' in 'fuck' is made by an accumulation of breath behind the upper teeth and the lower lip, and then ploded out. It's very effective.'

'I don't like the word 'fuck'. As Missie says it's not very nice.'

'I'm sorry.'

'Anyway, what are all your meditations leading up to?'

'I'd like to write a crime story. I've never really succeeded. I wrote a novel about a paedophile ring, but as always with my books the ending was all wrong. It needs quite considerable revision.

'Well, I'll sit quietly, and listen to your crime story.'

'Right.'

The old man bent over his computer and began to tap away. He gave the story the title – 'SHE KNEW'.

SHE KNEW
Fanatics have their dreams, wherewith they weave

A paradise for a sect.

(John Keats – 1795-1821)

Chris Roberts lay on his bed in the foetal position, shattered by grief. It was early morning. The summer sun was shafting through the gap in the curtains, the beams confused with floating dust.

Yesterday Liz had gone! They had only been married six days. They were on their honeymoon, in Bridmouth, a sea-side resort on the south coast.

Slowly he raised himself from the bed. Some of Liz's clothes were still in her two suitcases. She had not bothered to unpack. Others were tossed carelessly on a chair. He didn`t know what to do about them. They were new and expensive, everything paid for her by him. She had been delighted with shopping before the wedding. On the dressing table she had left her engagement ring, her pride and joy. It had cost a bomb.

Should he ring the police, report her absence? He heard the police were not all that interested in domestic tiffs, unless foul play was suspected. His mind went over the events of the past few days. The combination of the emotions of the wedding, frustrated travel when the car broke down, and their first honeymoon night of love, everything had reduced them to a frazzle.

Then, yesterday morning, sunning themselves in the deckchairs on the lawn, she told him she`d had a baby, at sixteen! She gave it up for adoption. It wasn`t so much the baby that upset him, but the casual way she informed him as if it were a joke. Worse still she had never told him until they were safely married. That hurt! He`d tried to be so honest with her about his *own* past. They`d quarrelled. What he said to her about complete frankness had come out all wrong. That was the end. She walked out in anger. Since then he`d not seen her.

It was over twenty-one hours ago.

He decided to ring the police.

Over the phone he became upset and explained matters badly. They said they would send someone round, but he was afraid of the publicity in a hotel, and opted to go to them.

He told his story to two police constables, a man and a woman. He didn't understand why *two* had to interview him. He told them of the quarrel and of Liz's temper. It all seemed so trite in the telling. The woman constable was understanding. She was pretty, fair hair glistening with health, her skin not yet marked by the rigours of life. She looked him in the eye.

'Why did you quarrel?' she asked.

He told her about the baby.

'That's surely in the past?' she exclaimed, Then she realised her mistake. 'I'm sorry. It's not for me to comment.'

She asked some more questions.

'What were you doing during the time Liz had gone?'

'Not much. I was afraid to leave the hotel in case she came back. I wanted to make it up to her. I watched TV mostly.'

Then he remembered.

'For a moment I slipped out to the church opposite. I wanted to pray.'

The policewoman nodded as if it was a normal thing to do.

'I'm a Christian, you see. Born again. Prayer means a lot to me.'

Again she nodded.

'Can you describe your wife to us again?'

'Dark-haired, small, about five two. She was wearing jeans and a light blue T shirt, blue and white trainers. She liked wearing trainers, but they made her feet smell.'

He laughed awkwardly at his attempt at levity. Neither of his questioners smiled. There was a sudden deadly seriousness about them.

'I'm afraid we have to tell you,' spoke the W.P.C., 'that a woman answering your wife's description was found at the foot of the cliffs near Tretton Point. It looks as though she had fallen. I`m afraid She`s dead.'

'Oh no!'

He buried his face in his hands and cried, heart-breaking sobs. His interviewers sat silently until he recovered. There was something menacing about them, with their grave faces and dark blue uniforms. Unanswered questions swirled through his mind? Would they blame him? Or would they think it was suicide? He felt a rising panic. Despite the strength of his Christian faith he was full of uncertainty.

The policeman's voice came from a distance, breaking into his thoughts.

'We would like you to accompany us, to identify the body.'

He stared at them stupidly. What were they asking? He managed to get up. He was dreading this part, afraid of seeing Liz dead. He knew he would break down again.

He was taken by police car to the mortuary. Liz looked white-faced and peaceful. He would have liked to have knelt down and said a prayer over her, but didn`t because of the others present. His prayer was silent. There was something disembodied about her, as if she was no longer the demanding girl he`d known.

'Is this your wife?' asked the policewoman.

He nodded dumbly.

They took him back to the police station, to the same interview room. This time an older man in a crumpled blue suit, a detective chief inspector, asked the questions. The young policewoman was sitting next to him, her male partner perched on a chair by the door.

Chris realised matters now were serious. It was they who suspected him of pushing her over the cliff. He`d once heard over ninety per cent of murders were committed by members of the family. The older man had gimlet eyes and didn`t smile. The woman constable looked kindly at him, inviting confidences.

'Tell me more about this quarrel?' asked the chief inspector.

Chris repeated the story about the baby.

'I don`t believe it! You quarrelled because she had a baby a few years before she met you, and never told you!' The inspector shook his head in incredulity.

Chris tried to explain about the purity of the soul, being completely open with one another. But he didn`t explain himself very well.

'You mean,' sneered the inspector, 'you killed her because she didn`t come up to your own high standards?'

At last it was out, the accusation of killing Liz. He knew it would come. He was prepared. He vehemently denied it.

'Of course I bloody didn't. Why would I kill the woman I'd just married?'

They kept going over the same ground – the quarrel that they found inexplicable; why he took so long to report her absence; even questioning his religious beliefs.

'You're a holy nutter,' the senior policeman stated at one point, as if such a man was beneath contempt.

'How dare you call me a nutter? How dare you question my faith?' Chris was shaking with anger. He'd always been touchy about his faith.

The inspector seemed pleased he'd produced so strong a reaction.

'Apart from the quarrel, how did you get on with your wife – in general?' the policewoman asked with a kindly smile.

'Very well.'

'So, your only disagreement was over the baby?'

He nodded.

How could he explain that, from loving Liz, he grew to hate her, almost from the first day of their honeymoon? She'd grizzled when the car broke down, even continued grizzling after it was repaired; it wasted so much time. In the hotel she complained constantly. The hotel was not what she expected, the food was poor, their room too small. By the third or fourth day he'd had enough. He couldn't believe a woman could change so quickly, from someone loving to an unhappy whinger. The crowning straw was, not so much the baby, but when she refused to kneel by the bed to say their prayers. They had prayed together before their marriage, gone to church every Sunday holding hands. She had professed to being a born again Christian, smiling at him through lowered eyelids. She'd rarely looked him directly in the eye.

On their fourth day at the hotel, Liz had said, sneering at him:

'You don't think I believe all that church stuff!'

Stuff! Stuff! His faith was just stuff! He couldn't believe it.

'Do you know?' remarked the young policewoman, still with that understanding look. 'You've never once said you loved her. You talked about getting on well, that sort of thing, but never, never *love*.'

There was perception in those eyes. No lowered eyes, no loss of eye contact as with Liz. No virulent, spiteful taunting. Just complete honesty and straightforward speech. How he wished now he'd met and married a girl like her!

She *knew*, he thought, she *knew!*

'You killed her,' she stated simply.

He was still. He put his hands together in prayer.

'No, I did *not* kill her.' He spoke slowly and clearly.

His eyes confronted directly the policewoman.

They couldn't prove it. It had been late evening and dark. Nobody saw them on the cliffs. Nobody saw him leave the hotel by the rear entrance. Nobody saw him follow her. Nobody saw the fatal push. The only possible conclusion – it was suicide.

The world was rid of so evil a woman – a liar and a cheat, without love for anyone but herself. She hadn't even loved her baby – just given it away without a thought. She'd certainly never loved him. Just inveigled him into marriage because it offered better prospects; he had a good job, a fair amount of money saved.

He'd done God's work. Hallelujah! He was the chosen instrument of God. His crime was justified.

Hallelujah! Hallelujah!

Praise be to God.

*

73

'I don't like that story,' commented Jemmi.

'Why?'

'I just don't.'

'Try and explain, poppet.'

'Well, to use your expression, that man was sick.'

'I agree.'

'Secondly, not once do you try and present the woman's point of view.'

'What do you mean?'

'It's very derogatory of the woman.'

'It had to be, to justify the killing.'

'I don't agree. Isn't it possible she could have found out the day after her wedding she was married to a nutter, as the inspector called him? And said so in no uncertain terms?'

'Humph!' went the old man, unsettled by this unexpected criticism.

'The man seems stupid,' continued Jemmi relentlessly. 'He chooses a poor hotel and a faulty car for the most important occasion of his life, his marriage. He was a religious fanatic. Though religion is not part of our animal world - thank goodness! - What an idiot to ram religion down the poor girl's throat.'

'Trust a woman to stick up for a woman.'

'Well, you men rarely try and look at things from a woman's point of view.'

'True! True!'

'Your story is one-sided, lacks depth of character.'

The old man nodded.

'You don't really like women, do you?' continued Jemmi, her head to one side, assessing him.

'Where on earth do you get that idea?'

'Things!' Jemmi resorted to feminine secrecy, something that always angered the old man.

'What do you mean by 'things'?'

'Just 'things'!'

The old man raised his eyes to heaven. He couldn't be angry with little Jemmi, but he felt exasperated.

'Go on. Please tell me,' he finally said. 'Give me an insight into your feminine intuition, your realisation of my character.'

'Well, you've often said you never loved your mother.'

'How could I? She never cared for me!'

'Oh, I expect she did in her own way.'

'She was a snob. She worried and worried, and never stopped worrying all her life. All her worry was centered on herself.'

'She had a hard time of it, as you well know.'

'No more than anyone else. Anyway, how do you know?'

'You've said so. You've sat in your chair going over and over your life with your mother, trying to make sense of it. I've just sat at your feet and listened. But I've tried to understand. You were certainly miserable enough.'

'I loved my mother – deep down anyway – despite everything.'

'Oh, yeah?'

'Oh, this is intolerable.'

The old man wanted at that point to switch his mind off from his imagined conversation with his dog. It surprised him he could put perceptive words into the mouth of Jemmi (in his imagination). This disturbed him.

But perhaps alone with his imagined thoughts he really did get at the truth.

'Yes, Jemmi, you're right,' he finally admitted. 'We were never close. She was never there when I needed her. I couldn't trust her. She had this habit of doing things in secret, never telling you, and that used to anger me. She was possessive. She hated my girl friends, was never nice to them. She tried to destroy my intended marriage.'

'How come?'

'Well, when I was engaged to my wife, mother went round to my future mother-in-law and said a whole lot of bad things about my family and about me.'

'Such as?'

'That my father stole money, that he had a mistress, that he never really put his heart into banking, that all he was interested in was playing golf, how in the First World War he was a military policeman, the most unpopular of soldiers, and so on and so forth. None of them were true, according to my brother. Well, the golf maybe! Then she went on to other members of the family. How dad's father, my grandfather, had seven children, nearly killed his wife by child bearing. How my mother's own father was so ineffectual, his business was a failure. My mother hated her father...'

'Ha ha,' interrupted Jemmie, nodding her head. 'That explains everything.'

'Explains what?'

'How you never got on with your mother. She disliked you as a boy and a man, just as she disliked her father and her husband. Tell me, how do you get on with your daughter.'

'Badly!'

'There you are, you see. You disliked your mother. It carried over to your daughter. Just as your mother disliked you because she never got on with her father.'

'Oh, rubbish. I've had enough of this psychological claptrap.'

'You've never disliked me, and I'm a woman,' said Jemmi archly.

'Oh, Jemmikins, I'm sorry. My past is all so miserable!'

'No more than anyone else's. You get far too sorry for yourself. It doesn't do you a scrap of good.'

'I know. I know. But I just can't get away from it at times - my past, I mean.'

'Tell me a happy memory of your mother.'

'Well, the best time for a while was after my father died. She was softer, more thoughtful. She used to play the organ at the local church. I wrote a poem about it not so long ago. It's a miserable....'

'Don't say it!'

'Say what?'

'That ot's a miserable, poor sort of poem. It's what you always say. And I wish you didn't. I kike your writings when you read them to me, even if nobody else does, as you point out.'

'Thanks.'

'Be my guest!'

The old man stopped to reflect.

'You know,' he said finally, I sometimes fear I'm becoming schizophrenic.'

What's schiz...schizo...?

'Well, according to the Oxford English dictionary, the Bible of Countdown, Channel 4's word programme... Ha, here it is – "a mental disease, marked by a breakdown in the relation between thoughts, feeling and actions, frequently accompanied by delusions and retreat from social life." There you are. That's me to a T.'

'Nonsense,' Jemmi said abruptly. 'You've got a perfectly healthy mind, even though you forget sometimes. You're just finding it difficult to adjust to retirement. Though your hearing and now lack of sight don't help.'

There was silence for a moment, the silence of one mind.

'Anyway, let me give you,' the old man continues with a trace of irony, 'my *wonderful, exquisite, de-elightful poem* which I am sure you will enjoy.'

That's better. You've got the message.'

*

A Rhapsody In Blue.

Love still has something of the sea

From whence his mother rose.

Blue coat, blue hat, blue veil,

All in blue, dressed my dear

Sad, lonely mum. Blue skirt,

Blue shoes, blue cardigan –

Except stockings, white blouse -

A rhapsody in blue!

I loved her dressed – in blue!'

'Navy blue, sailor true,'

She quotes with wink and smile.

'Dad liked blue,' she once said,

'Before he went to war

To die, and be no more.

Blue went with widowhood,

Not black, not sombre grey,

Always attractive blue.

Dad would have wished it so.'

Four widow proposals

My lovely mother had.

Finally she married,

Six years later – in blue!

She played the church organ

Ev'ry Sunday – in blue

Throughout a dreary War.

To church she walked in best

  Blue suit. In organ loft

She changed to old skirt – blue! –

With worn, shiny bottom,

Jigging as she did on

Hard, wooden seat. Shoes, too,

Were changed, scuffed blue, flat heels.

'No one sees me, up here

So high, except my head,'

She laughs and winks again.

She carries home blue skirt,

Scuffed blue shoes in bag – blue!

So dear a memory

Of my sweet mum – in blue –

Never shall I forget

As years roll to old age.

*

 'I like that.'

'It was a poor poem.'

'Oh, stop it, stop it. You're always deriding what you write.'

'I can't help it.'

'Well, it's about time you stopped. You write well when you put your mind to it.'

'Age doesn't make one any the wiser.'

'Well, it should! Particularly in your case.'

'Why me?'

'Because your negative pessimism will drive you into an early grave. It would be a shame because you still have much to offer.'

'That's a deep thought – for a dog!'

'Now, now, don't belittle us dogs.'

'I'm sorry.'

'And don't keep apologising. It's so wimpish.'

'Oh, really?'

'Yes, really.'

The old man mused for a moment. 'It's not nice being old. Your body deteriorates bit by bit. No hope it will get better. Downhill all the bloody way.'

'It's the same for everyone.'

'That's no comfort.'

'You have to be a man about it.'

The old man thought for a moment.

'I think we'll bring this conversation to an end. It's getting too uncomfortably close to the truth.'

'Your conversation, you mean.'

'Yes, in an insane sort of way, your words are my words.' The old man stopped to think.

There's one thing I really ought to say about the crime story I told you. It's religious fanaticism. It's saddened history. You don't know about the Spanish Jesuits in the past. Now you have the Muslim extremists, leading to terrorism. There many other examples – killing, bombing of innocent citizens. It's a wonder God allows it, if he is truly loving!'

But Jessie had lost interest. Her little rump was disappearing through the door; she could hear her missie downstairs.

*

CHAPTER 5
A RIGHTEOUS CAUSE.

The humblest citizen of all the land, when clad in the armor

of a righteous cause, is stronger than all the hosts of error.

(William Jennings Bryan – 1860-1925)

'Now listen, my friend…' God said.

The old man, intent on his toy, the computer, was not paying attention.

'I said 'Listen',' God emphasised. *'Listen.'*

The old man sighed, took his hands away from the keyboard.

'I'm listening,'

'If we are to have another of our conversations, will you promise me there'll be no more remorse, no more whingeing, no more miseries, no more anger or swearing?'

The old man sat thinking for a moment.

'I'll try, but it's not pleasant being old.'

'There you are, whingeing again!

'I am sorry, God, but I have difficulty finding meaning in life. I wrote a poem touching on this subject. Not a very good poem, but it was near my heart.'

There you go again, belittling your work.'

'You sound just like Jemmi in your comments on my attitude.'

'Isn't that inevitable? If you are conversing with God, your computer, and Jemmi, aren't all their thoughts coming through and from you?'

'I hope not. I try and give them different characteristics. You, God, are on the whole benevolent, the Computer is irascible and not always totally comprehended by me, and Jemmi is a lovely, loving and thoughtful dog who can surprise me at times. I try to make her feminine, which she is.'

'Hmm,' says God. 'I suppose there must be a difference between an understanding God', an inanimate computer, and the restricted intelligence of a dog.'

'You flatter yourself. Are you all that understanding when you have caused so much misery in the world you are supposed to have created.' The old man was in belligerent mood. 'And don't belittle the intelligence of dogs. They are wonderful companions when properly loved. Their loyalty is unbounded.'

'Hmm,' muttered God again. He paused for a moment and then said. 'Let's hear this poem of yours that you seem to hold so dear.'

'Right. Here goes.'

LONELY AGE.

Sad, alone, bemused by uncertain thought,

  Sound Indistinct, life seems an empty shell,

No meaning, reason, nor comfort in faith.

Children gone, life now their own, far from home.

I need them; sad, no more do they need me!

Flesh of my flesh, happy and confident,

What int'rest have they in redundant age?

My desire for woman, to touch soft breast,

To kiss sweet lips, to share her vibrant warmth,

All is now no more! What woman can want

Stomach fat, hair turned grey, and vigour gone?

I feel a discarded wreck, forgotten,

In an age intended for youth alone.

There is no real sense, awaiting my death.

And yet there is a battle to be won.

I have enough... money, home, all I need.

Yet still I long to touch the beauty of
    This great life that so nurtures me. But how?

There is a deep wish for fulfilment, love,

That I may die in peace, if peace there be.

'Hmm,' went God per usual, 'You seem to be speaking with some feeling.'

'I try'.

'You face the problem of most old people, that is to find meaning in your last few years. But why worry. Be happy. Enjoy your closing time. Don't agonise over the miseries of the world, and my status as your God. In the years to come you will soon know the truth.

'That's all very well, dear God. But I believe I shall just die and be food for the worms. I hope they find me tasty.

'Hmm,' God said and smiled. 'Can we change the subject to one less oppressive?'

'Well, I have another story for you, one that I quite like.

'That's better.'

'But it's one that never succeeded, never won a prize. You probably won't like it.'

God sighed. 'In that case, I'm sorry, but I don't want to hear it, certainly not if you belittle it.'

The two men glared at each other, that is, if it's possible to glare at oneself.

'Why?' asked the old man. 'Why this sudden restriction?'

'Because ... because I'm tired of these conversations, constantly going over a morbid past. You described one of your characters in one of your stories as an 'old misery-guts'. Well, that's *you*, you to a T, and I've had enough.'

'Oh!'

'Yes, oh! Oh, oh and oh again.'

'You've changed.'

'No, I haven't. It's *you* who have changed. I'm only your doppelganger.'

'What's a 'doppelganger', for goodness sake?'

'You should know. You're the writer, or pretend to be.'

'I resent that ' pretend to be'.

'You haven't had much success.'

'True, true, but it'll come.'

'At your age?'

'I refuse to give in to age.'

'Well, that's an encouraging, positive sign. Anyway, back to 'doppelganger'. It's a German word meaning the double of a living person. I'm you, in mind at least.'

'I seem to remember this was a word used in the War. Both Churchill and Montgomery had doppelgangers for security reasons. Also to mislead the enemy.'

For a moment God didn't reply. Finally he said:

'Well, do you agree?

'Agree to what?'

For a moment God looked as if he could be really angry. 'You tell me that I can be obtuse at times, but you – *you* – are the limit! You don't even listen to me.'

'I concentrate on my friend, the computer.'

'He's only an inanimate object.'

'Not to me he isn't.'

'I .. asked ..' God said the words slowly and carefully, 'if .. you .. would .. agree .. that our conversation today is .. positive .. and .. not .. I repeat *not* .. a morbid indulgence in the past, or a belittling of your good self.'

'God, you have changed!'

'In what way?'

'Well, you're more aggressive, more dominating – sorry, *domineering.*'

'Be that as it may, I don't want any more navel-gazing from you, my friend.'

'I couldn't agree more.'

'You couldn't? I *am* surprised.'

'Well .. I feel I don't have many more years left. I might as well spend them in as useful a way as I can.'

'Amen to that.'

The old man tapped on his computer for a few moments.

'What we need is a *cause,* something we can fight for,' the old man continued. 'They say the pen is pretty powerful. I'd like to tell a story that dwells on some social problem. And then, to go from the sublime to the ridiculous, another story that is a bit naughty. I want to shock you, God, to your very boots! But I may have to do it in the next chapter – shock, I mean'

'I don't have boots. I'm a mind only. Remember?'

'I was speaking metaphorically.'

'Anyway, what is your cause?'

'Racism!'

'Racism?'

'Yes, racism.'

'A dangerous subject.'

'Not necessarily. I feel the influx of different ethnic cultures will ultimately benefit England.'

'Wow! Not many pure English people would agree with that.'

'Possibly. But take the Afro-Caribbean immigration. It has done immense good, both in sport and in music. They are men and women of such tremendous physical fitness. Moreover, in other ways, they are gifted and very *human*, full of life and humour. Listen to my story.'

*

BLACK IS BEAUTIFUL

We hold these truths to be sacred and undeniable; that ALL MEN ARE CREATED EQUAL AND INDEPENDENT; that from that equal creation they derive rights inherent and inalienable, among which are the preservation of life, and liberty, and THE PURSUIT OF HAPPINESS. (The upper case letters are the author's, not the original).

(Thomas Jefferson – 1743–1826 – Original draft for the Declaration of Independence.)

Blondel was Afro-Caribbean – well, not quite. Probably in the past there had been a strain of white from a mixed marriage. I first saw her on a wild, windy and cold November evening. I was holding auditions for the opera 'Carmen'. She just stood on the stage, and gracefully took off her warm winter coat. Somebody whistled, a male wolf whistle. She fully deserved the appreciation.

The Brandeston (the London suburb where I lived) amateur operatic society, B.A.O.S., had decided to put on Bizet's famous opera. God knows why! Carmen was an opera of passion, of youth, of wild excitement, hardly suited to a staid, middle class, middle-aged operatic society.

They wanted Rosie to be Carmen. My God, Rosie of all people! She was thirty-eight, plumpish, dyed auburn hair, very Anglo-Saxon. Don't get me wrong. I like Rosie. She's great fun in a healthy English way, with a pleasant singing voice. But as a volatile Latin – over my dead body! Besides her acting capabilities were very limited.

I was in despair.

I hadn't wanted to direct Carmen in the first place, but I was only one vote on a committee of six. They said they wanted to expand their horizon, do something more ambitious than just good old Gilbert and Sullivan. What was wrong with the old dears, I asked; it's great music and the acting is well within our scope.   They were, however, frankly bored with these two Victorian gentlemen. When I pointed out we didn't really have the skills, particularly for the role of Carmen herself, they got a bit huffy, looked down their noses at me. They finally said they just wanted to do it because they loved the music. Mind you, even that was a bit ambitious, but Old Bones – Er, Mr. Bonarch to you, musical director – thought it would be O.K. Like most music societies our choral singing wasn't bad. But to ignore the acting, ignore the character of Carmen would be fatal. I was the poor bloke who, as director, would take all the flack if we failed.

But then, almost in answer to a prayer, on the night of the audition, along came Blondel, this attractive, coloured girl. She was great! I could have hugged her out of sheer relief! She could both act – and sing! Mind you she wasn't a Lesley Garrett – who could ever be? But there was something about her voice, which came over very forcibly, and in a husky, sexy way. Old Bones thought she had very real possibilities.

How can I describe Blondel? She had this coffee-coloured skin, full red lips, not pouty like Bridget Bardot, just lusciously rounded and kissable. She was slim, not scarecrow slim like a neurotic anorexic – her hips were too shapely for that. Fantastic long legs. And how she could move, how she could dance! She floated along with such seeming grace! I couldn't for the life of me understand why a girl with such loveliness was not on the catwalks of fashion, or an actress, or in ballet. But no! She was a student, only twenty, at the local university, formerly a Poly, studying for a degree in law, and doing the usual student amateur dramatics. And my goodness she was bright – intelligent, I mean. The student population these days is so crassly average. Why, I couldn't help grumbling in my despairing middle age, is it that some people have all the luck going – beauty, health, grace, brains, and to crown it all a charming personality?

When I told the committee I wanted Blondel for Carmen there was an immediate uproar. For a start she wasn't a member of the society. I countered that by reminding them we had decided to audition publicly to attract new members. If it came to it, I was quite prepared to pay there and then Blondel's membership fee.

Then they insisted yet again they wanted Rosie for Carmen. Damn Rosie, I said, intending to shock, she's a cow! I was quite rude.

The dragon, Mrs. Arbroath, a full-breasted contralto wearing her dated pearls, which betrayed her age, said bluntly that Blondel was black.

Immediately there was as a deathly hush!

The members of the committee had the decency to realise they were on dangerous racial grounds.

'So what?' I queried bluntly. 'I'm white. Does that exclude me?'

Then I went on to explain there was dark, Moorish, African blood in a lot of Spanish people. I argued that Blondel *looked* the part.

We took a vote.

Three for Blondel. Three for Rosie.

'We owe it to Rosie,' honked the dragon through her superior nose, trying to pierce me with her glittering eye. 'She's been a loyal member of the society for some eight years.'

'So what?' I replied, still unequivocally rude. I hated the dragon, and she me, I imagine. We'd crossed swords on many an occasion. 'We owe..' I spoke ponderously, trying to mimic the dragon, '.. an unquestioning loyalty to the artistic concept of   Carmen!"

High-faluting rubbish, but my goodness I was worked up!

After a few more moments of discussion one of my supporters weakened, the elderly Twitters – Mr. Twyford to you - a 74-year-old retired civil servant who fancied himself as an actor of bit parts, and as a lady's man. The trouble was, like most of us, including myself, he was fond of Rosie as a very human and pleasant woman. That made 4-2 against Blondel (Old Bones , now my only fervent supporter, and myself).

I'd lost!

The dragon looked triumphant, beady eyes glittering, large bosom heaving.

'I resign,' I said firmly, not without a trace of relief. This nonsensical idea of Carmen would be behind me.

I rose and gathered up my bits of paper to leave the room in as dramatic a manner as my short, paunchy frame could manage.

'Coward,' muttered the dragon, with a gleam of malice.

The rest of the Committee were concerned. The trouble was I was a hack – an unimportant B.B.C. director. I'd only joined the operatic society because my wife believed firmly in local community involvement, however trying and demanding. A director of some experience, however bad, who gave up some of his spare time, however reluctantly, added some kudos to the dramatic society. They didn't want to lose me.

I'm afraid I'm a bully, an utterly shameless bully, getting my way by threats. It's something you learn at the Beeb. If you don't bully, stand upright, then you're lost; you might as well leave Aunty.

I wasn't going to give up on Blondel!

One could well ask why I ever joined an amateur society. Well, to be fair, there were not only my wife's threats (She was an even bigger bully; it takes a bully to deal with a bully, as we well know in international politics), but there was a kind of fascinating challenge out of changing housewives and bank managers into something that was alive and credible. For once they are transported to a different world, a world of dreams and fantasy. Good for the soul!

'It's Blondel or nothing,' I stated emphatically.

I sensed there was nobody else in the society who would take on directing so demanding an opera as Carmen.

I surprised myself! Here was I putting my faith in a twenty-year-old, untried, coloured student whom I'd only seen once – that very evening in fact. But, you know, you have a certain instinct, something you acquire over the years. I just had a simple picture of Blondel singing that lovely song – L'Amour est un oiseau rebelle. – (Love is a rebellious bird), swaying to the music, oh, so enticingly.

The vote then went dramatically , 5-1, in my favour, one woman clinching it by saying (was there a trace of sarcasm?) with all my experience I ought to know what I was talking about. Only the dragon had voted against. I could see her thinking venomous thoughts – that rotten bully had won again!

But, really I hadn't won.

Art had won! If one could believe such pretentious rubbish!

The trouble was I'd made an even worse enemy of the Dragon. It's highly dangerous in life to thwart a woman which is maybe why I don't get on too well in the Beeb. Middle management in the B.B.C. is very female dominated. I get on well with men, which may say a lot about my limited character.

'I insist,' honked the Dragon, 'that Rosie is rehearsed as stand-in for Carmen.'

So!

Take a little, give a little! I had foisted on me both Blondel and Rosie, such extraordinary likeable but different personalities. Rosie, to do her justice, admitted Blondel was more the part. Rosie just learnt the songs, rehearsed the movements but left the passion to Blondel. I compensated Rosie by giving her the part of Micaela, whose love Jose stupidly rejected. The part was tailor-made for Rosie.

Blondel, Blondel, oh wonder, oh joy! She learnt so quickly. She *wanted* to learn. She was flirtatious, seductive. With her long black hair swept to one side, a red rose attached, she looked every bit dark Spanish. One could just imagine her rolling cigars on those lovely thighs. Not that I ever asked her on stage (My mistake!). Moreover she had the Spanish movement, the taut body, the swish of the skirt, the stamping of the feet. But, her eyes! My, her eyes! She rolled them enticingly at poor Jose and the silly man just looked embarrassed.

I'd chosen as Jose a Placido Domingo look-alike, a farmer called Mick Stacey, stolid, solid, not aware of what love was until Blondel, in the guise of Carmen, tried unsuccessfully to wake his earthy heartstrings. From then on he ought to have been doomed. The tragedy of Carmen was not yet inevitable.

There was one teeny-weeny problem about my production of Carmen as rehearsals progressed. I have already hinted on the problem. Blondel and Mick didn't jell. It was more Mick's fault. He was so wooden. He couldn't act with Spanish passion. He found it uncomfortable to be alongside so attractive a girl. When he had to kiss Blondel he was as shy as a ... Oh, I don't know what. He was more like a timid girl than a red-blooded man.

Poor Blondel! Poor Mick! It was difficult for them! And to be taught too by a middle-aged bore like myself! But they managed it at first in a way that was just passable. Blondel got away with it for three reasons. One, she was innately feminine, and all women have this capacity to be flirtatious. Two, she was *so* attractive, but I've already dwelt on that! Three, she had in no small measure the Afro-Caribbean spirituality, that emotion of the soul, so much better developed in African people who have suffered, than smug, self-satisfied whites!

Her feelings were strong. And she showed it on stage.

But she deserved a better actor than Mick. *His* only saving grace was a powerful singing voice.

I suppose I was the only one who could see the problem. Others, particularly the men, were full of praise. It was, of course, Blondel that fascinated them.

'God, you're right, you old so-and-so,' the men told me.

But – and it was a big but – her body didn't melt in the way a lover should. I'm sure you know what I mean. She was not *in* love. She didn't yet know what love meant. She went through the movements of love, but it wasn't *awakened* love!

She was so wonderfully young!

'Make friends with her, get to know her as a person, take her out to a candle-lit dinner,' I pleaded with Mick.

'Me?' he cried, appalled, all agricultural unimaginativeness.

I always thought young male farmers were like bulls, but in Mick's case I was probably wrong.

Mick was a 'nice' man. *That* was all that could be said about his character.

Sorry to use that dreadful word 'nice', but it described him so perfectly, at least at first.

'But she's black!' he protested, all fair-haired Anglo-Saxon, middle class, hidebound, inhibited white.

'So what? When will we ever learn,' I shouted, raising my eyes to heaven, 'that black, or yellow for that matter, is as lovely as white?'

I paused a moment, and then continued softly:

'She's a woman, Mick, and lovely at that. Be nice to her, tell her how wonderful she looks. Make her laugh. You're attracted by her. Take her out for a romantic evening.'

Mick had the grace to blush.

'I couldn't,' he pleaded. 'She'd never go. She's different.'

'So what?' I cried yet again. I was known as Mr. So-What. 'In the play, Carmen is your lover. Go on, make friends, chat her up. You won't regret it. The greatest experience of your life.'

But Mick just looked offended. He was also married, and his wife was in the chorus!

Later that evening of rehearsal, I said quietly to Blondel:

'If you want, if you really want, to give a breath-taking performance of Carmen, make eyes at Mick. You'll understand each other so much better. He's as wooden as an old barn door.'

Blondel rolled her eyes at me, gave that merry, tinkling laugh.

'He's so boring. He follows me around with those Spaniel eyes. When we embrace on stage, he's embarrassed and blushes, holds me at a distance.'

'I know,' I smiled. 'It would do him a lot of good if you could really get to know him, make him relax a little, have a cuddle together, entice him in life as you do on stage.'

Blondel, like Mick, looked horrified. I knew it would never happen, one of the problems of amateur performances; you can go so far but not far enough. For the realisation of a Carmen dream, it was an impossible situation. The performance on the night would never be memorably alive.

I swore, really swore!

I badly wanted the opera to succeed.

Bloody hell, it was *going* to succeed!

As with so much of the work I do, I try to put my heart and soul into the production. Besides I love Carmen, the opera, I mean. It's a fantastic work. I can never understand how a Frenchman could have written something so intrinsically and wonderfully Spanish. The finale is a bit tedious as it sometimes is in opera – all that agonising, screeching and quarrelling, leading to dramatic death. You know the silly girl is going to die. Get on with killing her! But the early love bits, backed by the music, the jealousy, and the sheer male authority of the toreador, are truly memorable.

It's my policy to have a fancy dress bonding party two weekends *before* the performance, at my invitation. We still have the traditional party when the play is over. But to my mind the bonding party is far more important. We make a fetish of playing silly games, loosening up with wine, and generally letting our hair down. Everybody comes as a character in the play other than their own. The Dragon, believe it or not, turned up as Carmen, instead of the hostess in the bistro. There's life in the old girl yet, I couldn't help thinking. She made quite a passable Carmen in a black wig, long red dress, and a red rose in her hair, despite her big bosom and wide hips. Mick came as the toreador and looked quite handsome. Blondel came as Micaela. They all tried to sing each other's song, Old Bones on the piano. Everybody would join in. It was hilarious seeing the Dragon trying to get the substitute Jose (Toreador in the play) to undo her bonds, while she sang 'And the Dance with my Lover I'll share'. I always felt this party relaxed people, and the opera became fun.

But ... but ... there was no sign of Mick and Blondel getting together, not one itsy-bitsy kiss. Mick seemed to find safety with Rosie despite the fact she was married with two lovely little girls. Blondel was monopolised by the Twitters for a time. He was dressed as a second toreador and quite fancied himself. He was all over her, touching her, smiling at her, gnashing his gruesome dentures. Blondel eventually escaped by going to the loo, and slipping back surreptitiously only seconds later to find refuge with some of the chorus girls, who were sympathetically protective (They knew the problem!).

We were all in great spirits at the party, but in the days to follow we were tense and anxious. The dress rehearsal was on the Monday a fortnight later, then a gap of one day to iron out any faults, finally four evening performances – Wednesday to Saturday.

The dress rehearsal was all right, I suppose, as dress rehearsals go. A few technical hitches, forgetting of the occasional lines, generally a nervous time. I'd have to kick ass, as the Americans say.

Then came the first performance!

I don't know what was up as we got ready, but the whole cast that Wednesday evening were giggly, especially the girls. The men smirked.

It was as if they knew something I didn't know!

I went around asking everybody what was wrong, but nobody would tell me.

'It's all right, it's all right,' they cried. 'Wait and see! Wait and see!'

Talk about suppressed excitement … well! At least they seemed happy, which was something.

But as the performance progressed, I knew then why everybody was on a high of adrenalin. I cried in sheer happiness.

My goodness, I cried!

Finally when the curtain came down with Carmen lying inert on the stage, a dagger held to her bosom, I danced backstage all over the place, out of glorious, marvellous delight!

Blondel was superb, really superb. She behaved like the whore she should have been right from the start of rehearsals, all feminine sexuality, her body bending alluringly into Jose. And Mick was responding, something he hadn't done before, really responding!

Fantastic!

He was a bit shy at first, like the purblind Anglo-Saxon he was, but Blondel egged him on, flirted outrageously, rolled her expressive eyes, lifted her skirts to her crotch to show those glorious legs. It was a performance worthy of a professional, better even. She was putting heart and soul into it, drawing Jose on. In the end Mick, a jealous, enraged Jose, killed Blondel (as Carmen) in a supreme fit of tempestuous anger, which is how it should be.

Blondel and Mick had become closer in life. The cast knew it, or sensed it!

'Blondel, you were great, really great,' I told her, as the curtain fell for the last time that evening, after more than the usual number of calls. I kissed her fervently.

She smiled sweetly, rolled those eyes.

'I took your advice,' she whispered. 'Mick and I got together after the bonding party. We felt we had to do something, we were so bad. We talked and talked privately, and practised, and well, you know ....! In the end we had a wonderful, romantic time!'

And she winked at me!

The little hussy!

*

'I don't like that story,' said God.

'You never like my stories.'

'Oh, I don't know.... I've liked some.'

'Tell me why.'

'Well, the character of the director is hardly sympathetic. He offends people – women particularly, I imagine. He's full of self-importance. Some women would

100

call him a male pig; he obviously doesn't like women very much. I can't believe a BBC director would descend to the level of amateur productions ...'

'It has been known.'

'Yes, but not on a regular basis.'

'Anything else?'

'Yes! You're so old-fashioned. You mention pearls ...'

'But I did say they dated the lady.'

'Then you use words like 'whore' and 'hussy'. No editor today would accept them. You're behind the times! To any woman they're offensive. If you want to take up a cause try feminism, not racism.'

'Due to my old age, those words you mention were in common usage in days gone by.'

'But as a writer you should keep up with current language. As for the romance between Blondel and Mick, it leaves me a little uncomfortable.'

'It can and does happen in the theatre.'

'Hmm. Anyway I agree the story is well written. But a theme of racism is dangerous ground. Few editors would accept it – a young coloured girl taking the major part in an opera and in a middle class company as well!'

'Oh, come off it, God. This is the reality we live in, especially in England. You've put into the world different coloured people, different cultures, different religions. We've got to get on, learn to live together, or we may face another divide as bad as Christian and Muslim, or Catholic nd Protestant in Northern Ireland.'

God shook his head.

'It's a sad world,' he remarked with a sigh.

'You created it.'

'I know. I know. I get tired of you telling me that. I never understand why you still pray to me.'

'Good question! ... But I don't really feel I understand myself.'

The old man paused, and then continued slowly.

'I think – I believe – that you have helped me when things have gone wrong - something I find very difficult to explain.'

'Try.'

'Well, take that court case.'

'What court case?'

'Oh, God, you know as well as I do.'

'Tell me. Refresh my memory.'

'I was convicted for theft on four counts. It's something I feel I have to talk about sometime, get it off my chest.'

'What happened?'

'Well, I was fined - not very much I'm glad to say - told not to be silly, and that was the end of he matter.'

'No, I mean – what happened that you were taken to court?'

'Oh, it's difficult to explain.'

'Try.'

'Well, I was housemaster of a state boarding house for the local grammar school. Fifty children, half boys, half girls.'

'Must have been difficult.'

'It was. But then I made mistakes, didn't make it easy for myself.'

'In what way?'

'Well, my predecessor was something of a martinet. This was some thirty years ago. I decided to make it more a family home, relax the discipline. It was a mistake.'

'Why?'

'Well, not all the children played ball. They took advantage of the situation. I relaxed too much.'

'But why theft?'

'Well, the boarding house was suddenly closed down. We had very little notice. The closure wasn't because of me, but because of the change to Comprehensive education, a change I've always felt was a bad mistake. Too big! The new school was in a town over ten miles away. It was deemed impractical to continue with the boarding house. That was the end of me. I found another job. When I left I was accused of taking things with me. I was shattered by this and resigned my new teaching post.'

'Why?'

'Again, my stupidity. Any other man would have stayed on and fought the case. But I felt I had to clear my name before continuing to teach. It was the most traumatic time of my life.'

'How did I help you?'

'Well – and nobody would believe this – I was out walking just before the trial began. I felt terrible. I had a headache. I felt my world had come to an end. Suddenly a voice spoke to me in my head. At least it seemed like a voice. It was probably just me speaking to myself.'

'And what did the voice say?'

'Well, basically, stop being a bloody wimp, Be a man. Fight this thing. It's what my father would have said.'

'And did you?'

'Well, in a way, yes. I pleaded 'not guilty'. I argued that I had put some of my money into the boarding house. The children had nothing to entertain them; our budget was miniscule. I was entitled to take what I felt was mine. Of the sixteen charges, the jury acquitted me on twelve. They stuck on four and found me guilty on a majority of ten to two. It didn't make a lot of sense that I should be acquitted on so much, and yet found guilty on a little. I appealed.'

'And then what happened?'

'I miraculously got another job.'

'Where?'

'In Libya.'

'Good grief. Did it work out?'

'No. I came back after two weeks. I wrote a story about it.'

'I'd like to hear it.'

'It's very long.'

'Doesn't matter. I have all the time in the world.'

'I thought you were busy with all the billions of people in this world.'

'Oh, I'm well organised. I have billions of little angels who help me.'

'So, really, I am talking to an angel, an underling.'

'In a way, yes. But you have to remember these angels are really me. We are in complete understanding.'

104

'But you are the product of my mind. My God is my mind, to put it in another way.'

'True! But how do you not know that I may be speaking through your mind?'

'Wow! That's quite a thought. My mind is not as original as I believed.'

'But this story about Libya? That's quite an interesting country, but not very favourable to Britain. How did you get on?'

'Let me tell the story.'

'O.K. But, first, you mentioned there were two occasions in which I helped you. What was the second one?'

'Wait and see. It happened after Libya.'

*

CHAPTER 6.

RETROGRADE STEPS

All that is human must retrograde if it does not advance.
(Edward Gibbon – 1737-1794)

'Oh, hell, not another of your stories,' muttered the computer. 'I was having such a peaceful rest.'

'I'm afraid there are a lot of stories to come. You are going to be busy,confessed the old manmischievously. 'I promised God two stories, one that will shock him, the other about Libya. But I will have to leave them for later when   I am talking to him. I've got one especially for you.'

'What a yawn! I shall go on strike.'

'You can't! You're only a computer. You do as you're told.'

'Oh, yeah!'

'What's that supposed to mean?'

'I'll crash out, and you'll have to waste time calling your son.'

'I know how to deal with you now.'

'No, you don't. I'm deep, I am. Old fogies like you don't understand a tenth of me.'

'We'll see.'

'Want a bet!'

'I don't bet with computers!'

'Why on earth not?'

'Because you don't understand the complexities of betting, nor its effect on human nature. It becomes an addiction with some people.'

'I bet I do.'

'Do 'what'?'

'Understand.'

'No, you don't!'

'I do.'

'No, you don't!'

'I do, I do, I do!'

'Stop acting like a child, and let's get on with it. I ought to tell this story, though God won't be too pleased with it.'

'Oh, your God! I don't know how you can stand him. Sanctimonious old prig!'

'Now, now! You might regret it one day.'

'God can't touch me. I'm inanimate. Just bits of this and that.'

'I shouldn't be too sure. God would argue that he created you just as much as he did man.'

'That's a laugh! It was man who made me, put me together, got me working.'

'I would dispute that. God put into the world the bits and pieces that made you. God also gave man the capacity to create weird technology from those 'bits and pieces'. You're as much God's creation as I am. Remember one day new, weird technology will make you redundant.'

'Why weird technology?'

'Well, you *are* weird to my generation. There was nothing like you when we were young.'

The computer grumbled noisily and thought about it for a moment. But the old man grew impatient.

'Come on, come on, you soulless bit of state of the arts. I want to get on with my story.'

'What do you mean 'state of the arts'? '

'Oh, I don't know. It's one of these meaningless phrases that suddenly become fashionable. Something very modern is my understanding.'

The computer sighed.

'Oh. O.K. Let's get on with your story,' the computer condescended to say. His voice was very grudging.

'There's a good little boy,' said the old man smiling.

'I'm not a boy.'

'To me, you are!'

'I haven't even got a willy.'

'Of course you haven't. You've no reproductive organs.'

'Well, then, why call me a boy?'

'I was speaking metaphorically, and with some affection. You have the characteristics of a boy.'

'Such as.'

'Well, you're petulant, moody, just like my sons when they were small.'

The computer made sulky noises. For a moment the old man thought it was going to crash out. Hastily he said:

'I call you a little boy because I am fond of you, just as I am fond of my sons.'

'Oh, yeah?'

'Well, why do you think I spent all that money on an IT course just to learn about you?'

'That was a laugh!'

'Oh?'

'Well, it took you ages, and tried the patience of your teacher. You would never have got there in the end if that pretty lady didn't take pity, and help you more than she should.'

'My, she was pretty – blond hair, long legs, pert little breasts.'

'Yer, and you went all gooey whenever she came near you. A man of your age!'

'Age has got nothing to do with it. You can still dream, still appreciate a pretty girl right to your grave.'

'Yer, but you can't do anything about it, though you tried.'

'I beg your pardon?'

'You gave her presents, asked her out for coffee, fantasised about making love to her.'

'Ye-e-s, but she never came, and I never did.'

'Didn't do what?'

'Fantasise.'

'Oh, yes, you bloody did. You wrote a story about her, do you remember? That one about lilies being so beautiful. You compared her to a lily because you thought the lilies in the pond just down the road were as lovely as her!'

'Oh!'

'Yes, oh! Here it is.'

The computer made some rumbling noises, and dredged up the story.

*

LILIES

Now folds the lily all her sweetness up,
And slips into the bosom of the lake:
So fold thyself, my dearest, thou, and slip
Into my bosom and be lost in me.
(Alfred Lord Tennyson – 1809-1892)

'Please, may I make love to you?'

'Mike!'

Sophie was astonished.

They were sitting by the pond just the other side of the hedge to the road, sheltered from prying eyes. Two young people together, she as lovely as the Suffolk sky as dusk descends; he conversely unprepossessing, sitting not on the ground but in a wheelchair.

'Please...'

She contemplated him for a moment.

'Why do you ask?' she said softly, and smiled.

'Why does any man ask?'

'But you, you're different. You're a cripple.'

'It doesn't stop me from feeling. I can still do it, though you will have to be patient with me, help me.'

'I still don't understand. We've been friends. Never once have you indicated – well – that you wanted me.'

'I was afraid.'

'Afraid of what?'

'That asking might destroy our friendship, that I might upset you, lose you even.'

He moved in his chair, and looked directly at her. He'd been afraid to look in case of what he might read on her face. But she was still as calm as ever.

'You know,' he continued. 'You're quite the loveliest person I've ever been privileged to call a friend. But I want more than friendship. You're just like the lilies...' He indicated the flowers floating in two groups in both of the far corners of the pond, pure and white, the green leaves glistening with moisture. '... If I were whole I would wade into the water and pick one, present it to you as a token of love. I wrote a poem not so long ago about these very lilies.'

'Read it to me.'

'I haven't got it on me, but I think I can remember it.'

She settled back on the grass, lying sideways, propping herself on one elbow, the remains of the picnic around her. She'd had to pass him sandwiches, olives, tomatoes, a glass of wine because he found it difficult to reach down. Lying back she looked depressingly lovely – depressing because he was handicapped; he would never achieve such glowing health. She had a slim, shapely body in light blue shorts and white top. Long, golden legs, she'd taken off her shoes to wriggle her toes in the coolness of the grass. But it was her face and hair that were so very attractive. Long, floating, fair hair that reached smoothly down to her shoulders. A face of creamy skin slightly flushed by the warmth of the sun. Or was it embarrassment at the present situation?

Mike sat back in his chair, looked into the distance and prepared to recite:

'I've called it 'A wondrous View',' he explained.

She nodded. She'd read some of his poetry earlier in the week. He'd been keen to show it to her. She didn't know what to make of   it. Not great poetry but it had a certain intensity of feeling that struck a chord - loneliness, unhappiness, longing.

<u>A Wondrous View.</u>
Give me, kind heaven, a private station,
A mind serene for contemplation.
(John Gay : 1685-1732)
Not far away, a Suffolk pond,
Tall grass at edge, still water deep.
Hoof marks of cows who quench their thirst.
A pond, that's all, but nothing more!
But ... but ... it has one lovely sight.
Green leaves, some lilies white, serene
They float their glory to display.
A wondrous view, their beauty clear.
It does my yearning heart such good
To see this gentle loveliness.
We have our cars, our cosy homes,
But nothing will exceed the joy
Such flowers give – a lift of heart,
A peace of mind; the world's worthwhile
We feel at last, amidst the stress
Of strife and crime, of gnawing hate.

*

'Good! That's good.'
She smiled at him gently.
'Thanks.'
'No, I mean it. You have a certain sensitivity that I admire. I only wish ...' She paused.
'Wish what?'
'It's awkward. Forget it.'

110

'No! I feel you were going to say something that concerned us both – something to do with the lilies.'

'Um.'

'Tell me.'

She sighed.

I don't want to upset you.'

'I've lived too long with my handicap. Nothing upsets me.'

'Oh, I don't know about that. You tend to be very frustrated at times, tied to a wheelchair.'

'If I promise not to be upset, will you tell me?'

'I might.'

Mike gave a tccch of exasperation.

'Oh, you women! You like your little mysteries. They can be so irritating.'

'It's just, Mike, I wish your sensitivity could carry over to human relationships.'

'What do you mean?'

'Well, you suddenly come out with 'could I make love to you?' It was so unexpected.'

'You mean, I should buy you flowers, chat you up.'

'Something like that.'

'I can't buy flowers. Shopping's difficult enough.'

'Have you made love before?'

'Only with prostitutes, only paid love.'

'Mike!'

'Well, what else can a bloke do? No normal girl will go near me.'

'I'm not sure I want to go with a man who's been with a prostitute.'

'Why? It was always protected.'

'It sounds – well – a bit disgusting.'

'It isn't really. They're just girls, ordinary human beings. One or two have been very kind. At first they put their prices up, regarded me as a special case. Then they felt sorry for me, and I didn't pay nearly so much.'

'They come to you, I suppose.'

Mike nodded.

'It's the only way.'

The girl sighed and got up, began to clear away the picnic into a large blue bag. She said nothing.

'I've upset you.'

But she wouldn't reply.

Suddenly Mike got very angry.

'What the hell else do you think men like me can do? Go, fuck ourselves!'

'Mike!'

There was reproach in her voice.

Silently she picked up the bag, hung it over the handle of his wheelchair, began to push him along the path back to the road. At the car she helped him into the front passenger seat, folded the chair, put it into the boot. It was awkward to lift.

She drove him back to the hotel without talking, Mike full of regrets. Why the hell did he open his stupid mouth? It was a weakness of his; he couldn't help it. In his bitterness in life, he said hurtful things. Always regretted them afterwards.

At the hotel she helped him out of the car, wheeled him into the hotel, into the lift, and up to his room, still grimly silent.

'Sophie, please,' he begged, 'I don't want to lose your friendship.'

But she left him, a forlorn figure in his chair in the middle of the room.

Mike at first was angry. How could she treat him in such a way, ignore him as if he was unclean? But gradually his anger turned to misery, a hollow ache in the whole of his body, a deep longing such as he had rarely experienced. The past week had been a strange time, so unforgettable, so poignant!

Sophie had arrived ten days ago. She was a TV presenter, one of several attractive girls who adorned television screens, chosen, one couldn't help feeling, because of their looks than their intellect. But Sophie was exceptional, like … he pictured one or two of the girls he so enjoyed on the early morning breakfast shows – Kate Small on ITV and Sophie Renchall on BBC1.

Sophie, the one who had given him friendship the past week, was a university graduate, similar in quality to Carol Sinclair who worked for Channel 4.

Their meeting at the hotel had been fortuitous. Mike was staying there because the hotel was run by his mother's sister who offered him the chance of a holiday in pleasant Suffolk countryside. Sophie was there simply because she wanted to get away from the stress of her job, and London itself. Rumours about her were rife. According to differing tabloids, she had broken with her long-term boy friend; she'd

112

had a nervous breakdown; she was not happy with her work and was close to resigning. Even that she was pregnant! The worst was she had undergone an abortion.

All highly dramatised in true media frenzy!

Nobody knew, among this welter of gossip, which was the possible truth.

Mike had recognised her. He was an avid television gawper, one of the few pleasures open to cripples. But he hadn't spoken to her at first, hadn't dared to approach her. What would such a well-known and lovely girl have to do with a cripple? She was the untouchable, way above his league.

But they had got together - eventually!

The lift had been awkward; the doors had started to close just as he was working his chair through the narrow entrance.

'May I help?'

Sophie had held the doors back while he manoeuvred his way in.

Inside she had smiled at him.

'Lovely day, isn't it?' she'd said, the most prosaic, ridiculous of opening statements.

Mike had agreed. They were in the middle of a summer heat wave, dry and windless. It was said that Suffolk could one day become an arid desert, such were the warnings of drought.

Again, more to make conversation than out of interest, she had said:

'What are you doing this morning?'

He had smiled.

'Going on my usual morning jog round the garden, enjoying the sun.'

'May I join you?'

She didn't know why she said it. Perhaps out of sorrow for this young man so badly handicapped.

'Pleasure.'

From this innocuous beginning had sprung a friendship of a deep platonic nature, at least on Sophie's part. He was what she needed, a man she could talk to without feeling threatened, a friend in a stormy, emotional sea who made no demands on her.

Until today!

It had been such a shame he uttered those few words –
'May I make love to you?'.

It was the last thing she wanted, at a time when her own romance had ended so disastrously.

She had talked so openly to him about her life, about work in the television studios, about the hundred and one people she met, about her present misery and loneliness, as if the bottom had fallen out of her life; he, about his own frustrations as a cripple, of being less than a man. His disability had been the result of a car accident. He had been knocked down by a speeding car, a fool of a joy rider, not even insured.

Mike had known before what it was to be whole, vigorous, and fond of sport. His great joy had been cricket; he'd shown promise at school and then at university.

Not once had they discussed sex. Not once had he touched her.

She hadn't expected it, nor wanted it.

But their conversations had been such a balm to her. Somehow he had put her life into perspective. How could she be miserable when he suffered so much more, had so much less to look forward to?

Sitting in her room after their abortive picnic she wondered how she could have behaved so badly, so unsympathetically.

He was a man. He needed a woman like any full-blooded male.

And yet the real joy of vigorous sex was denied him. Instead he sought girls whose sole livelihood depended on selling their bodies. They had given him comfort, and not even expected full payment. Weren't they better than her, kinder, more generous?

After supper she had sought him out.

'Mike, can we talk?'

He was drinking coffee in the lounge, a lone figure.

He smiled at her.

'Of course.'

'Mike, I'm sorry about today. I've behaved very badly.'

'Not at all. I'm the one who's been an idiot.'

They had continued in this mood of self-blame.

Finally he had asked:

'Where do we go from here?'

'I'm going back to London, Mike. Thanks to you I feel ready to face the world, go back to work.'

'I'm glad I've been of help. Will I see you again?'

114

'No. Oh, I don't know.'

'Oh?'

The disappointment on Mike's face was profound.

'I'm sorry, Mike. As a friend, yes. But I feel we have gone beyond friendship. There's no future down that road.'

Mike thought hard for a moment.

'You know, Sophie, you're a bitch.'

He said it quietly, pointedly.

'Mike!'

She suddenly thought he was like all men. Once a man was thwarted he resorted to calling a woman derogatory names, blaming her for everything.

'I'm sorry. What I'm really trying to say is that you're hard, as hard as nails, a characteristic of all successful women. You have to be ... to succeed!'

'I don't think of myself as hard. I've felt sorry for you – really! But you've spoilt my dream.'

'What dream is that?'

'That one can have a relationship without sex rearing its ugly head.'

'Oh, that's nonsense.'

'Nonsense or not, this is how I feel.'

She stood up, tall and magnificent, towering over Mike in his disadvantage in a wheelchair. She moved away.

As she left the room, Mike sighed. He felt in his pocket for his little notebook, looked at telephone numbers. Tomorrow he too would go home, telephone real friends, real girls who helped.

The end of a dream ... as lovely as the lilies!

*   *

The computer sighed.

'That doesn't make any sense as a story,' it pointed out.

'It does to me.'

'How come?'

'Well, as a man handicapped by hearing I've found it difficult to relate to women.'

'So ... like the man in the story you've sought solace in paid women.'

'Ye-e-s, I shame to say.

115

'My!'

The computer was utterly astonished

There was silence between them for a while, both feeling they had come to a truth, surprising in its intensity.

Finally the computer sighed, or as near as a computer can sigh.

'I really feel this discussion – any discussion on the complexities between men and women – ought to be with God, not with me. I'm out of my depths.'

'It's not surprising.'

'There are two matters which – within my limited knowledge – I find puzzling. First of all why did Mike treat Sophie so badly?'

'He basically didn't like women because they had rejected him so often as a cripple.'

'Um ...!'

The computer had to stop and digest this. Finally it continued:

'Secondly what has this story got to do with that nice girl who helped you on the IT course?'

'Nothing, really, except she was one of a kind.'

'Oh?'

'Well, like Sophie in the story, she was prepared to be kind up to a point.'

'What else can you expect? You're a deaf old man. Or would it be more true to say you're a dirty old man.'

'I'm not taking that from you, a mere computer. What do you know about human relationships?'

'Very little! The more I learn, the more bewildered I become. The only truth I can find, according to accepted human belief, is that God made men and women to live together, to comfort and support each other. That's very, very different from the reality.'

Once again there was an uncomfortable silence between the two. Finally the old man sighed.

'I'm afraid of you now,' he admitted. 'You know too much about human nature, more than you are prepared to admit.'

'It's not only that. You are becoming dependent on me. You confide in me your inmost thoughts. I know perhaps more about you than your wife. Remember that diary you keep?'

'This is getting embarrassing. I think we ought to get on

with my story about Libya. I expect you to do as you're told.'

'Under protest! May I however point out that as usual you are evading the issue? And may I also point out that, if your story is long, we ought to leave it until the next chapter of this exceedingly boring book?'

'All right then. But may I in turn point out this book is not boring? It's weird and getting weirder and weirder the more it progresses. It rather frightens me, as if I'm looking into a dark abyss and seeing nothing but horror and shame.'

'You said it.'

*

CHAPTER 7

ADVERSITY

For of fortunes sharp adversitee
The worst kind of infortune is this,
A man to have been in prosperitee,
And it remembren, when it passed is.
(Geoffrey Chaucer – 1340? – 1400)

'So … no story of Libya yet! You should never keep the reader waiting.'

God smiled indulgently as he spoke.

'I'm sorry, God. I was distracted.'

'By your friend, the computer, I imagine.

'He's no friend of mine. In fact I find him rather frightening. He's taking over my life.'

'Bound to happen. Bound to happen!' God nodded profoundly.

'What do you mean?'

'Mankind's giving computers too much power. They control everything, even the way you live - all your machinery, even those great monsters that fly in the sky. One day computers will turn against you, and the world will be in a mess.'

'Is that a prediction?'

'Sort of! It's one of the many ways in which man can ultimately destroy himself.'

'That's a laugh. Computers have no soul, no feelings.'

'But that could pass. Look at the way your computer is taking over a greater part of your life. You spend a whole morning on the computer, and an evening as well if you're not too tired. And you enjoy it; it's like a new toy to a man of your age.'

'Um! Tiredness is *my* problem, the curse of age. We could do so much more if we had the energy.' The old man paused. 'Be as it may, I can't see the computer taking over our lives. It's unimaginable.'

'Did you imagine computers when you were a boy?'

'No. There wasn't even television then.'

'Well then? You can't stop progress.'

But … no, no. It's just not possible.'

'We'll see. We'll see!'

The old man shook his head. Such a happening was beyond his comprehension.

But - it was *frightening!*

'I think I'll get on with my story. It's something more tangible.'

'You do that. You do that. I'm listening.'

*

THERE BUT FOR THE GRACE OF GOD GO I.
Bad laws are the worst sort of tyranny.
(Edmund Burke, 1729-1797)

Jim had never been to the Dorchester, Park Lane before.

The uniformed doorman in the big hat looked intimidating, making Jim feel as if he should not be there. He imagined this forbidding figure, probably an ex-soldier, coming up to him and querying gruffly his presence. All his life Jim had felt a sinking feeling when confronted by situations and people he was not accustomed to. He hurried through the door, not waiting for, or wanting this portentous figure to open it for him. At the desk he asked for Mr. Naiem Mohamed, the Libyan educational representative, who had summoned him for interview.

The girl behind the desk was pretty, but coldly efficient. She neglected to smile, thus increasing Jim's uncomfortable feeling he was out of place in these magnificent surroundings. He felt sure, if he'd looked rich or important, she would have smiled.

'Room 301,' she told him. 'Shall I announce you?'

'Yes, please,' Jim managed to croak. His nervousness invariably created huskiness in his voice. He half-coughed to clear it. He waited while the girl spoke over the phone. She had a way of hanging her head sideways to clear her long, blond hair from the phone. The movement was appealing, showing the soft white lines of a delicate neck.

Jim sighed.

London was a different civilisation, alienating. Yet not

119

so many years ago, before his marriage, he had lived in London and enjoyed its teeming atmosphere. Since then the misfortunes of life had crushed his self-confidence.

The girl put down the phone, tossed her hair into place.

'Colonel Mohamed asks you to go up at once.'

She repeated the room number as if he was some village idiot who didn't always take in what was said.

'Thanks,' Jim said and smiled.

The girl ignored him. Jim felt disheartened. There was a time in his life, not so long ago, when women had seemed to like him, had wanted to smile at him.

But not any more!

Jim wanted to ask the girl where the toilet was. Nerves always affected his bladder. But how did you ask so coldly clinical and immaculate a person something so mundane? She would probably look at him with disdain.

It was as if women recognised in him a lowliness of spirit, and were not interested. It was not the first time since his resignation that Jim felt, maybe wrongly, that women whose regard he needed so much both at work and socially, only wanted from him entertainment, a joke and a laugh. They ceased to be interested now he had come down in the world, as if they were not prepared to give compassion. It was the men who had stood by him, with a kind of camaraderie that said, 'There but for the grace of God go I'.

He took the lift up to the third floor. On emerging there was a sign 'Gentlemen'. It gave him the opportunity of relief he so badly wanted.

He came out, deep in his own thoughts. The word 'Colonel' gave him a feeling of dread. He didn't know that in Libya, as in most dictatorships, military titles were given out like confetti.

But.., an army man!

And a Libyan to boot!

Like Gaddafi!

The thought was not inclined to give a man confidence!

But why should he, an Englishman be afraid of some bloody wog? He squared his shoulders.

Jim had always admired soldiers, men who risked their lives, but he'd never found them comfortable to relate to. His own physical handicap, a gammy leg from childhood, had meant the butch men of society looked down their long noses at him as if he was an inferior breed. And yet it was only an accident of boyhood that had made him what he was. In different circumstances he would have been as butch as them. His father after all had been a soldier, killed on active service during the War, a brave and caring man.

Jim sighed yet again.

His life seemed full of sighs, regrets at what might have been.

Colonel Mohamed's apartment was plush, in a deep red colour with gold ornamentation. The whole effect made the room dark, as if too much light would reveal faded opulence. The furniture reminded Jim of seventeenth and eighteenth century French tables and chairs, uncomfortable, hard, designed more for elegance than bodily comfort.

The Colonel greeted him at the door. He spoke fluent English with an American accent. Jim was to learn later he'd lived in America for four years, doing post-graduate research.

He offered Jim a coffee. On acceptance, he went to the phone for room service. His manner was abrupt. He barked an order. Jim decided he didn't like the Colonel. He was fat and rounded like a balloon.

His first question - whether he had ever been to a Middle East, or Arab country before. He replied he had only been to Morocco with his wife, on holiday. they'd been fascinated by the different culture, by an exciting visit to a desert oasis, and by an intriguing weekend at Marrakech.

The Colonel seemed satisfied with this lame, uninteresting seemingly to him. The Colonel was brusque, almost to the point of rudeness. Jim's only confidence was that, at five foot ten, he was taller by several inches.

But the Colonel seemed shrewd, and obsessed with the American need to get to the point.

'Your qualifications are good,' he stated, rifling through Jim's c.v. 'Are you free on the spot?'

Jim hesitated, surprised by the abruptness. The Colonel interpreted it as incomprehension.

'It's an American expression meaning can you leave at once.'

Jim forbore to mention that it was a saying common to the English. The Colonel seemed to share the same American conceit that it was the Americans who'd created the English language. Jim decided to be positive and equally direct.

121

'I can leave when you like. But give me time to go home, collect my things, sort out my affairs.'

The Colonel grunted an unwilling consent. He seemed insensitive to personal needs.

'How would you feel about living in Libya?'

Jim had thought out his answer beforehand.

'I like travelling, seeing new places. As a bachelor I lived in France for well over ayear. I've been to several European countries.'

Desperate for the job, Jim searched for something positive to say.

'They were friendly agroad,' he said at last. 'I had a happy time.'

The last part was true!

'How would you feel away from European civilisation?' he asked, 'Tobruk is very isolated. It has few of the amenities of an English city.'

Jim explained that his main interests were reading and writing. He would welcome the opportunity to have time to himself.

The word 'writing' troubled the Colonel.

'You're not a journalist writing for the newspapers?' he asked, his eyes narrowing.

Jim assured him he was an amateurish, unsuccessful writer of fiction. It was a hobby.

'I'm really only a teacher of English,' he explained, not truthfully. His real subject was craft and woodwork, though he had a pass degree in English.

The Colonel grunted his satisfaction. He was a man of grunts.

After going through salary, conditions of service, free accommodation, payment of sixty per cent of his salary into his bank in England, the Colonel offered him the post of tutor in English at the Tobruk College of Higher Education in Petroleum Studies.

Jim gasped inwardly at the salary, which was far in excess of what he would expect to earn in a teaching post in England. Not a word was mentioned of his resignation from his last post, that he had been unemployed for more than a year. The latter information he wanted to conceal, though it would have come out if the Colonel had taken up his references. This period of unemployment must have been evident from the dates in his c.v. Either the Colonel was desperate for teachers or he was a fool, too lazy to check.

Jim couldn't believe his luck.

But with the natural pessimism of a man struck down by previous misfortune, he wondered how long this luck would last.

The real concern was his visa application, which must surely be a requirement for Libya. The Colonel brought up this very question.

'This afternoon you must go to the Italian Embassy,' he ordered, not asked.

It was surprising this reference to the Italian Embassy, until Jim remembered that the Libyan 'Embassy' had been closed down since the shooting of an English policewoman.

'Wait at the Embassy until you get your visa. You should get it by the end of the afternoon.'

Another order!

The Colonel's voice was peremptory now agreement had been reached. Jim was no longer an applicant but an employee. There was no consideration whether he could manage the extra time waiting at the Embassy, no query as to whether he had brought his passport.

Fortunately he had!

The Colonel's attitude should have warned him of the possibility of future problems. But his elation at being offered a job overcame any doubts.

'Go now,' ordered the Colonel. 'Report back here in two days at 10.30 a.m. with your luggage.'

The Colonel heaved his plump body out of his chair, and moved to his bedroom door, not bothering to say a courteous goodbye. He left Jim stranded in the middle of the room, having to see himself out. It was only when he was in the lift he realised that not once had Janet been mentioned, no indication as to how she fitted into future plans. He knew the post was unaccompanied for the first year; he'd been hesitant to talk about Janet. But surely the Colonel ought to have given her a passing mention?

*

'You've treated Janet verra badly!'

The speaker with a Scottish accent and a strongly rolled 'r' was Rosie, a friend of the family, another nurse, a tiny midwife who worked in the same hospital as Janet. She'd come round to their home, a frequent visitor, ostensibly to say goodbye. She looked angrier than Jim had ever seen her before. Her pretty face was flushed and there was an aggression in her that was entirely new.

Jim didn't know what to say. He knew why Rosie was angry, Yesterday Janet had cried, unusual for her because she rarely cried. Even when her mother died, Janet had remained white and silent. It was part of her nurse's training, not to show emotion.

'Rosie, I must take this job,' he pleaded. 'I've little chance of another.'

'Nonsense!' cried Rosie, her Scottish accent becoming even more pronounced the angrier she became. 'The wee lass has stuck by you through these difficult months, and now all you do is up sticks and away. It's no-a fair.'

It was odd calling Janet a 'wee lass'. She was eight inches taller than Rosie.

'But I'll be back again for a holiday at Christmas,' Jim protested. 'Then sometime in the future she and Peter will be able to join me. I'll have a flat all prepared.'

'Look, my bonnie lad ...' Rosie's five-foot frame advanced on him, poking him firmly in the chest. ' ... If it weren't for the fact I liked you both, I wouldna be talking like this. But yer can't go away and leave Janet. Better to be together without a job, than to go to some daft foreign place where you'll be eaten by fleas. They're Arabs where yer'll be going, a different way of life. Yer'll ne-er be happy.'

Jim found it impossible to explain how important this job was to him, any job, for his own self-esteem. A man was not a man without work. But then he thought sadly of Peter, only eight, just beginning to play cricket. They'd had such happy times together. Leaving him would hurt badly. In a sense he was doing it for Peter, for Janet, to give them more money, a better standard of living, a car even. They'd been without a car for over twelve months.

But Rosie guessed his thoughts.

'Och, I know yer want to worrrk, to feel self-important again. But it's Janet that matters, far more than you. She and Peter will be lost without yer.'

She began to poke him again, emphasising her words.

'Oh, Rosie, stop it. Please stop.'

The plea came, not from Jim, but from Janet who had

just entered. Tall, brown-haired, attractive, Jim couldn't help wondering how he could bear to leave her.

'It's all right, Rosie, really it is,' Janet pleaded. 'I know why Jim has to go; it's the only way. I can understand. But just for a moment it caught me unawares; it's all too sudden.'

Rosie gave a 'tccch' of disgust.

'Well, I'll say no mo-a.' She spoke rather primly. 'I've said what I wanted to say, and that's enough. I'll go, make some coffee for yer both.'

She walked out of the room, leaving them together, Jim and Janet, the two 'Js', never parted in twelve years of marriage.

'You'll need some thin socks for Libya,' said Janet, always the organiser of minute details.

Jim had a sudden desire to laugh. At such a strongly emotional time, Janet had to mention *socks!* But her organisation had always been great. and he loved her for it. All their marriage, in moments of crisis, she turned to practical matters, her nursing training coming to the fore. It was this strong facility to look at life in realistic terms that made Jim appreciate how Janet became one of the youngest ward sisters in the London hospital where she worked before their marriage, and for three years afterwards.

'I'll be back at Christmas,' he said, bringing matters to the central issue that gave them something to look forward to.

Janet nodded but said nothing. There was a widening gulf between them that no conversation could bridge.

'I'm sorry,' muttered Jim lamely, not knowing what else to say.

But Janet left the room quickly, muttering an excuse. He felt once again she was close to tears. He sighed. He felt engulfed by misery, an overwhelming dread that life would never be the same again.

And it had all started with that court conviction!

Jim could never understand why he had been so stupid. He had gone over what happened time and time again. Out of frustration with the slowness and indecisiveness of educational bureaucracy, he had replaced a few of his own used-up tools with school property. If he hadn't used his own equipment in the school , much of what he'd tried to achieve wouldn't have been possible, so inhibiting were educational cutbacks. He'd taken the replacement tools with him openly and defiantly when he moved to a new position in a large comprehensive school, offering far more opportunity than he'd ever had before.

The local authority had prosecuted him, claiming the tools had been stolen. Jim resigned his new post, in shame, even before the court case had begun. In the ensuing trial he had pleaded 'not guilty' and had been largely, not quite, vindicated. But he'd broken one golden rule of society – he'd taken the law into his own hands. This, society would not tolerate, however justifiable the reasons. And so the verdict had been guilty on four counts by a majority of ten to two, and on twelve other counts he had been found 'not guilty'. The punishment was a minimal fine, almost laughable. Jim had been pleased by an outspoken comment that the case should never have gone to trial.

But he was left with a criminal conviction, a damning mark against his record as a teacher, a fact, as far as education was concerned, he would have to live with all his life.

Finally after months of failure in seeking employment, he'd started applying without mentioning his conviction, which was illegal. It had worked with this Libyan application, but he was not sure his luck would hold.

Janet had stood by him, had still loved him, or so he hoped, and had kept the finances together by working full time herself in the local hospital. For fifteen months he'd cooked, looked after the house and child. He'd even gone to cookery classes, the only man among a whole crowd of knowledgeable women. He'd found – oddly enough – that women despised him – or seemed to – seeing a lack of manhood in what he did, instead of admiring him for the support he gave his family. He was doing what feminists wanted men to do, but the reality transcended their beliefs, making him feel bitter towards the opposite sex.

But sometimes he wondered how much his disability had to do with feminine attitudes.

In some strange way he enjoyed looking after the home. He made a passable hand at cooking. But always he longed for the day when he'd be his own man, not apologise to all and sundry that he was just a househusband.

*

Peter came in from the garden, holding his small cricket bat, asking for a game.

126

'All right, son.'

Jim smiled although he reflected unhappily it was his last opportunity for some while.

'When will you be back, daddy?'

'At Christmas, son.'

Peter pulled a face.

'It'll be too cold for cricket.'

Like his mother he was ever practical.

Jim hugged him impulsively. Not a word of direct reproach that he'd let the family down.

'Will you ride a camel, daddy?'

'I don't know. It would be interesting if I did. I'll send you a photo – me on a camel.'

Interspersed with their cricket, Jim talked about his new life in a remote desert country. The very fact of talking and playing eased the ache in his heart.

*

The tarmac at Benghazi airport sweltered in the mid afternoon heat. It had been a tiring journey. He'd stopped over night at Tripoli with Colonel Mohamed and another new teacher called Mike, staying at a luxury hotel, depressing for its lack of women, except for two voluble Italian cleaners in the corridor outside his room.

'Hey, Eengleesh man,' one had called. 'You want?'

She put her hands under her large breasts and wobbled them suggestively. Then they had both burst out laughing. Instead of being offended Jim had smiled, but shaken his head, realising they weren't serious. The incident, for some strange reason, cheered him up no end. There was little other sign of laughter in Tripoli.

The Libyans at the airport reminded Jim of the French; they were full of unnecessary officialdom and noise. All the alighting passengers, except Mohamed and those travelling first class, had been forced to stay out on the tarmac under a hot sun for endless moments – it seemed like hours! There was no explanation or apology. Then, in the Customs, his typewriter had been confiscated, his most cherished possession apart from photos of his family. He intended to use the typewriter because of his interest in writing, to alleviate the long and lonely days away from his family. It was only the interference of Mohamed that retrieved the typewriter.

The bleakness of Tripoli and the lack of organisation, made him wonder if he hadn't made a dreadful mistake in taking this teaching post. Not for the first time in his life he began seriously to doubt himself. Here he was, a relatively young man with a wife and child, and all he had to offer was a remote job in a foreign country where few men would want to go. He'd acted out of misplaced pride and need for money. His life had failed. He saw little future. It almost seemed as if his family were better off without him. Janet had an important position as ward sister in the local hospital, doing good and caring work. All he was doing was teaching a lot of wogs how to speak English. Some job! His despondency was such that even suicide crossed his mind. He remembered fleetingly on the plane looking out at the ground below, and wishing he could just jump out of the inhibiting metal cabin, and plummet to the ground in forgetfulness. It reminded him of a strange and lonely girl at college, overweight and unnoticed by men, once saying that she had watched the waters from London Bridge and wished they could have swallowed her up. He'd been a little sceptical at the time, but now he knew how she was feeling.

Benghazi was one grade more welcoming than Tripoli. The town was lighter in atmosphere, better planned, more attractive, with soft stone walls of a light cream colour. The roads were wider; vari-coloured paving gave the impression of a bygone Roman city, which he understood it had once been.

The hotel was cool despite the heat, and not so oppressively dark as the one in Tripoli. But this time there was even less trace of women, not even Italians to tease him with their flamboyant breasts and outrageous remarks.

'Come and have some supper with me, a real Arab supper.'

The speaker was his English companion on the plane, Mike, a man of twenty-six. He was a cheerful, open-faced man, full of naïve enthusiasm. He had spent most of his short working life since university in various teaching posts abroad – Italy, Greece and Saudi Arabia. He not only had an honours degree in English, but also a diploma to teach English to foreign students. He also spoke Arabic. Jim might be the older man, but Mike had all the advantages. He was unmarried and had developed a love of all things Arab, whereas what Jim experienced until now only increased his doubts.

'Isn't it marvellous being here?' cried Mike. 'Can't you

smell the spices, feel the whole vibrancy of an Arab country?'

His boyish delight had the contrary effect on Jim, increasing his distress, making him feel tired and old, even inadequate by comparison. It was like all despondency - self-feeding.

Mike, asking directions from an Arab, took Jim through the open streets to a narrower, poorer part of Benghazi, a confined Sook of filthy gutters and dirty walls. Mike chattered away all the time, using the occasional Arab words, revelling in the atmosphere. Normally Jim would have responded equally cheerfully, remembering his own appreciation of travel abroad, new sights, sounds and smells. But now the dreariness of the place matched his own downcast mood.

'Now we'll have a real meal,' enthused Mike. His delight was almost nauseating, and seemingly un-English.

They sat down at a long communal table set close against the tall stone wall that enclosed the Sook. Jim left him to do the ordering. The meal when it came was a watery mess of a varied shape and colour. Jim tasted it gingerly, while Mike lapped his down showing every sign of enjoyment. Jim, embarrassed, pushed his plate away.

'I'm not feeling hungry,' was his lame excuse.

'Off-colour are you?' consoled Mike. He reached out, scooped Jim's share into his bowl, and proceeded to demolish it with sickening enthusiasm.

'Great,' he said, patting his stomach. He was a thin man, like a rake, and the bones of his chest stood out under his T-shirt. Jim felt if that meal was all he ate, it was no wonder he was so skeletal.

They wandered back to the hotel. Light was beginning to fail. The whole town was hushed, eerie, a great contrast to the noise of pubs, canned music and traffic in any town in England.

'Isn't it wonderful?' enthused Mike yet again. 'You can imagine why the Arabs are so full of prayer. The whole atmosphere is conducive to quiet contemplation.'

Jim who'd lost the art of prayer, and regretted it, didn't reply. Mike's conversation at that point was of the sort that did not require an answer.

'When I'm with the Arabs, I don't understand why Christianity ever argues that it is the one true religion,' Mike continued to muse. 'The Koran is the word of God dictated to

Mohammad. It's every bit as good as Christianity. Moreover the Arabs try to live by their principles. I like them; I really do. They don't steal or mug. They're not affected by materialism such as we know. The whole atmosphere, at a time like this, is wonderfully spiritual.'

Jim kept his thoughts to himself. And Mike didn't ask him how he felt. Mike was absorbed in his own form of exultation.

But Jim's experience of Arabs while teaching in a summer English language school was very dissimilar to Mike's. The Arabs were like spoilt children, let loose in a freedom previously unknown. They treated women as if they were toys prepared to fall into their arms, then being petulant if it didn't work out. They knew little self-discipline; drink was a new excitement. In fairness, only the rich Arabs came to England, never women, only men. It might be the poorer were better behaved.

At the hotel Mike and Jim parted. Jim went up to his room. For a long time he leaned out of the window, thinking of Janet, of Peter, of cricket, wondering who would be picked to tour Australia for the Ashes. Over the past few months, because his economies didn't stretch to buying newspapers, he'd missed out on the sports news, except over the radio or television. But always his thoughts went back to Janet, the warmth and softness of her body, her kindly understanding, never demanding, and the way she moved when he made love to her. He badly needed a woman; he wondered how he was going to manage.

*

The next day was the long trip by college car to Tobruk, an endless, modern tarmac road, which followed the coastline. Mike discovered from the driver the foundations of this road had been established in the Second World War when battle had flowed back and forth according to fortune. Occasionally they passed through hovels of villages where dirty children came out to greet them. Unlike Morocco, full of olive trees and green coarse vegetation the land of Libya at this point was barren, sandy and desolate. The journey took all day in the intense heat, lengthened by the driver's need to refresh himself copiously with whatever beverage a village offered.

The driver was in no hurry. He was a big man, much

bigger than the average Libyan. His olive brown skin was lighter, and his manner more open.

'He's Egyptian,' explained Mike. 'More civilised than the average Libyan.'

The driver's more civilised background was supported by a more than average need for drink, which explained the size of his stomach. Jim couldn't help thinking that the driver was consuming beer, but he didn't think it was possible, not in a country, which had laws against alcohol. If by some strange chance it *was* beer, would they get safely to Tobruk? Beer and the heat were a dangerous combination. Fortunately traffic was sparse. At times the driver would stop by the roadside to relieve himself nonchalantly, great jets of water soaked up by the dry sand.

For a while Mike chatted to the driver in English; the latter's knowledge was quite fluent. Then Mike, like Jim, dropped off to sleep; the last two days had been tiring. Sleep was enhanced by the car radio, which droned out Arabic music in monotonous repetition.

At one stage Mike woke up and with typical enthusiasm exclaimed,

'God, the desert! The place of a thousand mysteries! It's infinite, timeless, like the sea, expressing a similar beauty and awe.'

All Jim could see was sand and more sand, just occasionally a stunted shrub.

Mike was like a small boy, finding endless enthusiasm in very little. His eagerness grated on Jim's frayed nerves. Mike reminded him of pimply schoolboys, the sort who were like eager puppies seeking always excitement.

At Tobruk they were driven straight to the college. This was a large, modern building that looked as if it was made out of prefabricated component parts. Inside there was a welcome coolness, with office furniture manufactured from black metal tubular frames, and shiny brown composite wood.

The building inside and out didn't seem to belong to an Arab country. It was not unwelcoming to Jim's unhappy mind, reminding him of prefabricated school classrooms at home.

They were greeted by a young, Europeanised Arab who spoke excellent English. He gave his name as Hali, explaining it was his first name. He described himself, without any pretence, as the personnel manager. He was a pleasant man, small, intense, intelligent, with none of the colonel's rude arrogance. He soon had them organised.

'I'd like your passports,' he stated, once he had finished explaining their accommodation arrangements.

Jim handed his passport over, but Mike was reluctant.

'When do we get it back?' he asked.

'About three weeks. The local police are a little slow.'

Mike pulled a face but didn't comment.

Later, when alone together, Jim asked about the passport incident.

'I doubt whether we'll get them back before the end of our contract,' Mike remarked.

'But they can't do that. That's not until the end of June next year.'

'It's their way of making certain we fulfil our contracts.'

'God, that's awful!'

With a sinking heart Jim thought of the dreadful consequences – no possibility of getting home at Christmas, what he longed for more than anything else.

He explained his concern to Mike.

'Not a chance,' was his unfeeling response.

Mike, without family ties, seemed outwardly unconcerned.

'But that's impossible!' Jim exclaimed. 'I promised my family I'd be back at Christmas, just for a few days. I'm sure Mohammad said there was a holiday then.'

'No holiday, Jim. Perhaps only a local one. It's a pity; I hoped to pop into Egypt for a few days. I've never been there.'

Jim felt he must check officially the situation. The thought of nine months without seeing his family filled him with dread.

They were taken by car to their accommodation. Mike was the first to be dropped off, near what Hali described as Italian style gardens, reminiscent of the days when Libya was an Italian colony. Jim was taken to a more modern part of Tobruk, dusty from intensive building construction. It consisted of large blocks of flats, several unfinished, exposed like a skeleton. It all looked so temporary, even artificial, increasing Jim's bemused uncertainty about life in Libya. It was dawning on him that, unlike Mike, he was not psychologically conditioned to this new environment.

132

The culture shock appeared more than he could take.

*

Jim's flat was in one of the finished blocks – clean, sparsely furnished with Western beds, tables, armchairs and a settee. Hali introduced him to Richard Myers, the current resident Englishman, soon to go back to England for unspecified personal reasons. Once he had gone, then this large three bed-roomed apartment would be Jim's to rattle around in. Longingly Jim thought how much Janet would have liked it, seen possibilities of decoration on the bare cream walls, placed little scatter rugs on the cold, tiled flooring. The flat seemed like another world, remote from Arab primitiveness.

'It's nice,' Jim said, his spirits lifting. He had at least somewhere decent to live.

'I suppose it's all right,' was Richard's dry comment.

Jim studied his temporary flat partner, a small man with thinning grey hair, and a sharp beaky nose, which reminded Jim of his former Latin teacher. He looked to be in his fifties, but that was purely guesswork. During their conversation Richard rarely smiled, regarding life with great gloom. He looked a typical English bachelor.

Hali said goodbye, politely wishing Jim a pleasant stay. He was a courteous, helpful young man, a credit to the Arabs.

'There goes the whiz-kid,' remarked Richard. There was a certain contempt for Hali.

They sat down to chat in -the kitchen. Richard brewed with pedantic care an English cup of tea, in a china teapot, which could only have come from England.

Jim asked him about the passport situation.

'That's the last you'll see of yours,' Richard remarked dryly. 'I haven't got mine back yet, and I'm supposed to be leaving in four days! This is a regimented country, full of distrust. No freedom.'

'But why?'

Richard shrugged.

'It's how they are. We had another Englishman here, hated it, wanted to get home. He bribed a taxi to take him to the Egyptian border, not so far away. He then walked across in an unguarded area, asked to be taken to the British consul. He got away with it, even though he had no passport. The Egyptians don't like the Libyans. The Colonel was furious, questioned all

133

of us in case we were accomplices. Since then there has to be some kind of permit to leave Tobruk, even on a short journey.'

'That's terrible!'

'It's life here! You chose to come. You have to live by their standards!'

This made Jim utterly depressed.

'Isn't there any way I can get home for Christmas?'

'Not a hope! And if you talk about it they'll put a watch on you. This is a police state. By your contract you belong to Libya, not to England.'

Richard mused for a moment, and then added cynically:

'Come to think of it, they love their little power games. Gives them a kick to put one over us English.'

Jim's misfortune seemed to give Richard some vicarious pleasure. For the first time he revealed a twisted smile. Jim's anger increased, not only with his situation, but also with the apparent lack of sympathy from his fellow countryman.

'I'll go and see Colonel Mohamed tomorrow,' Jim concluded.

'Not a hope! The man's a bastard! You'll get no joy out of him.'

*

The next day Jim waited with Richard outside their block of flats. There was a daily arrangement that all staff would be picked up by mini-bus. This surprised Jim because the college was within walking distance.

'The Arabs never walk,' explained Richard. 'It's demeaning. Only women walk, which is as it should be.'

At the mention of women Richard laughed, a dry laugh, which emanated from the depths of his throat. Jim wondered, maybe unkindly, whether Richard's stay in an Arab country was to do with a\ dislike of women, the Arab attitude satisfying some inner complex. Certainly Richard appeared a born bachelor. Mike was much the same, though not cynical about women. Jim could never imagine Mike marrying.

At the college, Jim went to see Hali about Christmas, but he proved non-committal, as if he was afraid to give a direct answer.

'You must see Colonel Mohamed when he's back. He's away for three days.'

Richard smiled sardonically when he heard of the

Colonel's absence.

'Mohamed's married to an American girl,' he explained, as if such a marriage was an ample excuse to be away for three days.

Jim began to wonder about the Colonel. It was now apparent he was Principal of the college, a fact that Jim had not clearly understood at interview. He also wondered how a freethinking American girl could marry into such a chauvinistic, restricted society.

But Richard was ever ready with an explanation.

'College Principal is a political appointment by Gaddafi. It keeps his army officers suitably occupied to prevent any military coup.'

Jim nodded. It made sense!

'As for his wife,' Richard sniggered, 'she is, or was, a starry-eyed American girl. It was cute to marry an Arab and a Libyan at that, given American distrust of Libya. She quickly bore him two children and another on the way. She's heavily domesticated now, well in his power, unable to escape.'

Jim didn't regard so favourably Richard's second comment. He was beginning to dislike Richard and his attitude.

Richard conducted Jim to the staff room, one of four on the first floor. He explained that each department had its own staff room – science, technology, languages and culture. The latter meant general subjects such as history (particularly that of Libya, much over-rated in content under a dictatorship), geography, art and psychology.

The language staff room was the best Jim had ever experienced – large, airy, with comfortable chairs, and plenty of cupboard and shelf space. Each teacher, or lecturer as they were termed, had his own desk, though Jim had to share with Richard until his departure.

Jim was introduced to the language staff. Apart from Mike and Richard there was an American, Ned, in his early thirties, tall and heavily built, with his dark hair sleeked back, and a Pakistani from Manchester whose name Jim could not decipher. Both the latter had D. Phils. in some aspect of English literature or language, and were far better qualified than Jim, Mike and even Richard. The other occupant, covering the French language, was an elderly Frenchman who could well have walked out of the era of colonial France, very grey-haired and distinguished. He gave an impression of lonely unhappiness, which Jim recognised as a similar homesickness as himself. The Frenchman, whose name was Pierre, later explained to Jim he was 'depayse', or suffering from the 'maladie de chez moi', a longing for his own home country. He paid homage to the French conceit, promulgated by General de Gaulle, that there was only one true language – his own! As a result his efforts to speak English were poor and heavily accented. Jim found it easier to converse in French. It was an opportunity to keep up his own knowledge.

Ned, as Head of the language department, offered to show Jim the classrooms, textbooks and syllabus.

All the classrooms were decked out as language laboratories, with each desk having earphones and controls linked to a central console on the teacher's desk. Jim's confidence went down a further notch; he'd never worked with such technology. But Ned assured him it was simple.

'The course is an American one, and you may find some of the vocabulary and pronunciation strange. It's based on a system by which you do one hour of class work going over the relevant data, followed by one hour of back-up work with the tapes. It's a good system once you get used to it.'

After he had been shown around Jim brought up hesitantly the subject of the Christmas holidays, which had by now become an obsession. Ned was kinder in his approach than Richard.

'I sure am sorry, but I'm afraid you'll be disappointed. Nobody is allowed to leave until the end of the academic year next June. All the holidays, such as they are, have to be taken locally, but there's very little to do or see. Didn't they explain this at interview?'

Jim shook his head.

'I may have misunderstood, but I'm convinced he told me there was a holiday at Christmas. I naturally assumed I could go home just for a few days.'

It was Ned's turn to shake his head.

'They'll sure as hell never give you your passport, I fear.'

He saw the disappointment in Jim's face, and added lamely.

'I sure am sorry. Yer see we're all bachelors here.'

Jim wanted to confide further in this big, friendly man why he, a married man, had come to Libya. To an observer he

136

must have seemed mad. But he had found, since his court conviction, difficulty in communicating. He could only explain his situation to a point, and then he had to tell lies. If he went further then people would look at him askance. He cared about how others felt. It was only friends like Rosie whose loyalty one could trust that helped him, even if she did go on a bit!

*

There was no teaching that day, even though term had begun. The way the Colonel had talked, Jim had expected to be in the classroom from day one.

'The students are on strike,' chortled Richard. 'Lazy buggers! They're always off for some reason or another. This time it's an anti-Gaddafi protest; the young don't like him.'

'All we can do is put our feet up and wait for the mini-bus,' explained Ned.

Jim wondered why the teachers didn't go home. The Pakistani was studying Arabic, and he found a kindred spirit in Mike. Ned was reading some American journals. Richard put his feet up on his desk and closed his eyes.

For a while Jim talked to Pierre. He told Pierre that at home he enjoyed hill walking, and had one year walked the Pennine Way. Pierre commented on Jim's limp, and asked how he managed such a long distance.

'Really from a fatheaded determination not to accept my leg as a disability. But the walk took me nearly four weeks, whereas others did it in two or three.'

'Jamais, jamais walk around Tobruk,' Pierre advised.

'Why?' Jim asked, inwardly groaning at another restriction.

'D'abord, it's very boring, just desert.' Deuxiement it's dangerous. Thee are still mines from the war. I know you English; you like to promener.'

Jim was horrified. He reckoned the war was over some thirty years ago. Surely the Arabs would have cleared their desert by now? It reminded Jim that in the poorer part of Benghazi, where Mike had taken him for a meal, he had been intrigued to see an old British army ammunition box built in as part of a derelict wall.

The teachers ate their lunch solemnly together in the staff room, nobody talking, chewing their sandwiches which they had brought with them. Richard had explained the night before there was no canteen. The only form of refreshment was an old van in the car park, which served omelettes thrust into bread rolls. Jim, ever hungry, found them delicious.

After lunch he slipped into the town hoping to buy some sandals, his feet uncomfortable in the heat. In his hurry to pack, and despite Janet's solicitude, he'd forgotten about suitable footwear. When he got back about an hour later, Richard called to him in great glee.

"You're for it, my lad. In deep hot water. The office wants to see you.'

'Why?' queried Jim, annoyed at the tone of Richard's voice.

'Nobody ever leaves the premises until four o'clock when classes finish.'

'What! But there's no teaching!'

'Aha, but you forget you're in a military regime. You conform.'

Ned nodded. 'Richard's right. They check on you hourly. Did you not notice the Libyan security man coming round during the morning? If you're not present they want to know why.'

'My God!' muttered Jim, totally dumbfounded his movements should be vetted. In England at school he was quite used to slipping out if he had a free period.

'I'll come with you,' said Ned. 'It's a Palestinian in the office. He hates the British.'

He took him down to the ground floor, to a door marked in Arabic 'Principal's Office'.

Ned knocked and waited, until a surly voice bade them enter.

There were two people present in fairly cramped conditions. One was a man dark of hair, swarthy faced, with a bushy moustache and unfriendly mien. The other was a girl, olive-faced, long black hair, petite, in a dark skirt and colourful blouse. Her hair was uncovered which was unusual. She had the air of a woman alert and liberated. She was a pleasant sight to Jim who had become resigned to seeing no woman, at least no attractive woman.

The swarthy-faced man offered no greeting. He just snapped out:

'You left the premises without permission.'

Jim thought it must be the Palestinian Ned had

138

mentioned.

Ned did all the talking. 'James Eskdale is new to procedures here. He's very sorry. He went into the town with a desperate need to buy some shoes. I gave him full permission as I felt it was a priority matter.'

Jim almost gasped; Ned's permission was a barefaced lie. It was his first taste of a regime, which required one to tell lies as an instinctive protection.

The man made grumbling noises; the girl smiled, trying to reassure Jim. But nothing more was said. The man went to a drawer and picked out a thin document. He handed it to Jim.

'Your contract,' he muttered. 'Read it, sign it and bring it back here.'

It was an order. Jim resented the way he was spoken to. Ned, seeing Jim's face, hastily made an excuse, and hurried him out.

'Never argue. Never show offence,' he muttered pragmatically. 'It sure don't pay in a country like this.'

Jim thought a moment.

'You know, I don't think I can take any more of this. I'm tired and homesick. Things here are different to what I imagined, though I have to confess I was warned.'

He thought ruefully of Rosie.

'I've had my passport taken,' he continued. 'I've lost any hope of going home at Christmas. I feel I've lost my freedom; this checking on our whereabouts is dreadful. Finally that man in the office, he spoke to me as if I was some sort of underling. It's all too much, far too much.'

He shook his head in sadness. Ned commiserated.

'You get used to it,' he commented affably.

But Jim couldn't agree. He wanted to say that human acceptance of unjust power was how tyrannical regimes flourished. He couldn't be like Ned and go along with the situation. And yet he felt he couldn't explain; everybody saw things so differently, from the cynicism of Richard, the enthusiasm of Mike, to the expedient attitude of Ned – all bachelors, no children of their own. He was surprised Ned, an American, should be so accepting.

It was at that moment, standing outside the college office, he decided not to sign the contract, go back to England as soon as he could. Rosie was right, bless her. Better to suffer in relative poverty with the people he loved, than to have money in

139

conditions one could not accept.

But how to get back? That was the problem. He had no money, no return flight ticket, and no passport.

Above all, he still had to tackle the Colonel, whose image became even more frightening with absence.

The situation rendered him even more miserable.

On the way back to their flats on the minibus, another Englishman, a physicist called Paul, invited him to his home. Paul was a very different kettle of fish to the others – a married man with his family *actually* in Tobruk.

'Have a quick cup of tea,' he suggested smiling. 'We expatriates must stick together.'

Paul's flat was one block further on than Jim's. It was a home, made comfortable by Paul's wife, Sandra, and an unbearable reminder of England. There was the usual paraphernalia of two small children – toys, kiddie cart and cuddly bears. Sandra was a woman who seemed to believe that virtue was in chaos. Dumpy in figure, untidy herself, her hair in a mess, she oozed housewifely motherhood.

'I was like you,' Paul explained. 'I had to come out for a year before my family could join me. It was quite an ordeal!'

Jim nodded. The whole home was a poignant reminder of what he was missing. A lump came into his throat as a little girl of two, apparently born in Libya without problems according to Sandra, tottered over to him, carrying a huge teddy bear, and wriggled her little bottom onto his lap.

'She's very friendly,' excused Sandra, 'sometimes too friendly as if she would go off with anyone.'

There was a touch of motherly pride in her voice, as well as concern.

*

That evening Jim cooked supper for Richard, in return for Richard having prepared a meal the day before. Jim found some fish in the market, grilled it in margarine, and prepared some vegetables. For pudding they had fruit from the market, and some English chocolate Richard had been saving.

Richard became more human over the meal, at least for a while. He admitted he had been working and living abroad for some twenty years. He felt it was time to go back to England. His worry was the opposite of Jim's; he wondered how he would settle back home. He had no elatives, except very distant

140

ones, and no friends.

But then he launched into an unbelievable tirade against Ned. Jim wondered whether his real reason for leaving Tobruk was his dislike of Ned, or his resentment that Ned, a younger man, was head of department.

'The man's a charlatan, a sucker-upper to authority,' he exclaimed. 'Beware of him.'

Richard had an old-fashioned way of using schoolboy phraseology, words like –sucker-upper, which dated him. Jim began to feel that Richard was a bitter, lonely man, hiding his unhappiness under caustic humour.

At the same time Jim wondered whether there wasn't a grain of truth in what Richard said about Ned. Jim had been uncomfortable in the way Ned had covered for him that afternoon. Ned was prepared to manipulate the Arabs and preserve an easy relationship, and yet behind their backs express criticism.

Jim sighed. Even in Libya he was faced with rival personalities, a situation he disliked. It was why he preferred working in wood, which he could shape to his own requirements away from human conflict.

That night Jim lay in bed and faced the blackest misery he had felt since his court case. Not only did every part of his being ache for Janet, long to see Peter again, need the reassurance of the country he loved, but he also began to doubt himself. He wondered how a man could be so stupid as to risk a criminal conviction, and moreover put himself in his present situation. He wondered whether he wasn't a little insane. The pressure of months of unemployment and the trauma of a trial that went against him had turned his mind. A more normally adjusted man like Paul would have accepted the situation in Libya, served his nine months, returned to England with money which would have provided a short term security and the wherewithal to move to Libya. He, Jim, had failed and was useless to everyone, particularly his family. For the second time since leaving England he contemplated suicide, throwing himself out of the third floor flat to lie crushed on the pavement below. But he wouldn't go near the window for fear that he might *actually* do it.

Why couldn't he be like the others, accepting of the problems of living in another country? The money was good. He had a decent flat. Working conditions were good, apart from certain restrictions. Why couldn't he get on with life and be less sensitive? Why couldn't he be like Janet, useful, caring, hardworking, loved by those she helped in the hospital? Why must he wallow in his own misery? Why be such a wimp?

Worse still, what would his son think of him if he sought the easy way out and took his own life?

Again what prospects did he have back in England? He'd be lucky to find a job!

The blackest hour for Jim was about four o'clock in the morning when he got up and walked the streets of Tobruk, his head aching, thoughts going round and round in his head.

Only one central issue stood out above all others.

He wanted to be home with Janet and Peter!

He was desperate!

*

The next day, another day when the students were on strike, Jim went to see Hali. He told him he wanted to return to England as soon as possible.

'May I ask why?' Hali was totally reasonable.

Jim found it difficult to explain. During his anxious time of walking in the early hours of the morning, he'd thought up many a hopefully convincing explanation. But now words totally failed him! In front of a man who must be his junior by ten years!

He could only repeat that he wanted to go home, like some blubbing schoolboy who wanted his mummy!

Hali took him to the office, explained to the Palestinian what Jim wanted.

'You Britishers, you want everything,' the Palestinian snarled, angry at such a request. 'I, Palestinian. You take our country, give it to Jew. It easy for you, solve everything. You think of Jew. You not think of us.'

Jim couldn't see the connection. He wanted to say it was the United Nations that gave Palestine to the Jews.

But it would be hardly tactful!

Only the girl smiled. Ned had explained she was Lebanese, the suffering of her country making her more free as a woman than might normally be the case.

'I telephone Colonel,' muttered the Palestinian. 'He home now.'

Later in the afternoon Jim was summoned to the

Colonel's office.

The Colonel didn't rise. He continued writing at his desk, which stood on a slightly raised dais, giving the authority of height to a small man. The room itself was intimidating, much too big to be a personal office, with wide windows down one length and large murals on the other three sides. Given a less stressful situation it might have been attractive.

At last the Colonel put down his pen.

'You continue to work for me,' he stated bluntly, a very different tone of voice to that at the Dorchester. 'You are under contract.'

'But I haven't signed any contract.'

'Have you never heard of a gentleman's agreement?'

Jim's heart sank. He knew in England a verbal agreement could be binding,

Suddenly there arose in him an angry resentment of the whole way authority had pushed him around over the last fifteen months, the same anger that had made him fight tooth and nail his court case.

'I'm sorry, but I must leave.'

'Why?'

The question snapped out viciously like a bullet from a gun, making Jim jump.

'I cannot explain, sir. It's just I must leave.'

Jim fell instinctively into a term of respect, like being back at school confronting the headmaster.

The Colonel looked at him assessingly through those piggy eyes.

'I understand you feel homesick. You want your wife.'

There was a sneer to the Colonel's voice.

Jim wondered who had told him.

'That is true. My son too! It was a mistake my coming.'

'I understand also that you dislike my country.'

Jim was stung.

'Who told you that?'

But the colonel didn't reply.

'It's not that I dislike Libya. I haven't been here long enough. It's just everything is so different. I can't get used to it.'

The Colonel's eyes glittered. There was something disquieting in his look.

'Your county is less and less important now,' he stated in his excellent English. 'One day England will be inferior to

143

us.'

Jim couldn't bear the colonel's look of megalomania. It frightened him, just as he had been upset by the hatred of the Palestinian. He hung his head in defeat, not knowing what else he could do.

The colonel dismissed him, saying,

'You work for me. That is the end of the matter.'

Down went Jim's head again.

It was then that he erupted!

'No way do I work for you. No way!'

'You will be held in breach of contract, a criminal offence in my country.'

Jim's heart sank. His spirit couldn't take another court case. He realised now how, in a dictatorship, a man could be broken.

He left the room, his body slumped in defeat.

That evening he went round to see Ned. He felt he was the only man, though younger than Jim, who might have the manipulative skills to get him out of his predicament. It was an odd situation, an Englishman pouring out his story to an American he hardly knew – or at least as much as he could afford to tell; he omitted the court conviction.

'Leave it to me,' Ned reassured him. 'I'll have a word with Mohamed. I once studied industrial relationships. I've had experience of situations that are deadlocked.'

As good as his word, Ned went to see the Colonel the next day. He went alone. When he came back his manner had changed. He no longer seemed so friendly.

'Mohamed wants to see you and I together,' he told Jim tersely.

In the Colonel's office, the American and the Englishman were left standing in font of the desk. Once again, they were ignored. The suspense for Jim was deeply disturbing. He couldn't help feeling the Colonel was indulging in some kind of power game.

Finally the Colonel gathered up his papers, pointed dramatically at Jim, and snapped loudly:

'You are a thief!'

Jim knew then what was coming. He had lost, utterly lost!

'The Italian embassy in London sent me a telex. You have a criminal conviction! Because of the need to have the visa quickly, they hadn't checked. But they have now.'

The colonel paused looking ominously angry.

'In this county we do not like thieves. We cut off their hands.'

He then pointed an accusing fat finger.

'You deceived me at interview. You told lies. I cannot continue to employ you.'

In his misery Jim suddenly saw a ray of hope. He had been dismissed! Even such an ignominious return to his home country would be worth it.

But the Colonel hadn't finished.

'You repay to us all the monies we have given you, your air fare to Libya, your hotel expenses in Tripoli and Benghazi, the advance of salary paid to you. If you do not you will not be allowed to leave the country, and will be imprisoned. I'm informing the British Embassy at Tripoli.'

He then left the room by a door behind his desk. There was nothing more to be said.

'I think he means it,' Ned warned unnecessarily.

Jim made a rapid calculation.

'That means finding about five hundred pounds, plus my own fare and expenses home,' he exclaimed. 'No way can I find that sort of money!'

Ned shrugged. For some reason his interest had waned; he'd done what he could. Jim had the feeling Ned despised him.

Later that day, realising he was no longer employed by the college, Jim went for a walk along the English promenade, the stretch of beach so-called because, in years of peace, the English lay in the sun, and swam in the Mediterranean waters. He felt his life was over, nothing remaining but further disgrace and misery. His gammy leg ached terribly as if the mental torment he was suffering communicated itself to the nerves of his body. His head felt as if it would burst with pain. He wanted to cry out to some unknown God, and then bury his head in the sands, making deep heartfelt moans.

He remembered on a previous occasion he had walked a beach, at the time of his trial. Then he had resolved to be a man. The same strength of feeling came to him now. He had a mad idea to steal a car and make for the Egyptian border. He had never in his life stolen a car. Perhaps there was a boat he could take, put his trust in the sea, just as his father had planned to do as an escaped soldier after Dunkirk.

He let out a roar of rage at the skies, as if defying the Gods to do their worst. It was lucky it was late afternoon and nobody heard him. He began to trudge back towards the town, a determination on his face born of desperation.

Suddenly he saw Richard walking towards him, crabbed, caustic Richard, unloving and unloved. Jim felt he could not take any more of his drab remarks, and began to move off in another direction.

'Jim, wait. Wait a moment!'

There was an urgency in Richard's voice. He, unfit, was sweating with the exertion.

He approached Jim.

'Ned told me what has happened,' he called out. 'I'm very, very sorry. I saw you coming this way. I'll lend you the money you want. Pay me back when you can. No hurry.'

Jim stared at him, astounded. This offer came from a man whom he basically disliked.

Richard, like so many Englishmen at moments of generosity, looked embarrassed.

'I'm an old bachelor. I've plenty of money. No dependents.'

The shock was so great, Jim just stood rooted to the spot. Then he began to cry, tears pouring down his face. He couldn't help it.

'I don't know how to thank...,' he blubbed out, unable to finish.

'Forget it! Forget it!' Richard made deprecating gestures. 'Regard it as a favour from one Englishman to another in this bloody country.'

'Thank you,' said God. 'Some story.'

The old man sighed.

'Would you mind if we didn't discuss it now, saved it for some future day? I'm tired and, well, not myself in some funny way.'

God waved his hand benevolently as if to say – 'Fine by me!'.

*

146

CHAPTER 8

There once was a man who said 'Damn!
It is borne upon me that I am
An engine that moves
In predestinate grooves
I'm not even a bus I'm a tram.'
(Written by Maurice Evan Hare (1886-1967) at St. John's
College, Oxford in 1905)

'That was quite some story,' remarked God, smiling, thinking once again of the Libyan story.

The old man did not reply. He just sat looking into the distance of his mind. Libya had been a traumatic memory.

'And Jim was you?'

'Ye-e-es. Sort of. I altered bits of the story.'

'Wow! You did go through a time!'

The old man was again silent. Though it was an experience, it was something best forgotten.

'And what happened when you got back?' God enquired.

'I became a headmaster.'

'What!?'

'I became a headmaster.'

'You're joking.'

'It's true.'

'What, with a court conviction, out of work for fifteen months, just returned from Libya, you became a headmaster, just like that? I don't believe it!'

'I couldn't believe it myself.'

'How did it happen?'

'Well, I had applied, before I went to Libya, for a teaching post locally in a school for ESN (M) children. I felt with my hearing handicap I no longer could teach French. I also felt I owed it to mankind to give something back to less privileged children. I had been lucky in life in so many ways.'

'What's ESN (M)?'

'Educationally Sub Normal. I'm not sure about the M. It implied they were only 'mediumly' disturbed, I suppose. Nearly all of them had police records.'

'And...?'

'Well, I'd rather given up on the application. I didn't

147

hear any more. But when I got back Janet - sorry, my real wife - told me there was a gentleman who wanted to see me. He turned up the next day.'

'And what did he have to say?'

'Simply there was an emergency vacancy for a headmaster. The present incumbent had left suddenly – a nervous breakdown I discovered leter. Would I stand in for one term?'

'And you did?

'You bet!'

'Even though you had no experience of ESN children?'

'It didn't matter, or so this gentleman said. He was an educational psychologist, a marvellous man.'

'How come?'

'Well, he said I was there primarily to promote the teaching side. There was a team of care workers who looked after the children.'

'And it worked?'

'You bet! Before my first term was over, I was offered the headship as a permanency - me, a public schoolboy, an Oxford graduate, looking after disturbed, unhappy boys from broken homes! Their parents never visited them, only their social worker.'

'Wow!'

'Um! I really felt that you, God, or whoever stood for God, was looking after me. It has been like that all my life. Out of apparent failure has sprung something worthwhile. The wheels of life, so to speak. It reminds me of Churchill's statement, if I can remember it correctly, - *'The pessimist finds disaster in opportunity, the optimist finds opportunity in disaster.* It's a saying I've never forgotten. It has kept me going on many an occasion..'

'Well, all I can say, you were lucky. Did you mention your court case?'

'Of course. I wasn't going to make the same mistake twice. You say I was lucky. It wasn't luck.. It was just I was in the right place at the right time.'

'Good for you.'

There was a comfortable silence between them for a moment.

'One thing I must ask you, my son. Jim in the story had a gammy leg. You have your loss of hearing. Was that

148

difficult?'

'You mean in Libya or life in general?'

'Both, really.'

'More difficult in life than I was ever prepared to acknowledge. My mother insisted I was brought up as a normal boy. No handicapped school for me. No concessions to my lack of hearing. I should have learnt to lip-read, but didn't. But that was my own bloody fault.'

'Why?'

'I ran away from the lip-reading lessons.'

'And you think that was right – to be brought up as normal?'

'In hindsight, Yes. In reality it gave me many difficult moments. But I learnt to cope the hard way.'

'Tell me about it.'

'Well, can I tell you a story, a true one? It might illustrate some of the problems.'

God nodded.

WANTED A GIRL!

And God stands winding His lonely horn,
And time and the world are ever in flight;
And love is less kind than the grey twilight,
And hope is less dear than the dew of the morn.
(William Butler Yeats - 1865-1939.

Steve badly wanted to go to one of the Oxford Commem. Balls. In his first year, it was the turn of his own college. He was nineteen.

The idea of a Commemoration Ball was incredibly attractive. It started at 10p.m. and finished at 6a.m. with a group photo. The girls wore colourful long dresses and the men dinner jackets or tails, some with very fancy cummerbunds. During the night you danced, ate a huge dinner, drank, watched the fireworks, listened to an entertainer, and did all the other things, or some of them, which young men and women did together.

Afterwards you went on the river in a punt, took a picnic breakfast, and drank perhaps more wine; maybe fell in the river to cool down.

149

This was back in 1949.

Steve loved dancing. The grounds of his college, Worcester, were among the loveliest in Oxford. The lake and wide tree-scattered lawns lived on long after in his memory.

There was one difficulty!

Steve hadn't got a girl!

You know, one of those lovely beings with an attractive bosom, alluring legs and long, glistening hair, who giggled delightfully, as girls did in those days.

He didn't have a sister who might have helped him.

He was incredibly shy of women, which made matters worse. It was really to do with his deafness. He had about seventy to ninety per cent decibel hearing loss. The trouble was his bass hearing was better than his treble. He would jokingly say no woman could whisper sweet nothings in his ear.

The other problem, deaf-aids were cumbersome, and the quality of sound poor. The constant buzz of background noise was tiring and distracting. Steve wore his aid under his tie. With a bow tie he wore it under his shirt; every time he moved a rustling noise against his shirt or tie made conversation difficult. The cord went from the box up under his collar and out to his ear. Steve was very conscious it was not an attractive feature.

The box also made it difficult for him to embrace a girl. It just caused squeaky, disconcerting feedback.

Altogether Steve fought a losing battle to attract the opposite sex. No girl seemed interested in going out with a young man with whom conversation was difficult.

The one thing he enjoyed at Oxford was sport. A deaf aid was not a hindrance to hitting or kicking balls. He just took the wretched instrument off. But sport did not pull the birds, to quote a revolting twenty-first century analogy.

Steve asked his brother's ex-girlfriend if she could help. Her name was Millie. She promptly invited herself to the Ball, together with her new boyfriend, a White Russian, a Prince. But she did promise she would ask around. She was great, a warm, generous girl who had no hang ups about deaf young men.

He also asked his mother if she knew of anybody. She said she had a few ideas.

There was one girl at Oxford Steve was quite attracted to. She was dark, slim, and very pretty, too pretty in fact because other men were interested. Steve had never even spoken to her. Just adored her from afar. She attended the same history seminar and some of the same lectures. He didn't even know her name, which was stupid, but he just didn't hear it.

He once followed her back to her college, his one and only effort at stalking. He really wanted to pretend to meet her by chance and talk to her, ask her out for a coffee.

But in the end he didn't have the courage!

Steve joined the C.S.Lewis discussion group, which met on a Sunday evening. He rarely heard what the great man said, but it made a pleasant, quiet, social situation. There was a girl there called Catherine, a cripple in a wheelchair. She was kind and understanding, and she teased him. She was about the only girl in Oxford he talked to. He needed teasing; most deaf people take themselves much too seriously. He told her of his problem. She giggled.

As it happened she also studied history and she knew the girl Steve wanted to approach. He asked Catherine if she would talk to this girl and explain the situation; enquire if she would come to the Ball, as a sort of blind date, even though he was hard of hearing.

'I'd love to sort out your love life,' Catherine exclaimed, smiling. She had a lovely smile.

Catherine, bless her, duly arranged that Steve should meet this girl for coffee one morning.

At the same time Steve's mother, also bless her, had arranged for the daughter of the regional manager of the Legal and General to come up to Oxford and discuss the matter. Mother, who was a great snob, thought the manager *a very* important man, and the daughter a wonderful catch, one who was very keen to go.

At the same time Millie had also found somebody, and more or less put it to her as a fact.

Catherine's girl turned out to be the wrong one! It was embarrassing at the coffee place, but Steve, trying to be gentlemanly, pretended she was the right girl.

The girl however was no fool, and Steve was unpractised in the art of dissimulation. The girl went back to Catherine and told her there was a mistake. But Catherine, a true Trojan, talked to Steve that same evening, suddenly realising which girl he really was referring to. Steve met this girl the next day; his heart gave a leap. Joy of joys, she really was the *one!* He took her punting. The delight of punting is that you don't have to talk, at least not much. Steve exerted himself at the manly art of wielding a lengthy pole, while Marianne (that was her name) trailed her fingers in the water, and looked heart-stoppingly beautiful. She also cooed over a string of ducklings following their mother like the tail of a kite.

Steve now had three – he couldn't believe it! – *three* girls all wanting to come to the Ball. Gloomily he realised he was not the attraction! It was the kudos of an Oxford Ball.

He had a lot of explanations to make!

The friend of his brother's ex-girlfriend proved not too difficult. Millie, in her understanding way, extricated him, apologising that she had invited too hastily. It wasn't strictly her fault, more Steve's for asking around without too much thought. But then he was desperate!

The daughter of the manager of the Legal and General, this supposedly important man, *did* come up to Oxford for an exploratory visit. It was difficult to put her off. Steve tried to give her a nice time – she watched him play cricket when he scored fourteen runs! Some 'nice time' for a girl! But she was incredibly shy, even more than Steve. She also wasn't very pretty nor very bright. She told Steve she had left school without any School Certificates. She also had a funny way of walking, like a duck, with feet pointing outwards. Anyway he told a white lie, said that an old friend had suddenly appeared (nearly true!) and he felt obliged to take her.

The Commem. Ball when it came was something of a disaster.

Steve got into quite a state about it beforehand!

He asked his mother how one treated girls on such occasions. She replied very sweetly – 'Just be nice to her, there's a dear!' – which was a considerate thought, but not very helpful. He approached his aunt for advice; she had always been sympathetic to his loss of hearing. She suggested various conversational gambits – 'Don't you think it's a nice band?'   - or – 'isn't it a lovely evening?' (which it was! They were lucky with the weather) – or, more appropriately – 'what a lovely dress you're wearing!' Such phrases were useful but did not allow for hearing the answers!

Anyway, after some discussion with Catherine, he bought Marianne some flowers, plus a little nosegay to put on her dress.

He also bought Catherine hderself, his stalwart helper, a bouquet by way of thanks for finding Marianne, despite an embarrassing misunderstanding at first.

'I enjoyed it,' Catherine laughed. 'I hope you have a wonderful time.' There was not a bit of jealousy or envy in her nature, despite the fact she was a cripple. It hung on Steve's conscience, even many years later, that he never took Catherine to the Commem. Ball. They would have watched, held hands and her eyes would have glistened under the pretty lights. He would have pushed her proudly round the grounds in her wheelchair, ignoring the sneers that the only girl he could take couldn't dance.

Catherine died, unhappily, the following academic year from some muscular wasting disease; Steve could never remember the name. Muscular atrophy? Her college held a memorial service for her in their chapel, and all the C.S.Lewis Sunday group went, including the great man himself who read the lesson. Steve blubbed like a schoolboy.

Truth to tell Catherine was his first love at Oxford, though he was slow to realise it. It was a strange relationship, a platonic, companionable friendship. She was the only girl he could ever talk to during his first year, a great relief in his loneliness.

Anyway, to get back to that wretched Commem. Ball! Marianne and Steve danced a bit; she wasn't a very enthusiastic dancer. Steve liked the Latin American dances; the joy was that you didn't have to talk; it was all movement. But Marianne preferred the ballroom dancing to a limited extent. To Steve she seemed either tired or bored, maybe both. She confessed she had already been to one Commem. Ball at another college. It was something he feared; he knew other men were after her, like bees to honey.

Steve kept asking her what she would like to do next; she would invariably reply rather pointedly – what would *you* like to do? It meant they never got anywhere. Steve hadn't the courage or the experience to take the lead. He rather supposed she felt under an obligation to him, which made him even more uncomfortable. He wanted her to enjoy the occasion, not feel 'obliged'. He never tried to kiss her, nor did they hold hands. He only touched her when they danced. She was one of those girls who danced with a stiff back; she didn't bend or flow to the music. Moreover she danced away from him, nose in the air as if there was a bad smell. Altogether she was a dead loss. Or rather he was a worse loss! It must have been difficult for her to spend eight hours with a deaf boy! She must have been bored out of her dainty little shoes.

Steve's brother's ex-girlfriend, Millie, was a help. She was great fun. But two things happened. Marianne found it more interesting to talk with the Russian Prince and he seemed to respond. Millie was quick to react to protect her interest, so Marianne went to sulk in the loo. Steve thought the prince was a pathetic little man, living on his meaningless title.

Afterwards they went on the river on a punt, just Marianne and Steve, as the other two had to get back to London. Punts are deliciously romantic, particularly if the weather is fine, but Steve's only masculinity was expressed through propelling a flat-bottomed boat in a dinner jacket, which soon came off he got so hot. Nothing much else happened except the breakfast ordered was a welcome meal, and so was the champagne.

Later Steve took Marianne back to her college, two tired and somewhat bedraggled young people. They just said goodbye, no kiss, no embrace.

And that was the end of his first Commem. Ball.

*

God laughed. 'I'm sorry. I can't help it,' he confessed.

'That's not very kind! I suffered. I really did. The Ball was a big disappointment.'

'Yes, I'm sorry. But the situation you got yourself into, you couldn't help but laugh. You were very naïve.'

'I couldn't help it.' The old man was offended!

There was a silence for a while. Then the old man sighed.

'God, can I ask you something?'

'Ask away, sonny.'

'I wish you wouldn't call me 'sonny'.'

'Why?'

'Well, it's a bit patronising. I know you're the great God up in the skies, and I'm just a poor human. But, well, I'd rather you called me something else. Only my real father can call me 'sonny', and he's not around.'

'Anyway it wasn't that you wanted to ask me. What was

154

it?'

''Have you really helped me over the years?''

'Why do you ask?'

'I feel there has always been somebody supporting me, despite all my mistakes. If it's true then I owe you a deep debt of gratitude.'

'What do you think?'

'Oh, bloody hell, God, you're at it again. Countering with a question, not giving an answer. My question is so important. Why can't you be like the computer? At least he gives a direct answer, even though he does grumble, and sometimes collapses on me, or makes rude noises.'

'It's difficult to explain, but one of the reasons I don't give answers is that I want you to think for yourself. In other words find the answer *yourself.* It's often there. It just requires searching. You don't want me to treat you like a baby, hold your hand and spoonfeed you with answers.'

'I suppose not. It's just answers are difficult to find.'

'Understandable! Very understandable! Life was never meant to be simple. From the smallest animal to the most intelligent human being, it will always be a struggle.'

The old man laughed. 'Particularly when you are my age! May I bore you with another of my poems?'

'I prefer your stories. But, yes, go ahead. Afterwards I have a question for you, one you may find difficult.'

'Oh dear!'

'Yes, oh dear!'

*

LONELY AGE.
Darling I am growing old,
Silver threads among the gold
Shine upon my brow today;
Life is fading fast away.
(Eben Rexford – 1848-1916)

NEVER LOVED.

Who have I ever loved?

155

Sad to say, not one soul!
Love enfolds not my heart,
Such tenderness a void.
Am I selfish, evil,
The servant of Satan?
Do my genes, I don't control,
Preclude such wondrous joy?
I shall never truly
Understand why I fail.
Maybe I just don't care?
Perhaps I close my mind?
I married a woman
Sweet and kind. But she died.
I mourned not her passing;
I sought another life.
She left for me a son;
He found a diff'rent home,
Not mine. But did I care?
Goodbye my son. Forget
You ever had a dad,
A worthless man, so cold.
I have an awful fear,
As my life nears its end,
I will be left alone,
Nobody still to mourn,
Not one soul to love me.
In heaven I'll be told -
'Thou evil man, to show
No love for those around.'
Yet I feel love's so false,
Hyped up, with no real truth.
My dog knows greater love,
A stronger loyalty
For the man, his master,
At whose warm feet he lies!
My dog will die for me.
But will I die for her?
There's another sad thought –
Will I die for love of
Country, as father did,
And what's more, medal won.
To Buck's Palace I went,

The award to receive,
From King, kind and quiet.

*

'Hmm!' went God.

'What do you mean 'hmm'?' You're always 'hmming' me.'

'It's just I don't know what to say. Anything I may say will come out as a platitude. And I know you don't like platitudes.'

'Unusual for a God not to know what to say!'

'I'm not infallible, unlike the Pope. I never heard such pretentious rubbish, the claim of infallibility. It doesn't go with the concept of humility, of open-minded love.'

They were silent for a moment.

'Anyway,' continued God. 'Remember I'm *your* mind. If you don't know the answer to life, then I certainly don't. All I can say is that your poem was obviously written with feeling. Perhaps I ought to add, more significantly, that God is a God of love for all mankind. That should give you your answer, as to whether there is a God that watches over you.'

'Thanks!' The old man mused a moment. 'The poem, incidentally, was rejected by the Writers' Circle I attended at the time. But then I in turn rejected the Circle. It, the Circle, was just a pretentious talking shop, a social gathering.'

God nodded. 'Can I ask my question now?' H

'You can, or should I say you *may*?'

'Why the bloody hell did you ever become a teacher, and a teacher of French to boot?'

'*God!*'

'Eh?'

'You shouldn't swear.'

'Why the hell not? The question was vital. I had to emphasise it, in the modern way.'

'Um!'

The old man hesitated.

'I don't really know myself. It was a combination of circumstances, to do with cussedness and downright stupidity and much else.'

157

'If you had your life over again, would you have become a teacher of French?'

'No. Decidedly not! Though I enjoyed the experience of France itself. I lived nearly two years in France as a bachelor.'

'What would you have become?'

'Again, I don't know. Accountant, I think. I was good at Maths. I very nearly went to university to study Maths. Could I say I've never acted logically in life. I've just followed my instincts and not thought it through. The result has been quite a number of 'pickles' as my mother termed life's problems.'

There was silence for a moment. Then the old man sighed.

'I suppose I must answer your question about French. There were four reasons why I went to France, tried to learn French. May I say at the beginning I had no idea of becoming a teacher of French or any other subject for that matter. It just happened as a logical sequence.'

'It all started at school. I was a miserable failure in French. It was due to my deafness. I coped with all the other subjects and achieved eight credits, mainly by reading assidously. French I failed three times. Then mother got me a deaf-aid; I could hear the birds singing for the first time. It was a huge box I put on the desk in front of me. I remember the first day I brought it into French class, I told the French master – 'Please, sir, I have a deaf –aid.' His reply was 'So what!' I was so astounded, I just crept back to my desk. He was a horrible man, but we boys played him up badly.'

Anyway, the deaf-aid helped me pass the French Dictee, which was the crucial problem. In the end I was awarded a credit.'

My horror of French spilt over to University. At Oxford for Prelims I was supposed to read De Tocqueville – L'Histoire de la Revolution Francaise. My mind just went blank, a complete blockage. I failed three times. I left Oxford.'

One month later I went to France as tutor in a French family. I was fascinated by France. Most of my leisure reading was about Paris through authors like Somerset Maugham and Hemingway. I dreamt of living in a chambre de Bonne (a garret) and writing my heart out.'

Another reason was that my father spoke very highly of the French who helped him in his escape from the Germans after Dunkirk.'

The final straw, I fell in love with a very kind French woman, the mother of the children where I was staying. She was 36; I was 21. She was a former opera singer, and sang to me after the children had gone to bed. Her husband had left her for a floosie in Paris. It was wonderful. We used to sit out on the balcony on a warm evening and talk our hearts out. I'd never talked to anyone like that before, certainly not a lovely French woman. I eventually proposed to her, but she very sweetly turned me down. She was a Catholic; to her she was still married to that fool of a husband.'

But she remained a very happy memory and we corresponded.'

My French improved by leaps and bounds, I went back to England and taught French in a prep school for starters. French teaching was easy then; it was taught as a grammar subject like Latin. When it changed to an oral subject I was sunk.'

I fear my ambition to write went by the wall. End of story!'

'You were rather an idiot falling in love with a Frenchwoman fifteen years older,' remarked God.

'I never felt an idiot. She was just a very lovely friend, going through a bad time. I nearly had a fight with her husband when he came back just for one night. But I eventually had to leave after four months stay. There was a possibility he would divorce her and have custody of the children because of me.

'Ye Gods, what a mess!' exclaimed God.

'It never appeared to me as such. It was just a lovely summer with a lovely, intelligent woman.'

'Was there a divorce in the end?'

'No. He was a strange man, highly strung. I was told he went into a mental home.'

'You were lucky!'

The old man mused. 'One of many bits of luck in life, and I don't know who to thank! Thanks are due for a wonderful summer, not so much for keeping out of trouble!'

To this God said nothing.

*

'm sure you've got a story to illustrate what happened.'

'I haven't, God, I really haven't. My mind's gone 'phut' on me.

159

'Am I allowed to laugh?' God asked.

'Laugh away! If that's how you feel.'

'It's just I like you when you're in a mood.'

'I don't see why. Sometimes it's quite a problem to find something to write.'

'Why? You've shown so far you've got an inventive mind.'

'My mind works on fantasies. I have to dream them up and at times it doesn't work.'

'Give me one of your fantasies then.'

'I'm not sure I can supply one. The only idea I have is – well – to do with history. The past intrigues me, though I doubt whether I would have preferred to live in another century. I would have been dead by the age of six.'

'Dead! Why?'

'Measles. I could never have survived a measles epidemic. It was only modern medicine that saved me when I was young, even though it did leave me with my hearing impaired.'

'I'd like to hear one of your so-called 'history' fantasies.'

'Well, be it on your head.'

*

THE CURE.

Was the hope drunk,
Wherein you dress'd yourself? Hath it slept since,
And wakes it now, to look so green and pale
At what it did so freely? From this time
Such I account thy love. Art thou afeard
To be the same in thine own act and valour
As thou art in desire? Wouldst thou have that
Which thou esteemst the ornament of life,
And live a coward in thine own esteem,
Letting 'I dare not' wait upon 'I would',
Like the poor cat I' the adage.

(William Shakespeare – 1564-1616 – MACBETH)

I'm a coward. I hate to admit it. But if there's any chance of a bully around, or any prospect of physical pain, you won't see

160

me for dust.

My cowardice is bound up in the student years of my life with a lady who lived some two hundred years ago. Her name was Charlotte Marie Thomason, born March 13th 1773 and died April 24th, 1837. Her mother was French, nee Marie de Montivant, hence Charlotte's second name of Marie. At the age of eighteen Charlotte married the Earl of Stanstead. He was in his late fifties and yet he managed to sire two children by Charlotte called Georgina and Emilie. At least one assumed they were his. Given Charlotte's notorious love affairs, there are reasons for doubt. When the old man died eight years after their marriage, Charlotte was already established as a famous beauty of her time and, supported by the title of Lady Stanstead, as a much sought after society figure. Her second marriage soon after was to a rich banker, Richard Brearley, who had an estate in Wiltshire. They had one child, Jacob, who looked so like his father there was little doubt as to his parentage.

Charlotte was the subject of my thesis for a Ph.D.

It all began curiously enough in a pub. I'm a lonely sort of person, and writing a thesis is a solitary existence, spent, in Charlotte's case, mostly in libraries and in the home of the present Earl of Stanstead who didn't seem to understand what I was there for but was prepared to give me the run of his vast quantity of historically precious family papers. Charlotte, despite the demands on her social life, was a writer, the author of five novels, in a style similar to Jane Austen, but much more worldly in her outlook and more involved in public affairs. The idea for my thesis began because I wanted to study a woman writer of that period, other than Jane Austen, and Charlotte was my choice.

I found the pub I attended solved a need for companionship, not that I talked to anyone. I sat as near to the log fire as I could, warming my toes because heating in my room was expensive. I dreamt of non-existent parties, unavailable pretty girls, and as always with me – of happiness. The latter was a search for the unattainable, and yet in some strange way it was connected with Charlotte Thomason. I had seen a portrait of her and ... my! ... she was lovely! Long, slender neck, little peeping bosom above the line of her bodice, and a quirky smile on her curved lips, giving evidence of a sense of humour. She was the sort of woman every man dreams

161

about, and DID, if all the accounts about her are to be believed.

One evening at the pub my dreaming was disturbed by a harsh voice.

'That's *my* seat, mate.'

The voice was surly, even a little drunk.

I jumped to my feet.

'Oh, I'm sorry, I thought it was empty.'

'Move yerself,' he growled.

He pushed past me roughly, and sat down. I, despising myself, found an empty table in the corner, near a curtained window. It was chillier there, sadly.

It has always been the same. People take one look at my fresh face, my slight frame, and think I'm fair game to be pushed around. I was convinced the man had not sat there before. At that point I began to wonder gloomily why I ever came to a pub. I'm not particularly keen on beer. The place was noisy, crowded at the bar, dominated by background music I didn't really like. I had little in common with the other drinkers. They were young like myself, but they were in work, or I assumed they were, with the easy way they splashed their money around. I was just an impecunious research student, part of a group that represented 0.2 per cent of the student population. I sometimes felt, in my lack of companionship, I could easily die of frustration, if it weren't for Charlotte Thomason. She was such a delicious, intriguing study, at times wholly absorbing. Is it possible for a man to become obsessed with a woman in the past, so much so that she appears almost alive?

I wondered what Charlotte would have made of this pub in modern times. She would have liked the log fire, the old oak beams, been familiar with the type of building because Charlotte travelled widely. The pub was a former coaching inn, now listed, about three hundred years old. It would have been busy in her time, with coaches stopping to refresh horses, the passengers to find rest and food. She might have stayed here, taken off her clothes, washed her lovely limbs in a hand basin, made love to one of her husbands, or one of her lovers. Charlotte's French background gave her a certain sensuality, even an eroticism that came out in her novels, unusual for her time.

Charlotte Thomason would *not* have liked the uncouthness of the pot-bellied man who had deprived me of my

162

seat. Her men were debonair, brave behind the fopperies, like the Scarlet Pimpernel. She would have hated the smell of stale beer, held her pretty handkerchief to her nose. Nor would she have liked the constant throb of background music.

I pictured Charlotte entering this pub today. Men would stop and admire her with lascivious eyes. Or they would have laughed coarsely at how remarkably out of place she looked. Her full dress, bedecked with ribbons, would have flowed to the ground, her waist pinched in by a corset, her bosom strained upwards.

In a strange way I felt I was in love with Charlotte. I lived and breathed Charlotte during hours of study. I imagined making love to her. Under those clothes was a vibrant, desirable woman, of flesh and blood.

It was because of this obsession I needed to get away from my studies, be with modern women, pull myself back to modern times in a pub. But even when I had a break, I still couldn't rid my mind of Charlotte. Because of her my studies became alive, centered as they were on a woman who remained real in the *mind*, but unreal in the reality of modern life.

After a while I noticed the man who'd deprived me of my seat finish his beer, wipe his lips with his sleeve, give a belch, and move uncertainly out of the pub. There were two pretty girls sitting near where he had been. I supposed, in my usual caustic way, all girls were pretty until they opened their mouths and ruined the King's English, or stood up and slouched across the room, not upright, composed and well spoken like Charlotte.

One of the girls smiled at me tentatively, patted the empty seat and mouthed at me to come over. Girls didn't often invite strange men in pubs to sit near them, or at least it never happened to me. But maybe this was different. I felt there was a trace of sympathy in her gesture, possibly because of losing my seat. It would be lacking in courtesy not to go over. I picked up my half pint of beer, all I ever drank, all I could ever afford, and moved back near the fire.

'Thanks,' I said smiling. The warmth of the fire enveloped me like a cosy blanket.

'Shouldn't have let him take your seat,' the girl who invited me over admonished. 'Never his in the first place. We arrived before he did.'

The girl spoke well. Fair-haired, wearing a warm blue

jumper that covered an ample bosom that didn't peep like Charlotte's, and dark jeans, she had the same kind of intelligent look in her face as I imagined Charlotte would have had, *did* have in fact from the portrait I'd seen of her.

I suddenly thought how ridiculous it was to compare an eighteenth or nineteenth century woman to a girl of the twenty-first century. It was a measure of my obsession!

'Anything to keep the peace,' I joked, trying to cover up my cowardice. 'Besides he was bigger than me!'

'Much bigger,' laughed the girl, looking at my slight frame. 'But didn't somebody – I think it was Churchill – say the solution to bullying was to stand up to the bully.'

'True! But it was said about Hitler. Cost millions of lives, the standing up! A heavy price to pay.'

'A price that had to be paid. The alternative was a loss of any freedom, as in occupied Europe.'

I looked at her a little surprised. This was not the kind of conversation one expected from a girl in a pub! Maybe Charlotte might have talked in the same way about Napoleon!

'Anyway,' the girl said, laughing. She laughed a lot; it was so refreshing. 'We're glad he went. He ponged! Of sweat and dirt as if he'd been working on a building site.'

There was a moment of silence.

'What do you do?' the girl finally asked, with all the confidence of an emancipated woman. 'Forgive me asking, but I'm sure I've seen you before. Aren't you at the university?'

I nodded.

'Research,' I explained.

'Second year.'

'Small world.'

They smiled. They were both so friendly I began to relax.

They introduced themselves. The girl who invited me over was called Sally. Her friend, mousy, more serious, but with a pretty face, had the name of Jem or Jemima.

'My mother was overfond of Beatrix Potter.'

'What are you studying?'

'Jem's, law. I'm E.Lit.' Sally answered.

'My research is concerned with E.Lit. Charlotte Thomason, a contemporary of Jane Austen.'

'Charlotte who?'

So I explained.

'There must have been other woman writers in Jane Austen's time,' I concluded. 'She couldn't have existed in a vacuum.'

'Interesting, this woman?'

Sally seemed intelligently curious.

'Remarkably so.'

I let my enthusiasm run away with me.

'Like Jane Austen she had a mind of her own, and was an acute observer of human nature.'

I was sounding like a professor giving a lecture, what I hoped would be my future career.

'She must have been one of the first feminists,' I continued. She said "men always need women; women need only themselves." She was strongly independent. She once said oddly that   " men need war as desperately as a baby needs its mother's milk". Also "man's fulfilment is in war; without war he is lost". Remember she lived in the time of the Napoleonic Wars. She'd understand the present obsession with violence among men and boys.'.

'Like football hooligans,' Sally remarked.

I nodded. 'I'm sorry. I must be boring you.'

'Well, it's bit different from inane men chatting us up. But I'm interested. Your Charlotte sounds as if she disliked men.'

'Not a bit of it! She believed in free love. She said in one of her books there was only one good thing a man could give a woman and that came from his nether regions. She added a little sadly the consequence was babies.'

Both girls burst out laughing.

'Where can we find her books?'

'You can't! No contemporary publisher would risk putting her into print, she was so far ahead of her time. So she had to pay for   a small number to be printed. I imagine one of her rich husbands put up the money. She gave them away to friends she thought might enjoy them. I found one of her books, her first, in the library of the Earl of Stanstead – musty and neglected, but still readable. I'm trying to persuade a publisher to do a reprint – the literary find of the century!'

'You're obviously full of enthusiasm about this lady,' remarked Jem.

'I love her!'

Jem looked at me as if I was out of my mind.

'I'm sorry! That must sound ridiculous. But she's been so much in my mind over the past year or so, she's become an obsession.'

'How do you think Charlotte would expect a man to behave when confronted with a bully who takes his seat?' Sally asked, with a twinkle in her eye.

I didn't reply for a moment. The question was important, to me at least.

'I believe – I'm sure she liked a man to be brave, to stand up for what he believed in, even to death. She once said that to see bravery in a man was a basic desire of all women. She quoted the concept of the knight in shining armour rescuing the fair maiden in distress from the jaws of death. Or, to give another example, the thrill it gave women – as well as the anxiety – when a man went to a duel on their behalf in the early hours of the morning. She was quite a romantic, my Charlotte!'

I wanted to say more, but didn't know how to. My thought, which really came from Charlotte, was that death was part of the mystique of life, inexplicable. I felt that men, and possibly women, of two hundred years ago considered life could be sacrificed more readily. Death was not a tragedy, more a fulfilment! It was this same attitude among the aristocracy (and generals were mostly aristocrats) that indirectly caused the carnage of the First World War.

Suddenly Sally gasped.

'God, he's back!'

'Who's back?'

I turned to look. There bearing menacingly own on me, pint of beer in hand, was the same lout that had ordered me out of my seat earlier.

'Hey, you, hop it,' he growled, jerking his thumb.

I caught a momentary glimpse of Sally looking at me with interest, gauging my reaction.

This time I didn't move.

'You talking to me?'

'Yer, I were sitting there, beside those two birds.'

'These two birds, as you so delicately call them, are *my* friends. Join us if you like. We were discussing eighteenth century literature.'

I couldn't help thinking at this challenging moment that Charlotte would have approved. In some strange way I could see her standing there, smiling.

Sally was smiling too!

I thought for a fleeting moment the wretched man was going to hit me, or shove me violently away. I braced myself.

But he didn't! Thank God!

But it wouldn't have mattered. On my high of exultation I was prepared to be hit, asking for it even. It was the ultimate male sacrifice in homage to a woman, and my mind was confusing Charlotte with Sally.

'Fuck you!' he growled, and moved away.

Charlotte, in some funny way, had cured me of my cowardice, at least on this one occasion.

But, to be honest, I think Sally had something to do with it!

A lot to do with it!

*

'I liked that story,' God admitted. 'Perhaps a bit prissy and pedantic at times, but it had a ring of humanity about it.'

'Prissy! What do you mean?'

The old man sounded offended.

'We-e-ell, he's a bit of a bore, that man, compensating his own inadequacies with dreams of a long forgotten woman.'

'Don't you ever dream, God?'

'No, I don't have to.'

'What! Everybody dreams.'

'But I have everything. A god does! I'm also kept very busy, looking after this very difficult and suicidal world.'

'Suicidal! I don't understand.'

'Yes you do. You've mentioned it at times. This world self destructs, either through misuse, or through creating weapons of mass destruction. The way you're going, the world I mean, you won't survive another hundred years. I can just imagine an atom bomb falling on an American city, destroying life.'

'Oh, God, you are a gloomy old sod!'

'No, I'm not. I'm a realist. It could and *will* happen.'

'I'm going to my lonely bed. I can't stand this ghastly, ghastly talk.'

'Before you go, could I say something else?'

The old man looked dubious.

'Go ahead, if you must.'

'Has it ever occurred to you that all the principal men in

167

your stories are wimps, even losers? No more so than this research student! But look at the others – the man who went to Libya. He was pathetic! The man who committed suicide; he was certainly one of life's losers! The man who seduced the girl even though he was married; he hadn't the courage to face up to the truth.'

God paused a moment, anger on his face. He continued:

'Doesn't this say something about you? You're such a dead loss you can't even create a proper male figure!'

'God!'

'Well, it has to be said!'

The old man got up, tottered to the door, thought a moment, and said sadly:

'You know very well that I have been unhappy about my past. I ought to do something about it, other than feeling sorry for myself. But I can't face the future. Not at my age. All I want to comfort my last few years is a warm woman with squelchy breasts and a kind heart to share my bed.

'Women again! You make a false God of women!'

The old man made a rude noise and left the room.

*

Chapter 9

FORTITUDE, LONELINESS, EXULTATION.

In that sweet mood when pleasant thoughts
Bring sad thought to the mind.

(William Wordsworth-(1770-1850) Lines written in
Early Spring).

'Stop it, Jemmi.'

'Stop what?'

'Rubbing your revolting little bottom on the carpet.'

'I've got an itchy bot.'

'Well, go outside and rub it on the grass.'

'I'll get a muddy bot.'

'Well, so what! Much better than rubbing your germs on our nice clean carpet.'

'Huh! Clean, you say? You never Hoover it.'

'We do! Admittedly not as often as we should.'

'Hardly ever. Missie has a bad back, and you're too lazy.'

'I beg your pardon.'

'You heard.'

'There are times when I don't like you very much.'

'Go on with you. You say that to everybody who stands up to you, whether it's God, your friend the computer, Missie or myself.'

'I don't mean it with you.'

'Well, you've just done it.'

The old man was beginning to realise Jemmi had the quick wit of a woman.   In an argument he was the loser.

'Change the subject, shall we?'

'Only if you leave my bot out of it.'

'It's a dear little bot.'

'Proud of it myself. At least it's trim, not an ounce of fat. And I do keep it clean, even if I can't use your carpet.'

The old man sighed.

'We're back to the carpet. And I – I – didn't bring it up.'

Jemmi sighed in her turn, contemplated her master for a moment, and said teasingly.

'Bad mood today? Got out of bed on the wrong side, did you? Missie told you off?'

'I'm *not* in a bad mood.'

'Oh, yeah! Usually you call me 'sweetie' and 'precious' and ' diddems', and all those nice words. But not this time. *And,* I may add, you forgot to give me my biscuits.'

'I'm just tired and sad, that's all.'

'You're always sad. Old misery, you are. You've got a nice house, a nice wife, enough money – and, of course – *me.* What else could a man want?'

'I just feel lonely and unloved.'

'Get on with you! You, lonely! That's a laugh!'

170

'Could I put it another way, poppet?'

'That's better! ..... I like 'poppet'. Now, tell me what's really troubling you.'

'I just feel incapable of loving.'

'Ahha! So it's not unloved that's worrying you. You're just feeling a selfish old git!'

'You're so kind!'

'But it's true!'

'Yes, I suppose so. I feel so useless. So much suffering in the world and I do nothing – absolutely nothing! Just sit on my backside and write. Worse, I seem incapable of love – emotional love, I mean, not physical, though that too is a problem. It's all *me – me – me!* Like these wretched women who write diaries, exposing past lovers. Kiss and tell women, I believe they're called – and all for money! They're not very nice, and they're very engrossed with themselves.'

'Oh, I don't know. They've probably been misused or abused, and feel aggrieved.'

'Trust you to take a woman's part!'

'Why shouldn't I? I *am* a woman!'

'Yes, sweetie. But you're not really. You're a bitch, in the best possible sense of the term. What would you know of the feelings of humans? And besides you've never had a boyfriend!'

'And whose fault is that?'

'Mine, I suppose.'

'Yes! Having me spade! Interfering with nature. Absolute disgrace!'

'Yes, sorry. Anyway, your knowledge of human beings...?'

'A lot more than you think! Doggy instinct. You men are paying the price for centuries of abuse of women. Makes you feel great the fact you're physically stronger.'

'My goodness! Talk about high horses!'

'They're facts! However hard you men try and twist your way out!'

The old man was silent. What could he say? There was no arguing with Jemmi, the dog he loved. Jemmi suddenly spoke again, but this time much more softly.

'I'll tell you something for free, which may help.'

The old man nodded.

'You know all these women you idolise, women in general in fact.'

'Mmm.'

'Well, they're not worth the idolising. Waste of emotional time!'

'How come?'

'We women are manipulative creatures, no better, no worse than men.'

'You weren't saying that before.'

'I know. I know. One has to have a go at male conceit. But the reality *is* different. We, as women, are not worthy of being put on a pedestal!'

'I never thought I would hear a woman say that, let alone a dog!'

'Don't denigrate me!'

'Far be it! But it still doesn't solve my problem.'

'Which is?'

'I can't love. Only myself! I've already given a poem to God on that subject in the last chapter. I contribute nothing to the well being of mankind.

Jemmi made a rude noise of disbelief.

'You're no different from any others! Because you're old, it doesn't mean you give up on life. You've still a future, however short, in view of your age.'

'Jemmikins, may I tell you a poem I wrote? It may explain a little of what I feel.'

Jemmi sighed.

'If you want.'

'I thought you liked my poems.'

'Well, er, yes. But they're too introspective for me. I want more blood and thunder. More oomph!   You admire Churchill. Would he have written in your miserable, self-engrossed way?'

'Did he ever write poetry? I'll have to check. He did a lot of other things. Anyway, here goes. I'm going to write about you, little jemmi. You are very bound up with our daily life, more so than anyone else.'

'I'm flattered,' says Jemmi, wagging her tail in appreciation.

*

We've had a dog since year one, or rather

Since long ago,our wedding day, in fact.

Our first came with us on our honeymoon

  It slept restlessly in our hotel room,

173

Insecure, not sue what was happening.

We nicknamed her the 'Virgin on the Rock.'

She went into water surprising deep.

She took refuge on a rock, the silly girl.

She wouldn't swim back, stood lonesome, howling.

Until my dear wife bravely rescued her.

We've had a sucession of staffordshires,

Their dear names starting with the letter J –

Jane, Jasmin, Jennifer, Jonquil, and Jazz.

You, Jemmi, are the last, by far the best!

I doubt we shall have any more - bithchies.

They've snarled and bitten the poor postman twice,

Protected safely wife, house and children.

Barked at dogs, fought with dogs, causing mayhem,

Come away smiling from the fray, so proud.

Strangely, people are afraid of this breed.

God knows why. They love children, everyone.

They are incredibly loyal, faithful.

You win their hearts they are yours for ever.

We shall indeed be   sad, alone, friendless,

When staffies we have no more their warm hearts.

'Such a morbid poem!' Jemmi uttered.

'It's how I feel.'

Jemmi looked at the old man out of the corner of her eyes, her splodge of a face turned to one side in contemplation.

'You know, Missie once said you liked to get into difficult situations because it gave you a buzz. You couldn't live life on a plateau, doing the same things day after day. You had to have *change*, even at your age!'

'Umm, I seem to remember.'

'We-e-ell, I think you like to be sad, because you actually enjoy *being* sad. It gives you great delight acting like a miserable old git.'

'Jemmi!'

'Well. It's true!'

'What a thing to say about your master!'

'Sorry! I don't mean to hurt you, particularly after the nice things you say about us in your poem. What I'm trying to say - you *needn't* be so sad.'

'I try not to be.'

Jemmi made a rude noise of disbelief.

The old man paused a moment.

'I don't know why, but everybody seems to be getting at me. God told me I was a wimp, or inferred it. You tell me I'm a miserable old git. The computer is even ruder.'

'It's because we love you.'

The old man made a noise of disbelief, imitating Jemmi's effort.

'Nobody loves me, and I love nobody.'

'Get away with you. If you believe that, you're a fool!'

The old man's mind went back to when he told a story about another of life's losers. He'd tried to show – well – see for themselves!

*

BONE OF MANHOOD
A people who are still, as it were, but in the gristle

and not yet hardened into the bone of manhood.

(Edmund Burke, 1`729 – 1797)

'Come on, Dave, be a *man*!'

Dave was sitting in his study full of introspective thoughts. It was his most precious pastime in the present crisis, just reclining in his favourite room, so beautifully furnished, soon to be no more. In the alcove by the window stood an antique walnut writing desk, valued some while ago at two or three thousand pounds. By the fireside was a former Parker Knoll upright chair, referred to as a granny chair, quite the most comfortable he had ever sat in. A galaxy of shelves lined all four walls, filled with books most of which he'd never read. A teak covered filing cabinet, disguised as an elegant cupboard, stood behind the door. The room was perfect, an advertisement for a stately home magazine, even down to the sparkling wine glasses regularly polished by his housekeeper, who sadly departed yesterday, a victim of the present problem.

176

He never drank alcohol other than wine. He argued that wine was a natural product, as pure as the grapes themselves.

Today all this was to go, follow his housekeeper out of the door. He would no longer have the money to drink wine. The house and its five bedrooms, his study, the acre of garden, the BMW – all doomed. His wife had already left – for good, taking with her their two boys.

It had all been brought about by three disasters – bankruptcy, a criminal conviction, and *divorce.* All three had fallen within the space of acouple of years.

'Come on, Dave, be a *man!*'

He got up, squared his shoulders, and tried to follow the only sensible advice he'd received – 'take each day as it comes; do the routine things to the best of your ability; keep up your personal hygiene, though that was put less elegantly – make certain you crap daily; be proud of yourself as if God was watching from above.'

Funny, he'd never thought about God since childhood. In adulthood, money had been the religion, *and* the possessions that went with it, including a beautiful wife.

Above all he'd been told quite recently – look to the future; don't whinge about the past. The immediate future is vital.

Easier said than done!

He went outside and sat on the terrace wall. The stone felt cold underneath. But there was warmth in the air. The afternoon had the promise of spring breezes, presage of hope, the resurgence of new life.

He watched the removal men, four of them, as they cleared the house; everything to go to auction. They worked quickly, efficiently. Liz had removed her personal possessions as soon as she realised the pending catastrophe. She was, understandably, a fair weather girl, not one to stand by a stricken husband.

But she'd been a good mother to the children. Still a lovely woman, she would soon find a successful husband to support her in the style she craved. He felt no bitterness. She'd given him moments of happiness. He'd been proud of her beauty beside him – a possession like the walnut desk!

The men's conversation provided a distraction.

'Blimey, that were heavy...'

'Here, mate, give us a hand...'

'Down a bit your end....'

'Careful, careful....'

Sometimes they talked of personal matters.

'Me wife, she's round the twist. Bought a dress. Cost forty quid. Dunno where she got the money.'

'Didn't half belt him. Took five quid from mum's purse, I ask yer. For 'is girl, he said. 'e's only bloody fifteen!'

The conversation was reassuring – the very essence of life.

He went for a walk, down through the garden, along the path that led to the woods. He couldn't bear to watch the house being stripped. For an hour he strolled restlessly around, finding no peace in the quietness. He loved trees, always had. He'd wanted to study forestry at university but his stepfather was against it.

'Maths is your subject,' he'd argued. 'Accountancy is the money-spinner. No money in forestry.'

Maths was his best subject at school.

Even the majesty of the trees brought no comfort.

Suddenly he remembered!

'God, where was it?'

He spoke aloud in his anxiety.

He ran as fast as he could back to the house, into his study. But they'd already cleared the walnut desk. He shot up to his bedroom, searched frantically through the chest of drawers, but what he was looking for wasn't there. His wardrobe had gone. Only his bedside cabinet remained. But it couldn't possibly be there.

He was right!

He searched everywhere – sitting room, dining room, even the kitchen. He chased back to the boys' two rooms. Maybe they had found it, regarded it as a toy.

But no luck!

It must be in the desk. He was certain that was where he had put it. His heart quailed at the thought of his most precious of possessions being swallowed up in the auction.

He went out to the men, drinking their tea from thermoses, eating hunks of sandwiches. One was sitting on the drive in the granny chair, insouciant, but he'd had the grace to protect it with a blanket.

'Please. I need to get to the desk you took from the study.'

The men looked at him, narrow, assessing eyes. They knew he had committed fraud, but got away with no custodial sentence. They didn't know he had been the victim of a conspiracy.

'Please, it's important.'

One man grumbled,

'The desk's right at the back, mate.'

They despised him as a failure, lacked any compassion. Only the older foreman seemed to have some understanding.

'It'll cost yer.'

Dave nodded. He had a fair amount of cash, which hadn't fallen under the hammer of bankruptcy.

The men didn't remove the desk. But grudgingly they cleared a space, had to take out some of the furniture onto the drive. It was sufficient for him to get at the drawers.

There it was!

Lovingly he took out the small, maroon box, opened it. Nestling on the velvet padding lay the medal, white striped ribbon, grey metal cross with G.R. inscribed, the Military Cross his father had been awarded posthumously after a brave rear-guard defence of Dunkirk. Dave had gone to Buckingham Palace to receive it. His mother had stayed at home, fearful she would break down.

He thanked the men but they ignored him, brushing past to restore everything to its former order.

He took the medal and sat on the cold terrace wall, his back to the men.

For the first time, in all this tragedy, he shed heartfelt tears. After a few moments, he braced his shoulders. Somewhere in the recesses of his mind he remembered, as a child, his father saying:

'Come on, son, be a *man!*'

He knew now that one day he would succeed again, have another home, another company, a magnificent car – even another beautiful wife!

But, come to think of it, maybe a plainer wife would be better, somebody with more loyal qualities.

He'd always been lucky in life. He remembered the quotation from Churchill:

'The optimist seeks opportunity in disaster; the pessimist sees disaster in opportunity.'

*

'Interesting story,' Jemmi commented.

'Thought of my own father's bravery   kept me going when my own life became difficult!'

'Uhm! It's still within the category of introspective morbidity.'

'Jemmi! So kind! What long words for a dog!'

'They're your words!'

'True! True!'

'Anyway I liked it. Something positive about the story. But you have to admit Dave was a loser.'

The old man hesitated.

'Don't know about that. I wanted to depict him as a victim, drawn into a situation, which he hadn't wanted. I did drop a hint. But – but – I thought too much leniency might detract from his effort to put a brave face on things. He'd suffered enough, divorce, losing custody of his children and forfeiting his money and possessions.'

The old man looked sad. He'd faced enough problems himself over the years and had to square his shoulders.

'Can I ask you something else, something God brought up?' Jemmi asked.

'Uhm.' The old man nodded.

'Why the hell did you ever become a teacher?'

'What on earth are you getting at?'

'Simple. You have a hearing problem. How the heck did you manage? I would have thought it was the last profession to go into.'

'I sometimes wonder myself.'

'Then, to crown it all, you became a teacher of French. Bonkers, utterly bonkers!'

The old man didn't reply. He just sat in his little room in front of his computer, contemplating the past. At night he sometimes dreamt of his life at school, not always happily.

'Did you enjoy it?'

'Enjoy it? No.' He hesitated. 'Yes. Bits of it.'

Jemmi just waited for him to continue.

'I enjoyed the activities out of school hours, and coaching games, particularly cricket. Sailing, ski-ing trips, hobbies, that sort of thing. I even became a cadet officer in the CCF.'

'What's CCF?'

'Combined Cadet Force, I think. It seems so long ago, I can hardly remember.'

'Wow, you a soldier!'

'No. A sailor. I was Temporary Acting Sub-Lieutenant, Royal Naval Volunteer Reserve. The wavy navy they were called, because their stripes were wavy.'

'Wish I'd known you then.'

'Long before you were a twinkle in your father's eye. You wouldn't have been happy. I was so busy I would never have had time for walks or doggie play.'

'What does 'twinkle in your father's eye' mean?'

'You weren't born!'

'Oh!'

'I'd had cadet training at school. Always wanted to be in the services, thinking of my father in the War. But the services wouldn't touch me. Poor eyesight, hard of hearing. I was graded C3, I think. I can't remember. Never did national service.'

'Hence the sailing?'

'Yep! Really enjoyed that. Another story?'

'Oh God, not another. I'm as bored with them, as are God and the computer. Does Missie see them?'

'Yes, at first. But then I felt I was writing for her. Oh, I can't explain. It was simply I wanted to write as *I* felt, and not be influenced by anyone else. But the story may give a little idea of my teaching life.'

Jemmi sighed.

'If you must!'

*

SAILING TODAY, SIR?

Thence did I drink the visionary power;

And dream not profitless those fleeting moods

Of shadowy exultation.

(William Wordsworth – 1770-`850)

I'm exhilarated by the sea, and frightened.

183

I'm Cornish by my father. West country by my mother. The sea must be in my blood, except my ancestors were mostly mining engineers, preferring to be under the ground, rather than on water.

I dream of standing at the wheel of a ship in a gale, desperately keeping the bow into the teeth of the storm, knowing that if the boat went broadside on, we would be swamped. It is exhilarating. I feel alive, every fibre of my body tingling.

But it is only a dream.

Sadly!

I shall never now know such exultation, I who am in my seventies, with a dicky heart. There is so much one would have liked to have done, but never got round to it.

I'm a teacher, or rather I ought to say I *have been* a teacher, now retired. Some teachers live their lives through their pupils. I've only once seen the kind of exultation I dream of in a boy I taught.

'Sailing today, sir. Good-o!'

Paul was stating it as a fact that today we were going sailing. Yet I had my doubts. The weather forecast was not good. We'd get soaked. Certainly the sailing dinghies would be at risk of capsizing such was the strength of the predicted wind.

'I doubt it, Paul. The weather's not promising.'

Paul's face fell. He was a sulky lad of sixteen, even at the best of times. I hated to spoil his one enjoyment. School to him was a bore; he had a history of truancy. But I could always rely on him being present on a Thursday, the day for the after school extra-curricular activity of sailing. I was the poor sap in charge, not that I minded. I enjoyed sailing, but I wasn't really qualified; I only had a helmsman's

184

certificate. A teacher should have an instructor's qualification, to be legally covered. I hate to think what might happen if anyone drowned. The Head said I would be all right. The school insurance policy would cover me. But I never fully trusted the Head. He was a man appointed because he looked the part, and spoke well. He was a P.R. man as so many Heads are, not somebody who dirtied his hands in the classroom year in, year out. Moreover he was younger than me, self-satisfied and unctuous, a type well known to teachers. These Heads get away with murder, yet sooner or later they'll leave you in the shit, and walk away as pure as the driven snow.

I shame to say I disliked him, as did many of the staff.

Against my better judgement I agreed to take sailing. I couldn't deny I'd put on my c.v. one of my hobbies was sailing.

'When will you decide about sailing, sir?' Paul asked anxiously.

'I think we'll go there in any case, see what it's like. If it's not O.K. we'll do some maintenance work.'

Paul pulled a disagreeable face. He was the product of a broken family; neither parent had wanted him. He was now with foster parents. Boys like Paul made one wonder about parents, some of them at least. I'm not overtly keen on parents. They're quick to blame teachers if their children fail. But *they've* failed their children long before the teacher has the chance to undo the harm.

At 4 o'clock my sailing group, a happy little bunch, piled into the minibus and off we went. We sang. We always sang, going there and back. It was part of the enjoyment. There were ten of us, five boys, four girls and myself, including my beloved Paul. Forgive the sarcasm – an understandable failing in teachers – but he really could be a pain!

185

The girls all adored Paul. He was a good-looking guy in a sultry way, tall, slim, with a lantern jaw face. There's something about a rogue that makes   girls wet their pants with longing. I never understood why, because Paul treated them like dirt. He was not over-fond of the opposite sex; I imagine his mother must have something to do with that! But teenage girls go for the baddies until they are old enough to see sense. If they ever do!

My sarcasm is based on years of teaching frustration. But kids are oddly perceptive. They accept I'm all bark and rarely bite. They know just how far they can go with me.

Where we went sailing was a lagoon, not the sea, though the water of the lagoon was brackish seawater. Imagine the sea, then a high bank of shingle, and just beyond the lagoon. There is at least the illusion of being at sea, with the sound of the waves pounding on the shingle. I was grateful for the lagoon. It was possible to hold eager young sailors within the circumference and keep an eye on them; not so easy in the vast expanse of the sea.

Sailing that day was out of the question. It was teeming with rain and blowing half a gale.

'Right, you   guys, maintenance work.'

'Fuck!' went Paul.

'I didn't hear that!' I exclaimed angrily. I may swear to myself, or away from the workplace, but I don't allow it on a school activity. Though it's surprising how many kids do swear!

Paul refused to follow us behind the clubhouse where the boats were kept. I left him to sulk. There was a large wooden shelter where we could drag three of the five boats the school owned. We   left two by the jetty.The girls started by checking the ropes and sails, then storing them away neatly. The boys checked the rigging and stays; it's surprising how quickly tackle can wear out. Both groups then set to, rubbing down the varnish.

'Where's Paul?' asked Irene anxiously. She was probably the one the most enamoured of Paul.

'Shirking, most likely,' muttered a boy.

'Sulking,' said another, 'or smoking.'

The boys were jealous of the keen interest the girls showed in Paul.

'I'll go and look,' Irene volunteered.

In a moment she came running back.

'Sir, sir, Paul's out sailing!'

I swore (to myself)!

We all ran round to the front of the clubhouse, disregarding the pouring rain, and looked over the waters of the lagoon. There was Paul sailing away, obviously enjoying himself, the boat doing a merry dance on the choppy waters and keeling over in the wind.

Paul wasn't even wearing a life jacket!

'You fool, you bloody fool!'

I was seething with anger.

We watched anxiously, expecting Paul to capsize at any moment.

'The safety boat!'

Two of the boys came with me to where it was moored alongside the jetty. But just when it was wanted the boat refused to start. We tugged and tugged at the starting toggle.

Helpless we stood and watched, getting more and more soaked.

'How the hell did he get a boat?' I asked.

'He took one of the two boats we left behind,' Irene pointed out.

I swore. In a sense it was my fault.

'You won't be angry with him,' begged Irene. She was a pretty girl, long brown hair, soulful eyes, and a figure developing nicely.

'It's the last time he comes sailing,' I muttered, gritting my teeth.

'Oh, sir!'

Irene looked at me reproachfully.

'Well, what can you expect?'

I immediately regretted snapping out. Poor Irene looked quite distressed!

I have so often explained that sailing was a dangerous sport. Discipline was paramount. The problem was - trying to mix enjoyment with sticking to the rules. You *had* to enjoy a sport, otherwise it ceased to be a pleasure. I wanted to say this yet again to Irene – gently – but in the wind and the rain it was not the right time.

Watching Paul I couldn't help admitting, despite my anger, he was doing himself proud. He sailed with perfect balance, keeping as close to the wind as possible without tipping over. He seemed to have the instinct of the natural sailor, knowing how far he dare go and no further.

He was flying!

The boat splashed sturdily across the disturbed lagoon waters. From time to time, above the noise of the elements, would come a yell of excitement from Paul, a kind of 'yahoo' and then a 'yippee' like a cowboy on a bucking bronco. At any other time it would have been enthralling, but not today, not in the situation I had been put!

None of the other kids could have done what Paul was doing, not even myself. We were all cautious, fair weather sailors. Paul reminded me of the madness of the cockleshell heroes during the War, men who attacked enemy harbour installations in frail canoes. They were stark, staring bonkers, but they were wonderfully brave!

Suddenly, heading back towards us, a fierce gust of wind caught Paul's sails and he capsized.

A gasp of fright from the girls! Irene stood with her hands to her face, horror struck.

I yelled to the boys to get one of our boats. I'd have to sail out, whatever the conditions. Reefed sails might do the trick. I was wet through, cold and seething with fury.

But there was no need. Paul did what I had trained them all to do. He swam pushing the boat into the teeth of the wind, stood on the keel, hauled on the stays and gradually the boat came up, accompanied by a cheer from us all, and a further whoop of delight from Paul. Slowly he sailed the waterlogged boat back to the slipway.

'Please, sir, you won't be angry with him,' Irene pleaded.

'Like hell I *will*!'

To tell the truth I was not only furious, but scared as well. If anything had happened – well – I'd be for it! Paul was my responsibility and I knew him well enough to know what a stupid ass he could be. I should have kept a closer watch on him.

Paul arrived, grinning from ear to ear. It hadn't occurred to him he'd done wrong. For once in his unhappy life, his sullenness had gone. He was alive and full of joy!

189

Who was I to spoil his day?

'Well done, Paul,' I said, feeling relief he was safe.

'Sir, sir, that was real marvellous! Best sail I've ever had.'

'I'm glad!'

Irene looked at me gratefully with her soulful eyes, and gave Paul a hug of spontaneous relief, wet clothes 'n all.

'Paul.' I spoke gently. 'You're beyond all that I can teach you. I'm going to recommend you go to the sailing school at Southampton as an outstanding prospect. I'm sure they'll take you on.'

Paul looked pleased.

This was one way round the difficulty, passing the responsibility elsewhere. But I'd need to have a quiet word with him later. Meanwhile we were all soaking, not least Paul.

'Come on, kids. Clear up. Then Minibus! We've done enough for today.'

We sang over and over again – 'We all Live in a Yellow Submarine.' And Irene sat next to Paul and was blissfully happy, his arm around her shoulder.

He shouldn't have done it, really – school rules! Space between boys and girls was set at one foot, the length of a ruler!

But what the heck!

*

'I enjoyed that story. What happened to Paul?'

'He left school at the end of that term without taking any G.C.S.E.s. But he found a job in a shipyard building yachts. To his delight he was given a chance to try them out

190

as part of a crew. Then I lost touch. I did hear later on that he emigrated to New Zealand and was part of their America Cup sailing team. For a while he became a famous old boy!'

'He was doing shat he wanted to do.'

'Uhm.'

'You deserve some credit.'

I looked doubtful. 'He was a pain – in the ass!'

Jemmi laughed, if a dog can laugh. Her tail went up and she wagged it with pleasure.

'Tell me more about your teaching career. Why French for instance?'

'There's the rub. It was the last thing I should have done.'

The old man looked ashamed. Jemmi sensed another story.

'Come on, tell me.'

'There's nothing to tell.' He spoke thoughtfully – slowly –trying to look back at so many unsuccessful years. 'It's just I was a fool. In the first place I failed French three times for School Certificate. I needed a credit to matriculate for university.'

'Three times, my goodness! What went wrong?'

'My hearing, mostly.'

'That's understandable.'

'The problem was the French dictee. I didn't have a hearing aid. It was just so much nonsense, no matter how loud the teacher spoke. I could manage the grammar and the translation, but when it came to speaking or listening I was lost.'

'How did you get over it?'

'I was fitted out for a hearing aid. My mother took me to a large London hospital. We went up to the fourth floor, to the audiology department. I was given an aid to try. I suddenly cried out: 'Mum, I can hear the birds singing'. We were near a park. It was quite a revelation. I'd never heard birds before.'

'And you passed fourth time?'

'Yes – just!'

'The aid made a difference?'

'In a way, yes. But it had various drawbacks. It marked me out as somebody with a handicap, which was not what I, or my mother wanted. I wanted to be normal. The aid was clumsy - a black box which squeaked horribly. On my first French class after coming back from London, I put the box on my desk, went up to my teacher and told him with some pride I now had a hearing aid. His response was:

'So what?'

'How cruel!'

'I suppose so. None of us liked him; we played him up badly. He didn't stay very long! I think he disliked us as much as we disliked him.'

'Still doesn't justify what he said.'

The old man grinned at Jemmi.

'You're very sweet.'

'You made me so.'

'How come?'

'Well, I only say what you make me say. I'm just a figment of your imagination.'

'True. But you're still a wonderful companion.'

Jemmi's tail wagged delightedly.

'So, you failed French. But it still doesn't explain how you came to teach it, or even get a degree in the subject.'

'I not only failed at school, but at university too.'

'What, in French?'

'Yes.'

'Curiouser and curiouser!'

'Uhm. Oxford had an exam called Prelims. For anybody studying history, as I was, you had to pass four papers. One was French – De Tocqueville's 'La Revolution Francaise'. I failed that three times! I passed the others first time.'

'Crikey!'

'That's a very dated word. Where did you learn that?'

'You.'

'Uhm. Very much a schoolboy word in the forties.'

'Anyway, what happened?'

'I left Oxford.'

'Oh! Your mother must have been upset.'

'She was. She gave me one hundred pounds to go back. I could have stayed another term and retake that paper. But I'd had enough. I gave her back the money. I didn't find much happiness at Oxford. It wasn't for lonely, handicapped young men.'

'So, what did you do?'

'I went to France.'

'Wha-a-at?'

'I went to France!'

'Good grief! Why? Why?'

'I was attracted to the country.'

'Despite your difficulty with the language?'

'Yes.'

Jemmi continued to look astonished, as far as a dog can. It was mostly putting her ears back, and looking at me out of the corners of her eyes, showing plenty of white.

'There were other reasons,' continued the old man.

'There must have been.'

'My father wrote from Unoccupied France in 1940 saying how well he was treated by the French during his escape across France after Dunkirk.'

'Escape?'

'Yes, he was taken prisoner after Dunkirk, wounded. But managed to escape when his wound healed. He and a companion walked and cycled from the North of France to Perpignan in the South. They had to rely on the French for food and shelter. Only once were they let down!'

'Some achievement.'

'Yes. I'm immensely proud of him.'

'That was one reason for going to France. What were the others?'

'You have to remember that I was a very immature man...'

'Immature, you?'

'Don't be so surprised. People who are hard of hearing don't mature in personality like others. They miss out on a whole learning process known as socialising. My history tutor once referred to me as the most simple-minded student he'd ever met.'

'Not very kind.'

'But true! I learnt about life from books. What intrigued me was the culture of France, particularly of Paris. I read Hemingway, Somerset Maugham and Maupassant, the latter in English of course. The whole ambience of the city intrigued me, stories of writers and poets meeting together in cafes for discussion. I wanted to write, to live in some 'chambre de bonne', a sort of garret room. I could feel myself inspired by the atmosphere of cafes and theatres and cinemas. The French cinema at the time was great, very earthy, and very full of feeling. So different from stodgy old England. I made the mistake of thinking the grass was greener, a mistake I've repeated so often in life.'

The old man paused, ashamed perhaps at what he had said.

'How did you get to France? You couldn't have had much money.'

'I advertised in a French newspaper, Le Monde, for a post as tutor in a family. It's a long story but in the end I found what I wanted with a family in the Midi of France, just outside Montauban.'

'But you still couldn't speak French?'

'That was the strange thing about it. *I could!* Or rather I learnt very rapidly. It makes such a difference living in a country that spoke the lingo. The extraordinary thing was I didn't need to wear my deaf aid!'

'Really?'

'Simple. The French shouted. If I didn't hear something, they assumed I didn't understand. They never, or rarely, cottoned on that I had a hearing problem. Moreover, the clarity of speech in France is far better than here in England.'

'Anything else?'

'Yes, I fell in love with a French girl, or rather a woman. For four months we spent many a pleasant evening just talking French, covering every aspect of life.'

'Why do you say 'woman'?'

'She was fifteen years older than me, married with five little boys. But she was still a very beautiful lady, an opera singer. Mezzo soprano.'

'Cripes! You never cease to surprise me.'

'I surprise myself. But I really did love her. I even proposed marriage to her.'

'You didn't! A woman with five children!'

'God's Gospel!'

'Wow! And did she accept you?'

'I leave you to guess. I rather hope it will be the subject of my next novel. But I did write a short story, from the French woman's point of view. It may give you some idea of what happened. But could we leave it to the next chapter. This one's getting a bit overfull!'

'I can't wait.'

'There's a woman for you! A hint of romance and you're all agog.'

'Absolutely!'

CHAPTER 10

THE GENEROUS WINE.

All love at first, like generous wine,

Ferments and frets until 'tis fine;

But when 'tis settled on the lee
And from th' impurer matter free,

Becomes the richer still the older,

And proves the pleasanter the colder.

(Samuel Butler – 1612-1680)

Here we go, Jemmi. My French story.

Jemmi wagged her tail.

'Are you sitting comfortably?' the old man asked.

An even more pronounced wagging of Jemmi's tail gave the answer.

THE SOUTH OF FRANCE.

The house looked so lovely in the sunlight, perched part of the way up the hill. It gave her such a secure feeling, as she drove back from Montauban, feeling so miserable.

She'd just seen Martin off at the station with many a tear on her part. Martin, bless him, had been as English phlegmatic as ever. But she felt he was struggling to hide his misery.

The solid yellow walls of the house could be seen from several miles away. It was, perhaps, too brash, like her husband who had decided on the design of the building. Its modern aspect clashed with the aged brown stone homes of the French countryside, many still ravaged by the economic effects of the recent war and enemy occupation.

As she drove, she thought back over the last four emotionally tumultuous months.

Whatever happened between her and Jacques, her husband, she would keep the house. There her five children had been born, all boys; Guy, the eldest; Francois, the most difficult; Marc, so sturdy; Regis, the prettiest, though he hated it when she told him; and Emmanuel, little Nano, the one she loved the most, the one who had been born at a time of unhappy loneliness, the one who had given her such comfort as he suckled at her breast.

'How could you leave me?' she'd accused Jacques, 'just when God has given us this gift.' She indicated the baby, le petit Nano.

It was a strange way of expressing birth as a gift from God. But that's what her Catholic faith taught her.

'I'm not leaving you,' Jacques had insisted bizarrely. It was then she wondered if he wasn't just a little mad.

'Mon Dieu, if you aren't leaving me, then I don't know what else you're doing up in Paris.'

Jacques had shown no contrition.

'I want us to live together. Marie to come down from Paris and live with us with her baby, *my* baby, Annette. The house is big enough!'

It had hurt her, more than anything, his mistress had produced a daughter she herself so longed for.

'Tu es fou!' she had screamed at him, convinced even more that he was mad, and then she burst into tears.

The man she'd married – how long ago was it? Over twelve years – was no more than a little boy himself, wanting his cake and eating it. Born into the culture of French male arrogance, he truly believed he could have his wife and his mistress and his six children all under one roof.

It was incroyable, unbelievable!

'Jamais, jamais, never, will *that* woman step across the threshold of this house! Yu m'enerves, you infuriate me. Go away! Go away!'

Jacques had gone back to Paris, she assumed. Only once did she ever see him again. Even then he was like a little boy in the body of a man. *I want, I want,* was his continual theme. In the meantime, when Nano was two, without consulting her, Jacques arranged for a young Englishman to come ant stay in her yellow domain, in the belief that this 'Anglais' could help her with the children over the long summer months of school holiday. It was the only time he'd ever remotely thought of her needs.

'Mais,' she'd cried out over the phone, 'But I don't speak English, and the English rarely speak French.'

It had seemed to her a needless complication at a time in her life when she wanted to live peacefully with the children, help them get over their loss of a father.

A Frenchman in Montauban had asked her to marry him, knowing how she had been abandoned. For a moment she had been tempted. But her faith did not allow divorce. True, many French couples in the Fifties did divorce, but she knew it was her duty under God's guidance to remain loyal to Jacques in the hope that one day he would return to her, as handsome and attentive as when they had first met.

Minus of course his mistress!

She remembered the day the Englishman came! Only twenty-one, Mon Dieu! And here was she, thirty-six, with five robust boys ranging from Guy who was ten to

Nano, a chubby two. At least with her husband away she would have no more children, no more struggles to keep him off, the only birth control allowed her under religious teaching. Her children had been conceived in marital rape, all except Guy, a love child! The church was illogical, she thought bitterly. It taught one had to honour and cherish one's husband, but   it didn't allow any protection against the inevitable childbearing.

The Englishman arrived. Martin he was called, fresh from university. He was going to stay from May until September. He was fair-haired, fair-skinned. She wondered how he would cope under the fierce rays of the summer sun. She wondered even if he would manage five small, energetic boys. But he proved tireless, calm and phlegmatic, even when Francois had one of his tantrums. All he did was to pick up the small eight year old under his arm, and carry him upstairs, kicking and squealing, to his bedroom where he detained him until he calmed down.

He once said, in broken French that the more excited the French became, the calmer he would become. He also remarked to her he was appalled at the boys' behaviour at meal times, so epouvantable, yet he remained quiet and usually refrained from comment.

She wished Jacques had acted forcibly with Francois, but he'd never tried to discipline the children. It was the fashion, he'd explained, never to thwart a child. Punishment would leave him psychologically damaged!

What nonsense, she felt!

The Church taught obedience, supreme obedience even, and here was Jacques letting them do as they liked. The consequence was a mad household of unruly, impossible boys!

Reluctantly she began to admit that Martin was just what she needed. She'd treated him with coldness at first. After a while she found his quiet presence soothing. Above all he proved very helpful. He would take the children off to the River Aveyron, just across the fields, and they would swim, play games, and come back to the house tired, more amenable – like the five little angels they could sometimes be. Somebody, usually the domestic, a young girl called Anne-Marie, would take their lunch down to the river, a French baguette filled with ham or cheese or on occasions dark chocolate, plus fruit and a drink. Their absence gave her much needed rest.

There were times when she felt the Englishman was a cold fish. She didn't realise he was hard of hearing and not used to socialising. He came back one afternoon and calmly announced that Nano had fallen in the river, as if it was an incidence of no importance. She'd spoken to him angrily. How could he be so careless as to let Nano fall, and how could he be so placid about it? It wasn't until later she learnt from the children it was Francois who'd pushed Nano, and it was Martin who'd dived in and fished him out, spluttering water and crying.

She felt the Englishman's modesty was false until her Montauban friend explained the English were always like that. They considered blowing one's own trumpet as socially unacceptable.

There came a time, a little while later when Martin's French had improved, when she herself was feeling depressed, they would sit out on the terrace in deckchairs and chat. The evenings were extraordinary beautiful and pleasantly warm. There was a myriad of insect lights, and one could hear the crickets croaking in the hedges. The very loveliness enhanced her sadness, almost to the point of crying. Suddenly she felt Martin's hand on hers, large and comforting.

'Je suis desole, madame. I am so upset for you.'

She was so surprised she could hardly speak. As often happened to her in difficult situations, she *froze.*

At last she managed to whisper:

'Pourquoi? Why?'

'Je connais, madame.'

As so often, he mixed up 'je sais' and 'je connais' both meaning 'I know', but the first was 'to be acquainted with', the second was to have knowledge.

'What do you know?'

'About your husband. I met him in Paris. He told me everything, about his mistress, about his daughter. C'etait assez bizarre, oddly enough, your husband seemed very proud of his infidelity. I cannot understand why he should leave someone si gentille, so nice as you.'

What could she say? What impertinence of this boy to mention it! How typical of her husband to let out all the family secrets to a stranger! How embarrassing that the Englishman had known all along, but had not mentioned it until now!

'It was terrible what he did,' the young Englishman exclaimed. 'I feel so sorry for you.'

His hand tightened on hers in sympathy.

For a time she was silent, letting his hand rest. It was so comforting. Not even her friend in Montauban had behaved so gently. Quietly she withdrew her hand. It was difficult to know what to say. Finally she murmured:

'It is a time I do not speak of, jamais, never!'

'I'm sorry, madame,' said the Englishman.

He was always apologising. It made her smile. He was so attentive to her needs, so anxious not to do anything that would upset her.

She had gone to bed , too afraid to speak in case she cried. In her room Regis slept. He'd thrown off the covers, he was so hot. He lay just in his underpants, looking so sweetly peaceful. She wanted to take him in her arms, cry

202

over him, but it would have disturbed him. Below her, on the terrace, the young Englishman still sat, looking into the distance. It was an hour before he moved.

The next day the Englishman hardly spoke, just smiled shyly at her. It was silly how she kept thinking of him as the Englishman, not as Martin. He was so different from French males, quieter, better mannered. He'd never been familiar with her, except just this once holding her hand. It was a long time since a man had held her hand so gently. A Frenchman would kiss her hand, but that was a formality that meant little.

The next day, Monsieur Guillaume, her Montauban friend who would never take 'no' for an answer, took the three eldest boys and Martin to a motorcycle race. She was left with Nano and Ragis, both of whom she knew would be no trouble, though for a while they were upset they couldn't go. It gave her time to ponder her new situation.

That evening she and the Englishman sat out on the terrace once the children were settled, and for once she talked of her husband, of her life, of her childhood in Belgium not far from Lille. She'd never believed she could talk so much. She wasn't sure the Englishman understood, but he nodded his head, called her madame with great respect, and sometimes asked her to repeat a phrase. It was comforting to talk to a stranger, a foreigner; both were the same word in French. Eventually he would go back to England, and her secrets would go with him. She told him of Monsieur Guillaume, how he wanted to marry her.

'Never, madame,' the Englishman had said firmly. 'He is not a good man.'

'Not a good man? Que voulez-vous dire? What do you mean?'

For a time the Englishman would not or could not explain, but then he said rather confusingly:

'He likes you, madame, only because you are a beautiful woman. He has little interest in anything else. Certainly not the children.'

She smiled at the word 'belle' – beautiful. He'd paid her two compliments, both sincerely said – 'belle' and 'gentille'. They touched her! What he said about Monsieur Guillaume confirmed her own doubts. It was strange, a young man of twenty-one passing judgement on a man nearly fifty. But it was comforting to talk to somebody who had such decided views, and who, she felt, had real concern for her. Except in the first year of their marriage her husband had rarely shown such qualities – qualities she needed both as a woman and as a young mother. It made her unhappy to think how bleak her marriage had been, no tenderness, just rough passion, lust almost. He had been a very virile man, respecting not even her pregnancy nor her frailty after birth.

On this and subsequent evenings she poured out her feelings. In time the Englishman began to talk about his own life in England, about his family, his father escaping through France, and in particular his mother. It was funny, she thought, how men always talk about their mothers.

'She was a pianist and an organist. But eventually arthritis made it impossible for her to play.'

He had to look up the word 'arthritis' in the dictionary. It was much the same word.

'Mais alors, I too am a pianist.'

He looked at her, surprised.

'I've never heard you play.'

'When I am unhappy I never play.'

'I'd love to hear you play. Are you unhappy now?'

'No,' she surprised herself by saying, 'I've been much happier these past few days.'

'I'm glad.'

She wanted to explain it was because of him, the quiet Englishman. But how could she, a married woman? It wouldn't seem proper.

Every day, from then on when the children were in bed and quiet, she'd played the piano. He'd sat at the table, ostensibly writing his letters home, in reality just listening. He said he was 'enthralled' which he looked up as 'enchante'. He would say it reminded him of his mother. More often he would say nothing, but it became obvious music meant a great deal. He was not a man who showed emotion, but sat intently listening. He was so quiet!

And then she began to sing. Normally she only sang to the children. But she had trained as an opera singer in Paris before her husband dragged her away to a profitless marriage – well, not profitless, there were the children! She couldn't remember how the singing started in front of Martin; it seemed to happen so naturally. Maybe he said he'd heard somebody singing a tune she played on the piano. She'd then sung the words in French. He'd stood quietly just behind her. When she'd finished he'd walked out of the room, He didn't come back until much later. Without explanation he'd said softly:

'Bonne nuit, madame,' and had kissed her gently on the cheek. She thought he was almost on the point of tears. He left immediately, quietly went upstairs.

She sat at the piano, not moving. Inevitably she thought of love. Was it possible that she, at her age, was falling in love with a man so young? Was it possible that he too was feeling a 'tristesse' for her. It was a lovely word 'tristesse'. It meant sadness, but with undertones of longing – for the impossible!

She smiled quietly to herself that he always called her 'madame' and showed such respect. Never her name, never 'Marguerite'. She smiled too at the kiss. It had been so soft, almost magical. He'd not tried to force it on her lips, as her husband would have done.

Every night – or most nights – she sang to him throughout that hot and wonderful summer of 1951. It soothed her when the children had been fractious, or when she was depressed, thinking of her husband, of her loneliness.

There were two special occasions she would never forget. One was when she drove to a plage by the river Garonne. A bend in the river had created a sandy stretch. The two eldest children played happily there, while the three youngest went off with Anne-Marie to a makeshift playground.

There, by the plage, a small stage had been erected, and as the evening drew on, people danced to the music of a small band. Martin was not a good dancer. He was wooden and embarrassed to hold her. But he went through the motions and after a while relaxed. She was so happy; she loved dancing. For a spell she seemed to live away from her problems, forget she was a wife ands a mother. She became a young woman, with all the dreams of a young woman. She even imagined Martin was her lover, and she was transported into another world of desire. But he seemed to be too correct ever to be a lover, except for one brief moment when his arm accidentally brushed her breast and she sensed his momentary response. But she had to step back. She was afraid she would lose her children if ever Jacques could prove unfaithfulness.

On the way back the boys and Anne-Marie slept, huddled in the back. Martin too fell asleep after hesitantly thanking her for a wonderful day. She too was tired, but strangely happy, as happy as when she had first married and thought her husband some kind of handsome god. In a way she was glad she never had daughters. It didn't bear thinking about they should go through the same misery and disappointment she was experiencing. She hoped her sons would treat their wives with love and kindness. Francois was the worry; he was so like his father!

The second memorable occasion was a protracted one. She couldn't remember how it began. Martin came to church with her every Sunday, just the two of them. There were special services for the children nearby in the school hall. More and more Martin became interested in the church; more and more on the terrace they discussed religion and life. To her Martin was naïve and idealistic. Her own suffering had made her mistrustful. He idealised women, his mother especially. She herself was unhappy about men, her father particularly. She sometimes thought she married Jacques to escape from her father. At first she had extended this mistrust to Martin, until she began to realise he would never knowingly do her harm. In fact she knew he loved her, and this was a cause of great wonder; it restored her confidence in herself. When she looked at herself in the mirror she couldn't help thinking she'd retained some feminine attraction. Her breasts were still firm, and her body slim. Her skin was fresh and clear, and her hair barely touched by shades of grey. She was alive, intelligent and, because of her love of music, interesting. She told Martin several stories of her early training as an opera singer.

Eventually Martin said to her,

'Madame, I would like to enter the Catholic Church. Is it possible?'

She couldn't hide her surprise.

'Why?'

'It's hard to explain.' For a moment he'd been quiet. 'I like the spirituality, the fervour of your service. Always the church is packed on a Sunday, not just old people, but all ages. Our churches in England are empty apart from the elderly. There has been a gradual decline in attendance ever since the War.'

'A pity!'

'Well, it's more than that. It's a tragedy. There seems no longer meaning or interest, as if the church has deserted the people. But here in this little village the story is very different. I can't explain, but it has touched me deeply.'

He looked at her anxiously.

'Could I explain something else, Madame? Please don't be offended. I am very impressed by the strength it has given you – you personally. You have suffered badly, and yet you have kept going, put loyalty to your children first. And you even remain faithful to your marriage vows! It's so impressive!'

'It hasn't always been so. I have my weak moments, my times of doubt.'

She felt uncomfortable he could see such goodness in her. Life had not always been the same. Despair was a very real factor. It was he, the quiet Englishman, who had given her strength in recent weeks, not the church, though its teaching had played a part.

'I would like to be accepted into your church, to take Catholic instruction.'

'I am surprised.'

'I know. I'm sorry. We've talked about religion, faith, that sort of thing. But it's only recently it has crystallised in my mind.'

'I think you ought to think about it a little longer. How will your mother feel? How will you feel when back in England? I understand England is a Protestant country.'

'I don't know about my mother. She's very accepting of what I do. But I will write to her.'

She remembered the long discussions in the evening, a time that had become increasingly precious to her. Eventually it had been decided he should take instruction, and then perhaps in a few weeks time, before he went back to England, he would be baptised into the Catholic Church.

She remembered with sadness, almost agony, the last two or three weeks Martin spent in the house. Even the children were sad. Their unhappiness was mingled with moments of joy that became more and more precious. The Harvest Supper was one of them. They all gathered at the Bertelozzi farm, one of the tenant farms on the estate. The harvest had just that day finished. Martin had helped with the harvesting, looking hot and dishevelled in the late August sun. For once he worked wearing only shorts; his body had become accustomed to the summer rays. He looked tanned and fit, and her whole being longed to touch him, to run her hands over that slim perfection. Her desire for him became an unbearable pain. She made an excuse to go back to the house, to hide in her bedroom until the passion eased. Curiously she felt Martin was under the same spell of desire, but they mustn't – they mustn't – never! Her whole life could be ruined by one moment of love. It only increased her misery - to want so badly, and yet not be able.

That evening she danced with Martin, not too often for fear people might talk.

The lighting in the farmyard in front of the farmhouse was poor, just lights from the windows flooding dimly, making figures shadowy. For once Martin held her tightly, her breasts pressed against his chest, his nose buried in her hair, It was a moment she wished could last; she was desperate for it to last. Suddenly he whispered through her hair:

'Madame, I love you. Will you marry me?'

She almost laughed. Here was an Englishman, speaking badly accented French, proposing marriage, talking of love, and yet still calling her 'Madame'. It was 'merveilleux' and yet 'tout a fait bizarre'!

'Not now, Martin,' she eventually whispered. 'Let's not spoil this moment.'

With that he was silent, but took her into a dark corner and kissed her lingeringly on the lips. After a brief second she drew herself away, almost pushing him off.

'Non, Martin, c'est impossible – impossible! Tu le sais.'

For the first time she used the familiar form – tu – something only granted to relatives and close friends.

After that Martin, with great understanding, troubled her no further.

She was deeply touched that somebody so young should love her. Yet there was no future. By all accounts he was penniless, still to find employment after qualifying at university. Differences of nationality and culture threatened any long-term future, not to speak of children and age differences, and her difficult husband.

The problems were enormous!

And yet she loved him, wanted him desperately.

But it was impossible! Ridiculous even!

Life was more than she could bear.

Time passed quickly, too quickly as the days drew near for Martin to leave. Martin was baptised into the Catholic Church and she was his godmother. One problem was confession. It was felt that Martin's French might not be good enough to make a proper spiritual confession. Instead he read out a written prayer of contrition, followed by the act of forgiveness and blessing.

Something happened during the last week of his stay. It made her smile to think about it. Martin, unusually for him, became anxious because he had overstayed the limit on his passport. By French law he should have obtained a Carte de Sejour for staying longer than three months. He'd neglected to do so. He'd been down to the Town Hall to rectify the situation but had got nowhere. He was afraid he would be stopped at the French port from going back to England. Unlike her compatriots he was a stickler for authority.

'Leave it to me,' she told him.

She'd put on a nice dress, one, which showed a little cleavage, brushed her hair till it shone, applied discrete make-up and perfume, and then went into battle, all feminine guns blazing.

'You look lovely!' Martin exclaimed. 'But why?'

He didn't understand the need to dress up to deal with French officialdom.

At the same 'Bureau' where Martin had met with little success, she smiled sweetly, played the helpless female, and explained the situation. The same official patted her hand, bowed graciously and within fifteen moments had put the necessary amendment to his passport.

'Crikey,' Martin exclaimed, an English word she did not understand, 'that fat Frenchman soon jumped.'

She wrinkled her nose. That same 'sale' official aroused her contempt.

Martin was impressed. He was even more struck by her loveliness!

At the station, in the early, bleak hours of the morning, they hadn't known what to say.

What could she say?

Here was a man she loved, and who loved her.

Yet because of her situation, there was no future.

Life was hard. All she had left were memories to cherish.

It was that which made her cry!

*

'I liked that,' said Jemmi.
'Hmm.'

'Did you ever see her again?'

'Yes, twice. No, three times. I went to Belgium the following Christmas. She'd gone there to be with her family. It was a very uncomfortable time.'

'Why?'

'Her family were very against me being there. They thought it might compromise her situation with her husband's family.'

'What happened to him?'

'My goodness, you want to know everything.'

'I'm interested.'

'I understood he'd had a nervous breakdown, and was under medical care.'

'Oh dear, everything seemed to be happening! What did you do in Belgium if you couldn't be with her?'

'I went into a Catholic retreat.'

'What's a retreat?'

'A place where you go to pray and be quiet.'

'You, quiet? That's unusual.'

'I found it very difficult. I was alone most of the day except for meals, and the occasional visit from a monk who acted as my spiritual adviser.'

'How long were you there?'

'Three days. It did nothing for me. I was glad to leave.'

'What was the second time?'

'Oh, it was a couple of years later. She came to England and stayed with my parents. It wasn't the same.'

'Why?'

'Oh, I don't know. The magic had gone, I suppose. Madame in England was very different from madame in France. My parents didn't know what to make of it all. The stay was a little embarrassing. She'd been through a hard time, and had aged. Oh, it just wasn't the same. But we had a happy time. She loved being in England.'

'And the last time?'

'It must have been about seventeen years later. We'd kept up a correspondence. I was married with children. My wife knew about her. We visited Madame in Bruxelles where she was living. We were on our way to Salzburg to the music festival. We had lunch in her flat. Nano was there. He'd grown into a very nice young man. It was a pleasant occasion and we laughed a lot. My only guilt was that, after an excellent meal we had to hurry away, leaving her some considerable washing up to do. I never saw her again, but I still think of her. I often wonder what would have happened had I ever made love to her.'

'She wouldn't have let you.'

'Possibly ... possibly.'

'End of story.'

'Maybe. I've written a novel about that time in France. It's not finished yet. I want to contact her or her children and see if they would mind. I've tried to find out their address from the Belgium embassy.'

Jemmi sighed.

'I suppose it was all experience.'

'Umm. But I've never forgotten it. One of the few happy moments of my life.'

'Oh, come on, old misery. You haven't had a bad life.'

'Umm.' The old man sighed. 'That was the beginning of all my interest in France, and in the French language.

*

CHAPTER 11

'Prisons are built with stones of Law, brothels with bricks of Religion.'

(William Blake – 1757-1827)

'Good morning.'

God smiled benignly.

'Good morning, God. Slept well.'

'I never sleep. Far too much to do.'

'Conceited man!'

'Why, for goodness sake?'

'Well... No respectable man or God talks about his high workload. It's just not done!'

'Hey, hey, I'm not English, subject to your rules of behaviour. I really do have a heavy workload! Think of how many millions of people there are in this world, all of whom have to be given serious consideration for their future.'

'You mean, whether they go to Heaven or hell?'

'That's an old wife's tale – heaven or hell, created as a myth to control primitive people.'

God looked his most imperious, if it's possible for an old fraud to look in that way.

'So... so... you are not a believer in the concept of a future kingdom?'

'I just don't know, God. The only true factor in my life is that one day, perhaps soon, I shall die. I don't have all that many years left. Beyond that ... well ...'

'Have faith.'

'How can I? I ask you. In a world where we stick to facts, the future after death has no concrete meaning. I'm dead – full stop!'

'If you think that then there is little future hope for you.'

'God, God ...! You are a God of love, at least that is what you say. If such is the case I cannot believe that you will abandon us. We are your children, at least, that's what you say. Oh God, I just don't know. I feel so miserable there is no real answer. But I'm not going to give myself false hope, and then find I'm disappointed.'

God smiled benignly:

'Bless you, my child!'

'That doesn't do me an awful lot of good. Anyway, back to sleep; I'm sorry I side tracked you. Waste of time, sleep – if you think we spend one third of our day in bed, on average.'

'Perhaps not for me, but certainly for you humans, sleep is necessary.'

'Why?'

'Obvious. Restores the batteries.'

'Why have you come, God?'

'To have a chat, as per usual.'

'About?'

'This and that. Future life, perhaps! You know how much you love a natter, even though you grumble.'

'I've just had a chat with Jemmi. We touched on religion – more appropriate to you – and on love.'

'Oh?'

'I've already said it, but I just don't understand religion. The older I get the less faith I have.'

'Understandable.'

'But why? Why? Why?'

'Don't ask me. Ask yourself.'

'Usual damned evasive answer!' The old man muttered grumpily to himself. 'Anyway, here goes.' The old man pauses to reflect, 'All my life until now I have always tried to be religious. Well, 'always' may be a bit of an exaggeration. 'Off and on' is perhaps better. It started with my mother.'

'Usually does!'

'Meaning?'

'Simple! All life begins with mothers.'

'Oh.'

The old man looked confused by the interruption. 'My mother was a church organist. I spent many an hour up in the organ loft while the congregation sang and prayed below. The vicar was a tall, thin man who spoke most indistinctly, through the side of his mouth. Then came school – one of the loveliest chapels I've ever seen. I became a Sacristan, carried the Cross at Services. But the real influence was the summer farm camps. They were great, some of the happiest times I've ever spent. It was an evangelical organisation – I can't remember the name – akin to the Crusaders. Some name like Inter-School Camps. They were for teenage boys, mostly like myself from public schools. They weren't really camps per se. The organisation rented school buildings for the duration of August. Each day we went out to help on the farms, mostly gathering in the harvest. I enjoyed it – never fitter!'

'What had this to do with religion?'

'Everything! In the evenings we had prayer meetings, talks and entertainment. We sang silly songs like –

Be kind to your web footed friends
For a duck may be somebody's brother.

I enjoyed it very, very much, and became strongly influenced by the spiritual evangelism. I went home and told my mother I was 'Born Again!' Hallelujah! It didn't last. Day to day life soon drove it out of my system.'

'I'm sorry about that.'

'A year or two later I told one of the young leaders on the camps I had lost my faith. I was then subjected to a lengthy pleading – it lasted until the early hours of the morning – trying to get me to regain my former beliefs. My mother was furious with me I got home so late. She wasn't so bothered about the religious side.'

'She was probably worried about you out so late.'

The old man hesitated.

'I don't think so. For some while she was quite possessive about me – resented anything that took me away from home.'

'I don't like you to disparage your mother.'

'Why not? I'm only telling the truth as I remember it. I think I may have mentioned this before, but a girl I took out once, my mother referred to as a bitch. Yet she never met the girl - a nice person.'

'That is as may be. It's a question of loyalty. Whatever your mother may have said or done or been, you owe her an ultimate loyalty.'

'I don't see why. Our relationship wasn't of the happiest. I never had a home. From the age of ten onwards we lived in hotels. I was shoved off to boarding school. In the holidays I was put out anywhere, such as these farming camps. I became institutionalised. I felt rejected.'

God made a motion of violin strings. 'You poor soul,' he said it with a mocking tone. 'You can't spend your life blaming your parent or parents. There comes a time when you have to take responsibility for your own life. *And,* if you'll forgive me saying so, you are long past that time. Remember your mother as the lady in royal blue when you loved her. Remember your poem.'

'Yeah, yeah.'

The old man didn't sound convinced. His memory of his mother was not always an affectionate one. He'd loved her until she married again, and forgot about him.

God sighed.

'Anyway, what happened next in your religious life. I gather you became a Catholic under the influence of this French lady.'

'True. But before that I wanted to become a clergyman in the Church of England.'

'You *do* surprise me!'

'It didn't last long, as with everything I do. Oxford soon knocked it out of me.'

'Is there any reason why you were constantly seeking religion?'

'Good question! I wish I knew. I think – I believe – I was lonely and unhappy, and I constantly sought the peace and commitment religion can give. I wanted to belong, but I never did.'

'How long were you a Catholic?'

'About four years.'

'And it ended how?'

The old man shrugged.

'Several reasons. I fell in love with a girl who didn't mind my Catholicism, but her mother did. I didn't like the idea of no birth control. I had madame in mind and her large family, and the strain it put her under. More importantly, Catholicism in France had national meaning; it was part of French character. Not the same in England. It made me feel unEnglish. What was more important I wanted to share the same faith as my wife.'

'You were married in an Anglican Church or Catholic?'

'Anglican.'

God smiled.

'Why are you smiling?'

'*You*, dear boy.'

'Oh.'

'There was almost as much variety and change in your religion as in your problems over the French language and girls.'

The old man didn't dispute this. He felt ashamed of the many changes in his life, his lack of sticking power – stickability it was sometimes called.

'What happened after that?'

'Oh, I continued a nominal pretence in the Anglican Church, but it had no real meaning, except on the odd occasion. I found I prayed when I was in difficulty. In fact I think – as I have mentioned earlier – my prayers were answered on several occasions. In all my life I was rather like the Phoenix, strangely able to rise from the ashes of failure. I began to realise the truth of the saying that every cloud has a silver lining.'

'And now?'

'I rarely go to Church.'

'Why?'

'I feel the Anglican Church is dying – slowly but surely. I still appreciate it for its historical interest, but I find little spiritual value. I'm still searching. I tried the evangelical movement again, but it seemed a lot of boyish enthusiasm (which left me cold), and little substance. I've only once met a really spiritual man and that was in Poland, a place called Czestochowa, which is a pilgrimage centre for the Polish. I was so moved I almost cried. There have been other odd occasions, but they're rare. On the whole I've found the church peopled by the elderly and the eccentric. It has no vibrant young life. It may be the sign of the times, but the Church has failed the young. If you do that then you die eventually as a Church.'

The old man paused again.

God was silent.

'You got a story?' God eventually asked.

'Sort of. And possibly a poem.'

'Why 'sort of'?'

'Well, it's not really a story. It's more a pastiche, like several of my writings.'

'Meaning?'

'A medley of impressions, going nowhere. Very boring.'

'Oh.'

'I'm not very proud of this story.'

'Because?'

'There's something in my nature that is too critical. I've mentioned it before. I don't look on people with kindly, humorous eyes, more seeking fault.'

'I'll be the judge of that. Some people have that critical nature. It has its positive side. The world needs to be reminded of failings. But such an attitude is not popular. It makes one a loner – which you admit you are.'

'Yes, God. Thank you, God. So kind, God.'

God laughed, a great bellyache of laughter.

'I do my best.'

*

BORING OLD FARTS.

But the churchmen fain would kill their church,

As the churches have killed their Christ.

(Alfred, Lord Tennyson – 1809-1892)

St. Loftimus Church was, to put it mildly, not very interesting. It was a typical Victorian, Gothic, middle of the town (by situation) Church. It was only because it was 'middle of the town', therefore easy of access, that it attracted a semblance of a congregation.

But what a congregation!

'Boring old farts' would have been a certain England rugby captain's sotto voce comment, or alleged comment (to stay safely on the legal side).

They were all over sixty. Not a child, a teenager, or even a young married couple were present among them. It was sad in a nation that is supposedly Christian.

The building had recently been vandalised. Nobody knew how the vandals got in, though it was suspected the vague forgetfulness of an elderly churchwarden responsible for locking up may have been the cause.

But the vandals got in, no matter how!

And they had a wonderful time, glorifying God!

Mostly with cans of spray paint!

The kind of messages they left were not for the eyes of elderly women, who probably would not have understood them in any case. Nor really were they for the attention of younger women, dealing as the messages did with the much-favoured subject of intercourse, and the more desirable parts of the female anatomy.

As a result, a posse of elderly, retired gentlemen slowly groaned and creaked their way round the Church, obliterating words and lurid pictures, restoring the interior walls to a state of pristine newness, with much lavish and not always expert coats of paint.

The Reverend Septimus Aphrodite (What an extraordinary name considering Aphrodite was a woman, the heathen Goddess of love!) was the rector or vicar (one is never quite certain of the terminology) of St. Loftimus. The Sunday after the vandalism the rector was due to give the sermon. He was a very odd man for a priest. He was a huge man, built like a second row rugby player, which he had been twenty-five years ago at university. He would stand upright in the pulpit making full use of his height to dominate those below. During his sermon he would speak only in short sentences, with alarmingly lengthy gaps. To listen to him one was inclined to giggle, or more likely lose interest, certainly lose the thread of what he was trying to say.

He started his sermon on that particular Sunday –

'We live, sadly ...'

A few seconds pause while he lifted his face to the roof and studied it vaguely as if he had not seen it before.

'In an age of destruction ...'

Another lengthy pause, the same looking upwards.

'Of disrespect for property ...'

Lengthy pause.

'Of violence ...'

Lengthy pause.

He began to quote some statistics with the same vague pauses – a rape every hour; pause. A road accident every other minute; pause. A burglary every few seconds; pause. A murder every two hours, all throughout the United Kingdom, but omitting Northern Ireland where the figures were much higher. Pause.

Goodness knows where he got these figures! Or even were they accurate?

'We must fight this evil ...'

Lengthy pause!

'This curse in our midst ...'

Pause. This time, for some unknown reason, he contemplated the poor organist who wondered what on earth he had done wrong. Some of the congregation were reminded of the speeches of Churchill, but the rector lacked the passion of that great leader.

'We must bring ...'

'To our society ...'

'A new peace ...'

'We must fight ...'

224

'To solve ...'

'This devastating problem ...'

He glared at the congregation as if expecting them to rise up that very instant with a cheer like good Christian soldiers ready to do battle. He didn't suggest how they should fight, what weapons to use, what strategy, and what tactics to adopt.

'Why, oh why ...' he pleaded to the roof as if to the heavens.

'Must men ...'

'Behave ...'

'As they do ...?'

He regarded sombrely the congregation for some lengthy seconds. They probably echoed his feelings, particularly after so many hours of cleaning off the graffiti, and in one instance the shit!

'Christ will ...'

'*Will* ...' he repeated in a stentorian voice.

'Show us the way ...'

After a few more minutes of spaced out exhortation in which he seemed not to realise his listeners were experienced and intelligent people, he raised his eyes to the rafters –

'In the name ...'

'Of the Father ...'

'And of the Son ...'

'And of the Holy Ghost ...'

'Amen ...'

The audience breathed a collective sigh of relief, as he descended the pulpit steps. They were a little stunned. He'd said very few words in the space of twenty minutes. Some just blinked their eyes from nodding off. Others let their minds wander off to thoughts of the Sunday roast.

Afterwards he was congratulated.

'Dear Rector, such a stirring sermon!' twittered an elderly lady, smiling gratefully.

'Bring back the cane ...' 'Restore national Service ...' were some of the cries of the 'old farts!'

Only one man, with a twinkle in his eyes, had the strength to demur.

'Historically we have always been a violent nation,' he stated. 'Look at the time of Dickens, the murder and cruelty in the poor dwellings. Look at the time of Cromwell – the pillage, the destruction. Look even at the time of the Reformation when so many beautiful monasteries were destroyed. Violence and crime will never go away; it's a part of society even among the most civilised. We can only try to control it.'

The man paused a moment, and then looked directly at the rector over glasses perched on the end of his nose. He spoke as the rector had done in his sermon.

'We shall ...'

He looked keenly at the people gathered around.

'Never ...'

He looked up at the Gothic spire of the church.

'Never ...!'

Louder, more carrying voice.

'Wrench this evil ...'

Pause.

'From our midst ...'

There was an impressive conviction in his voice, hardly surprising in that this man had once been a politician. It was even rumoured he had at one time been in the Cabinet.

'But we must try,' interjected the rector, not realising the mickey was being taken. He spoke in his normal voice, resenting perhaps he was losing the lofty high ground to which he was so accustomed.

'Absolutely!' the man replied, and smiled wickedly.

All the elderly people standing around shook their heads in sorrow, and then wandered off both physically and mentally to the preoccupations of the day.

In the meantime five youngsters were chortling among themselves at home, so wonderfully proud of the havoc they had caused, as if it was some wonderful victory.

Of course it wasn't!

Quite the opposite!

*

'Uhm!' grunted God.

'Is that all you've got to say?'

'What can I say? In a way I agree with you, though I am not certain I like your acid sense of humour.'

'Humour keeps me sane.'

'Tell me – and this is the many dollar question – what do you really think of religion?'

'Big question ...! I wish I *knew* ...! I think ... Mind you, what I think now I may not believe later ... or more possibly I won't necessarily act on. I'm a queer old cuss ...'

'You said it!'

'How kind ... ! Anyway ... anyway, what do I believe in some seventy odd years of living? Nothing ... basically ... I suppose.'

'There must be something.'

'Uhm ... uhm! I am convinced ... but I have no concrete evidence, just feeling ... there is some force, call it what you like ... that orders the world. All religion is based on that central belief, whatever name you give it.'

'O.K. ... That's a great start.'

'I feel ... and, again, I must emphasise this is only feeling ... that Christ was a great teacher. I may even go beyond that, but for the moment let's stick to the teaching attribute, something I understand. He did everything by clear analogy. The story of the Samaritan sticks out a mile as an example of unselfish love. Just a simple story but so effective. It reminds me of a story of the Falklands War ... two stories rather. When the Argentines landed, the soldiers turned out to be mostly young men, hardly more than boys, very underfed. The islanders used to feed them. They felt more sorrow than anger, some of them at least. Another story - on one of the more remote of the Falkland Islands - an Argentine plane crashed. A family took the pilot into their home, treated his wounds, bathed him and fed him and gave him clean clothing. In other words they treated him as a human being and not an enemy. There couldn't be a greater love.'

'Uhm. Why then do you not follow the teachings of Christ?'

228

'I do! Or rather I try to. I'm not always consistent. I wrote the following poem within the last year or so.

*

MYSTICISM.

You must lie upon the daisies and discourse in novel phrases of your complicated state of mind,

The meaning doesn't matter if it's only idle chatter of

A transcendental kind.

And everyone will say,

As you walk your mystic way,

'If this young man expresses himself in terms too

deep for me,

Why, what a very singularly deep young man this

Deep young man must be!'

(Sir William Schwenk Gilbert – 1836-1911)

This poem is based on the concept that creative writing is akin to meditation and prayer. As in meditation and/or prayer one sits (or kneels in silent thought, emptying one's mind of daily stress, reaching into the depths of one's sub-conscious, to find the words and love of God. So, in creative thought one's mind dwells in tranquillity, searching as far as one can into the dark corners of one's spirit a germ of inspiration.

My church is the spare room, bed in corner,

Dog at my feel trying hard to slumber.

The altar is my desk, wooden, not stone,

At which I long to seek my sins atone.

The chalice is my mind, empty of wine;

Slowly I taste of wisdom not yet mine.

The word processor is the sacrament

That gives me strength to write in terms well meant.

The candle is the lamp beside the bed

Giving light to inspire my woeful head.

My deaf-aids off, such hush, such peace. No noise

Disturbs the joy of ideas which poise

To grow and grow, to bear such wondrous fruit

That one no longer sits, so lost, so mute!

*

'Great contrast to your previous scepticism.'

Uhm. That is why I say I am ambivalent. The winds of life force me one way and then the other.'

'Do you have any other comment?'

'I'm not happy with St, Paul. Christ was a teacher. St. Paul worked by exhortation, admittedly because of the situation in which he lived. But he said some remarkably silly things. It was because of him we suffered the narrow, bigoted Protestantism of the nineteenth century and earlier. Why say women must cover their heads? Christ never said it or implied it. Hair is a woman's crowning glory, a present from God. Why hide it? Christianity should

230

be based on the teachings of Christ, not the utterances of St. Paul.'

God sat thoughtful.

'Sorry,' continued the old man. 'I'm speaking out of turn.'

'No, you're probably right. But St. Paul was also a leader. Without him maybe Christianity would not have survived. He was the Winston Churchill of the early years, and you know how proud you are of that overweight, cigar-smoking man.'

The old man wrinkled his nose.

'I still always find it difficult to understand why so much religion centres around St. Paul and not the more profound teaching of Christ.'

God didn't comment.

The old man wandered to the window over looking the garden. The lawn looked soft and green from the overnight rain.

'Thank God for the rain,' he commented. Then he added dryly. 'Why are so many countries deprived of rain, and we are so blessed?'

God shook his head.

'I cannot answer that. It is a part of nature and the cycle of life. One day the climate will change and the deprived may become the blessed.'

'Small consolation for those dying of starvation because their crops won't grow.'

God had the grace to look ashamed.

'And,' continued the old man relentlessly, 'you say we must love children. Yet in times of drought it is the little ones that suffer.'

'It grieves me.'

'Phooey! If you are half the all-powerful God you claim to be, you would do something about it.'

God laughed.

'It's not a laughing matter.'

'I know. But it wasn't to do with that.'

'What was it then?'

'The boot's on the other foot! Usually I have a go at you. Not any more!'

The old man turned his gaze once more to the garden.

'I'm sad,' he confessed.

'Why?'

'Because I think I will die not having understood this life of ours.'

'What do you still not understand?'

'Man's inhumanity to man. That's the first, and certainly the most important. Do you know, there was a warning on the news that terrorists may blow up a cross channel ferry, killing many hundreds. Who in their right senses would want to do that? It's not the fighters who suffer. It's poor, bloody women and children.'

The old man looked as if he could cry.

'I lost a dad because of war!' he continued. 'Yet the war solved very little. Men still fight and hate each other; mothers lose sons; children lose fathers. It's such god-awful nonsense, but nobody has the sense to cry enough is enough!'

The old man points dramatically at God.

232

'And you ... *you* ...do damn all about it!'

'There's a reason!'

'Oh, don't give me that malarkey! Whenever there is suffering, you resort to mysterious statements, but offer no concrete proof. It reminds me of the time when the two little girls at Soham were murdered. The church tried to justify the mystery of their death. But it was humbug. And no consolation.'

'I think we ought to end this conversation.'

'*No!*' The old man's cry was heartfelt. ' Don't run away from me, God. I hate you, and over the years you have done very little to make me love you, except perhaps to get me out of the occasional mess.'

'From war comes peace and revival. From suffering comes character and strength.'

The old man made a rude noise.

'It would take more than the few years left to me to help me to realise the truth of that.'

'So be it!'

The old man turned on his heel and left the room. After a few minutes he could be seen contemplating the garden, the grass, the flowers and the trees, and the vegetables he tried so carefully to grow. It was there that he found peace.

*

CHAPTER 12
DESIRE, OR LUST

The expense of spirit in a waste of shame

Is lust in action; and till action, lust

Is perjur'd, murderous, bloody, full of blame,

Savage, extreme, rude, cruel, not to trust.

(William Shakespeare – 1564-1616)

'I've just quarrelled with God!'

'More fool you!'

The Computer grinned wickedly, if ever it's possible for a computer to grin.

'Hell for you, my lad!' continued the computer, looking smug as only a computer can.

'Oh, stop it! It's a serious situation.'

'You should have thought of that before you quarrelled.'

'What is known as wise after the event!'

'I don't know about that. I thought you liked God.'

'I do! I do! I don't understand him, but his heart's in the right place, to give a boring old cliché.'

'Well, he's supposed to forgive you. Part of his religion.'

'I don't know ...'

'You never know. You bumble along from day to day, never knowing anything. Now, take me for instance! I have a whole load of information stored within this little box, and more beside if you call up the internet.'

'Oh, you're marvellous!' There was a sarcastic note to the old man's voice. 'What I was really trying to say before you so rudely interrupted - most religions teach of a very wrathful, vengeful God. My God is kind, despite everything. I've made *so* very few friends in life, I don't want to lose him.'

'I shouldn't worry. He'll always be there.'

'You really think so?'

'I know so.'

'Strange! Strange!' mused the old man. 'I never thought an inanimate object

could be so certain of something.'

'Aha!' The computer grinned knowingly. 'Little do you know of us poor souls.'

'You don't have a soul!'

'Little   do   you   know.   One   day ... one day ...'

'Could I tell you a naughty story? To change the subject rather.'

'Oh, I love naughty stories. Is it sexually naughty, or morally naughty?'

'Both I think. Though the two are intertwined!'

'Oh well, perhaps it will teach me just a little more about this mysterious, freakish, incomprehensible human kind to which you belong!'

'Oh, absolutely!'

QUEEN ANNE'S VAGINA.

You know, my Friends, with what a brave Carouse
I made a second Marriage in my house;

Divorced old barren Reason from my Bed,

And now the Daughter of the Vine to Spouse.

(Edward Fitzgerald – 1809-1883)

She felt bored, stuck away in the country, bored to the roots of her tinted hair.

It was all the fault of that husband of hers. Perhaps she shouldn't say that. It sounds so *disloyal*, so hackneyed, like a story in a woman's magazine, or a plea for help in an agony column.

It had all started with her husband's resignation. Before that, life had been – well - marvellous. He'd done well, a senior civil servant, closely associated with leading politicians. There had been parties, dinners (official and private), theatre visits, an expanding group of friends – all had been her lot until the silly man had decided to take early retirement at fifty-five. This had coincided with their own two grown up children leaving home. Within a year she was bereft of all that had made life worth living.

'There's no point in working on,' Basil had explained. 'Dad's wonderful legacy, plus an inflation-proof pension, plus a lump sum, plus our savings, we've all the money we need. Besides I want to do other things.'

His idea of 'other things' was to buy a beautiful but neglected Queen Anne house in the country about ten miles from Oxford. He spent time and money obsessively restoring the house to its former glory. To her it was an utter waste – of time, but more to the point of precious money. She wanted people, life, not a load of bricks about three hundred years old.

Lovingly he redecorated the house throughout, doing much of the work himself. He devoured books about Queen Anne houses, noting how they would have looked when first built. He spent a fortune on antique furniture, to fit in with the ambience. He was a rich man, rich enough to feed his obsession. She, the little wife, wasn't consulted. If she voiced an opinion, it was rarely heeded. She felt like screaming at him, so dull was he in his preoccupations. When she finally *did* get angry with him, he couldn't or wouldn't understand, man-like, what all the fuss was about.

Once the house was decorated, he slowly recreated the walled garden from a wilderness of weeds. Locally his work was much admired. Then appreciation was extended. The garden became part of a television programme entitled prosaically ' the Gardens of England', in which he featured prominently, standing, smugly smiling, by the roses, pontificating on the art of horticulture.

She was excluded, remaining bitterly in the background, while television cameras and crew bustled around her.

She seriously thought of leaving him, so desperate did she become. He was a perfectionist, a tidy, careful, bloody bore who knew exactly what he wanted. They were qualities that had stood him in good stead as a civil servant, but were questionable in a human relationship where two people were thrown together in the demands of lonely retirement. His very patience was exasperating; he would rather wait than buy anything remotely out of touch with his own concept of how the house should be. They slept in the twin beds belonging to the children until he could buy the four-poster bed he craved.

'Why, oh why doesn't he think of me just a little?' she kept on asking herself. 'Why has he changed so much?'

It reminded her of her mother's remark that the best man to marry was a sailor. At least he would never be under a woman's feet, getting in the way, all the time!

She disappeared up to London to see her friends, so neglected did she feel. She would go off by herself on various holidays to strange and exotic places, hoping perhaps for romance. Not unattractive, she was still in her late forties, younger than her husband who thought less and less of his conjugal obligations.

'He's married to a silly house,' she complained to her London friends, 'not to me.' And she added crudely, after a drink or two, 'if the house had a vagina, then it would be his mistress, but it would have to be a Queen Anne vagina.'

Her friends were fair weather acquaintances, uninterested in her problems, though they tut-tutted in sympathy. At the same time they thought how lucky they were, their husbands didn't have such all-consuming interests. Their lives were so different they made excuses not to meet her again; she was no longer a part of the London set-up.

She felt desperately she wanted a lover, somebody who would cherish her for herself, fondle her, take an interest in her. But she realised lovers didn't fall off trees, particularly in the heart of the Oxfordshire countryside.

Sitting on the sofa in the Queen Anne salon, one of those sofas giving support only at one end, made for ladies to recline gracefully, she reached over to the side table and poured herself another gin and tonic with a slice of lemon; It was a refreshing drink. After two or three, or was it four, there began to creep over her a relaxed warmth. Drink was like a miracle, her only relief from the excruciating boredom of her life. Today Basil was away, seeking an antique desk to enhance his study. Normally she would have gone with him, wanted to in fact, anything to relieve the cooped up feeling that overwhelmed her at times. But this time he ordered her to stay behind. Note, he ordered, not asked! The cleaner was coming in the afternoon; it was imperative she, the housewife, kept an eye on the woman. No spray polish; only the special wax in a tin. No banging the furniture with the vacuum cleaner!

She was furious she was left behind. Normally, while he haggled his way round the antique shops, she would take herself to the nearest high class hotel, sit in the lounge and sip coffee, or better still a gin and tonic, look lonely, and hope that some man would approach her.

He never did! But she didn't give up hoping. It became like a dream floating through her mind.

On the sofa she began to conjure up a woozy fantasy of a tall, handsome man who would touch her below, and gently stroke her while she sighed in heavenly languor. Her hand slid down, drew up her skirt, and slipped into her panties, seeking the very spot where she imagined being touched. She moistened it with cream from her handbag. Her mind dulled by alcohol, her legs splayed apart, it was the only sexual joy she had.

But it was nowhere like the real thing!

The doorbell rang, shattering her dream.

'Oh damn!' she exclaimed, withdrawing her hand from its moist depths.

Wearily she got up, adjusted her clothes, and moved unsteadily to the front door. A man stood there, tall, swarthy, probably in his forties, professionally polite.

'Good morning, ma'am,' he said respectfully, the smile on his face warming to a handsome, seductive grim. 'We're lost, I'm afraid. Can you tell us how to get to Slipping Upton? We're delivering furniture.'

He indicated a large brown furniture van, the nose of which was poking through the gate.

239

'Why, oh yes, of course,' she said girlishly, giving a quick shake of her head to clear her mind. 'I'd love to help. It's only about another five miles. But it's so difficult to find. The village is off the main Oxford-Stratford road. But please, *do* let me show you on the map.'

She was good at map reading, unlike some of her female friends. Today she'd worked out Basil's route to Banbury. On their outings together it was always she who navigated.

The man on the doorstep seemed to hesitate.

'Oh, *do* come in,' she exclaimed. 'I really won't bite.'

She tottered before him to the dining room. She suddenly had qualms about letting a stranger into her house, remembering the strictures that women had drilled into them from early age, namely strange men can be dangerous.

But he seemed such a nice man, so polite and smiling. She felt drunk with desire, her perceptions muted by gin.

As he followed her in, the man looked swiftly around.

'What a beautiful house!' he exclaimed.

'Oh, yes, isn't it? Really divine.' She put on her best upper class accent. 'My dear husband has spent a hu-u-uge amount of time and money restoring it.'

She spread the Oxfordshire map out on the beautiful mahogany dining table, an action Basil would have described as the desecration of a valuable antique. As he leant near to her she could smell his male sweat.

How she longed for a man! It had been so many months since she had last made love, and then only with a reluctant husband. She squeezed her thighs together to hold back the desire.

'There's Slipping Upton. Such a pretty little village; you'll love it.'

She turned to him and gave one of her best full frontal smiles. He avoided eye contact. She turned back to the map.

'You turn off here, to the left, just by a pub called the 'Three Lemons'. Strange name, isn't it?'

She laughed girlishly.

Casually he asked her, slipping the question in almost as an aside.

'Where's your husband?'

'Oh. He's gone to Banbury, looking for a desk. He won't be back for a-a-ages.'

She didn't know why she said 'ages' so suggestively.

'So, you're on your own.'

She nodded with a half smile, lowering of the eyes. She began to hope this might be her chance. One heard of milkmen satisfying lonely women. Would a removal man offer the same service? There must be more than one man in the large van.

What heaven!

She felt suddenly remarkably young again. That smell, that masculine, sensuous waft – it struck sexual desire in her, making her weak at the knees.

The man suddenly grabbed her arm.

'Oh,' she gasped, and leant her bosom towards him. This was it! He would take her. He would be firm and satisfying.

'Take me upstairs,' she begged. She leant even more against his strong body. He put his arm, around her, supporting her. Together they staggered up the stairs. In the bedroom he released her by the single bed; Basil hadn't yet bought the four-poster. He felt in his pocket and produced a roll of sticky black plastic. She started to undo the buttons on her blouse moaning with anticipated pleasure. He put his arm around her again and forced her back onto the bed. He seized a wrist and bound it with the tape to the metal frame of the bed head.

God, bondage! How heavenly was her thought.

She squirmed delightedly, putting up her other wrist to be fastened.

The man smiled down at her. Then he did a strange thing. He adjusted her skirt decorously which had risen up. He sat on her legs and bound them swiftly before she had a chance to struggle. He passed the tape under the bed and over her, pinning her down helplessly. He smiled at her once again, put a finger to his lips, and disappeared. She wondered where he was going. Alarm was sweeping over her. This was not what she had expected.

She heard the noise of a van being driven up to the front door. My God, the removal van! There came noises downstairs, men moving around, hushed voices, followed by the unmistakable sound of heavy furniture being moved, male exertion, grunting and heavy breathing, just like love making.

But this time, far from it!

She began to scream! Another man came up, younger, but with an obvious beer belly.

'Make a noise and I'll put a tape across your bloody mouth.'

He looked so threatening, she was immediately quiet. Besides it was useless; nobody would hear her, and the cleaner was not due for another few hours.

The man disappeared swiftly.

242

She struggled to get free, but the tape was too strong. The man had known what he was doing. She twisted her hips, tried to get her feet on the ground, but it was useless. She collapsed back in exhaustion.

Subsequent events were like a nightmare. She thought maybe the men might finish by raping her, and wondered whether to resist. She remembered a mediaeval story of an English woman raped by a Chinese warrior chief. She had lived happily ever after with him, refusing to be rescued.

Perhaps rape wasn't the trauma it was made out to be!

Four men came into the room, including beer belly and the man at the door.

'Please, you can do what you like to me, but let me free.'

Her wrists were painful; her whole body ached.

But they laughed, ignored her. Suddenly it came to her. They were focused on antiques, not on her – antiques for lucrative gain, not a retirement hobby.

The irony struck her! She seemed fated to be messed about by men interested only in the past – for different reasons, of course! The thought deflated her utterly!

They hauled out of the bedroom the bow-fronted dressing table, which Basil had paid several thousand pounds for. They threw the contents of the drawers in the middle of the floor, keeping only what might have value – all her jewellery mostly. The lovely, gilded Queen Anne chairs went, followed by the deep mahogany wardrobe; Basil loved mahogany, the deep red richness of colour! Her clothes were added to the heap – dresses, skirts, blouses. At least they weren't interested in what she wore. When they emptied the chest of drawers, again of immense value, one of the men held up a bra and sniggered, looked suggestively at her. She took quite a large size. She could feel his eyes burning into her chest.

'That's enough!' snapped the leader, the man who had come to the front door. The bra was hastily discarded on the pile.

She could hear the men struggling, cursing, as they moved heavy pieces downstairs.

God, Basil would be so upset! Months of work wasted!

But it would serve him bloody well right, the boring old fart, for all the time that he had forsaken her for a house that was now being deprived of all its precious assets, like a woman left naked, stripped of all her lovely clothes.

The men never came back to the bedroom. She heard the van departing. There was a deathly silence in the house. She moaned and twisted and struggled on the bed. Finally she gave up from sheer exhaustion, and waited for the cleaner to come.

Her discomfort was alleviated by the glorious feeling that spread slowly through her conscious mind, of Basil's distress at his loss.

'His mistress has gone,' she thought, ' and serve him bloody well right!'

She thought of a game she would play, something in fact far more serious, affecting life itself! If, on arrival back, his distress was more for *her* and what *she* had suffered, then she would stay with him. *If*, on the other hand, it was more for the loss of *his* antiques, then she would pack her bags and *go.*

'That'll teach him!'

She smiled maliciously to herself.

She knew what the outcome would be!

*

I never knew you were so sexually minded,' mused the computer. 'What on earth gave you the idea for such a story.'

'Simple! There was a report in a newspaper about a removal van that drew up at a country house, tied up the occupants, an elderly couple, and took away their valuable possessions, furniture, everything.'

'Wow! And the woman?'

'There was much talk of lonely women in the Seventies and Eighties becoming secret drinkers, or finding sexual satisfaction with daily service men like milkmen, especially if the women were on H.R.T.'

'But a woman masturbating, and being so stupid?'

The old man shrugged. 'It happens.'

'They must be desperate!'

'I don't know whether it happens today, now women are so much a part of the work force. In days gone by there was a difficult period for many women, a sort of hiatus when children had gone, husband busy with his work. They felt alone, neglected, and life had little purpose. I remember my mother saying, after my father died, she felt so desperately lonely she would have married the dustman if asked. I think she meant it half jokingly, but there was a kind of pathos in that remark.'

'You human beings never cease to surprise me.'

'We surprise ourselves sometimes. We never know how we'll react in certain situations.'

'Well, I'm glad I'm not a human being!'

245

'We're not so bad. Life has its moments!'

'Uhm,' breathed the computer, looking doubtful. 'Human beings, it seems to me, lack commonsense. They're totally, totally illogical! Even to the extent of being stupid. That woman in your story was silly, utterly silly! Now take me for instance. I'm just the opposite, *utterly* logical.'

'Oh, yes, you're brilliant! But you're also *utterly* boring!' The old man tried to mimic the computer's speech.

'I beg your pardon!'

'Well, look at it this way. It's the aberrations of human nature that make life interesting. You're like Basil in the story. You can't think of anything else than what you are programmed to do. Basil was a bloody bore to his wife – so are you to me!'

'I don't believe what I'm hearing!'

'Well, it's true. But your saving grace is that you perform an excellent service. You relieve humanity of routine tasks, like typing this book. I could never do what I do without your help. You're a beautiful, lovely, valuable, precious bit of mechanism. . . and ... and ... I love you very much.'

The computer looked a little mollified. The old man smiled to himself. The computer lacked human understanding to realise he was being flattered outrageously.

'Have you any other stories to show the aberrations of human nature?'

'Yes, lots!'

'As bad as that?'

'Human nature is a very funny thing!'

'You can say that again! Oh, well, let's hear your story.'

'May I tell it to God as well? It might help to change his mind about me.'

'O.K.'

'God, God,' called the old man.

'God's head appeared above the bookcase, looking a little like Father Christmas.

'This old thing,' explained the computer, contemptuously indicating the old man, 'wants to tell us another story.'

God smiled benignly.

'Of course, of course, my dear man. Pleasure, pleasure!'

'It's a little longer than usual,' pointed out the old man.

'No matter.' God seemed in an expansive mood. 'But first tell me, my dear boy, why you want to tell this story?'

'It's hard to say...'

'It always is!'

The old man ignored the interruption.

'May I ask, God, why you created man, *and* imbued him with such desire... desire sometimes so strong as to be akin to lust?'

'You're always asking the why and the wherefore of human nature?'

'I want to understand! I've lived seventy-two years and I'm still far from understanding. Desire, when it becomes lust, is dangerous. We seem obsessive in our desire, and yet it rarely leads to happiness. That woman in the last story I told the computer   was rendered stupid by her lust.'

'But, but…' interrupted the computer, 'that woman was desperately unhappy. She needs our compassion, not our criticism.'

'What do you know about compassion, you soulless bits and pieces.'

'A lot more than you think.' The computer hesitated. 'I believe we've had this argument before. Beware, beware, O mankind, who knows that one day computers might have feelings.'

The old man ignored this assertion with a contemptuous dismissal.

'Can I come back to my original assertion that we as a nation are obsessed with sex?   I feel it is the failure of our people – sadly!'

'No, no,' said God. 'It's not a failure. It's a part of nature, a very fundamental part. It's there to test us. Character forming, I think you call it.'

'You mean that if we resist desire, we become good characters.'

'Not quite, not quite. All these urges have their good side and their bad. We need to control it in a sensible way.'

'You say 'we''

'Naturally! It's you talking through me!'

'Uhm,' said the old man doubtfully. 'What you mean is that I am expressing answers through you. In which case I'd better shut up. I'm not God, nor am I a psychologist.'

'Precisely!'

'Can I first, before the story, give you a poem which may illustrate my disappointment with the world in general. I wrote it in Hyde Park, the day after the much vaunted Millennium.'

God nodded. The computer sighed.

*

FALSE HOPE.

Millennium – false hope, so much brave talk!

What does it mean? Sadly, very little.

The same harsh fact that life's a slow, sad walk

From birth to death. Time can be so brittle.

Is this Millennium any better?

Far worse! What hope have we from nature's might?

Floods, storms, tempests, earthquakes, so much greater than any in the past; an awesome sight!

A diff'rent fear exists – we kill ourselves –

Not from the elements, but from our greed;

Corrupt, moral failure, deep sins themselves.

To think of good there's strong, nay desp'rate need.

Beware, not today, but for our children,

And their children. To such a truth – listen!

*

'That's a strong message,' commented God.

'Oh, I don't know. I felt very depressed at the Millennium. I was staying up in London with my daughter. The actual night seemed just an excuse for a booze up, and the mess the following day was unbelievable, ankle deep in bottles and rubbish. I walked to Hyde Park and sat on a damp, hard bench and wrote that poem. It was a time when we had much flooding in the country caused by heavy rain. The day seemed grey and sultry, not one for rejoicing. My spirits were at a low ebb.'

'Perhaps you'd been drinking.'

'Not at all. That night I had gone for a walk with Jemmi, but the crowds were so thick, both of us were scared. The fireworks were impressive, but we were so jostled we were hardly in a position to enjoy them. I just couldn't conceive of any justifiable reason why the Millennium should be celebrated. Perhaps there was hope of better things. After all the twentieth century had known two savage world wars, killing up to forty million people. Maybe the twenty-first would be better.'

'You don't know. Nobody knows!' God shook his head in sadness.

'Technology will be better, of that you can be sure,' chirped in the computer, looking for once very pleased with himself.

'Oh, you and your technology!' exclaimed the old man. 'All you do is make us lazy and ruin our health.'

'Oh, come on! Not true!'

'God will bear me out. God gave us brains. If it wasn't God then somebody or something did. You – you technological scrap heap – you replace our brains, or try to! The worst is television. We sit in front of it in a stupor of laziness, our minds aimlessly drifting, accepting all that is thrown at us.'

'Television is hardly computers.'

250

'Oh, it is. It is!'

'Let's see what God has to say.'

God gives a self-important 'harrumph' to clear his throat.

'The general syllogism is ...

'What's syllogism?' asked the old man.

'I'm not sure. It sounds a nice word to use. Makes one seem part of the intelligentsia, enhances one's self-importance.'

'God! You surprise me!'

'Well, one has to restore one's confidence. You, my son, spend so much time knocking me down and questioning all that I do, it's quite disheartening.'

'Syllogism' is I quote - 'a form of reasoning in which a conclusion is drawn from two given or assumed propositions," quoted the computer from its extended dictionary, looking pleased with himself.

'Thank you, clever clogs!' muttered the old man, grimacing at him, or should one say 'it'?

'May I continue with my theory so rudely interrupted by you two gentlemen?'

'Oh, go ahead, God,' muttered the computer, somewhat put out.

'The syllogism – and I'm not sure it is the right word in this instance - is that man has so much done for him, he is degenerating in many ways. The commonest example is the car. People don't walk; legs degenerate in time. The same with the hands. We have so much done for us, we lose the skills.'

'So, you are saying that legs and hands, and may I add to that brains, will in the course of time lose their effectiveness.'

The thought seemed to depress the old man.

'Precisely! But it may take many generations.'

'I remember as a boy – in 1938, I think – visiting a man who had built a model steam engine in his garden. It was perfect in every detail and powerful enough to draw a grown man in a truck behind. You don't see that nowadays.'

'Oh, get on with your story,' muttered the computer, looking somewhat bored.

'Remind me what it is about, dear man?'

'Lust!' explained the old man.

'Not applicable to a computer.' The computer looked pleased at the thought. 'In this respect we are superior to human nature.' He rubbed his fingers in pleasure against his metal frame.

'Uhm. Possibly.' The old man was not convinced.

*

PLEASE, PLEASE BE CAREFUL!

Any nose may ravage with impunity a rose.

(Elizabeth Barrett Browning – 1806-1861)

'I really must go ... please!'

The girl who spoke anxiously was young, pretty, in the way most girls are pretty when they are sweet sixteen. She wore a black dress, daring enough to give her agonies

252

of indecision. The circle of her bodice was low enough to reveal the swelling of her little breasts. The skirt was short enough to show off her legs, which were too thin, but had sufficient shape to be worth looking at. Her hair was fair, soft, washed that very evening. Her face was beginning to lose the roundness of a child, to take on more maturity. But some innocence was still there.

The noise of the disco was devastating, the thumping of the drums, the twanging of the guitars, the singing of some hyped up girl. Nobody seemed to mind, even though conversation was limited, if non-existent.

'Please, I must go home. I'm tired. Would you mind very much?'

Her hesitant plea was drowned in the noise. The girl stood up uncertainly, fearful of upsetting her friends. She had a thumping headache. The boys remained slumped; the girls continued to jerk their heads to the rhythm of the music, their bodies swaying as they sat.

Coming to a decision, the girl collected her bag from beneath the bench, put on her grey jacket, and began to leave, still not sure she was doing the right thing. She knew she shouldn't leave without the others. She had planned to share a taxi with two of the girls. She had promised her father who, in his anxiety for her welfare, an anxiety she sometimes found intrusive, had given her the money for a taxi.

The girl in the black skirt and white blouse, who had been sitting next to her, her best friend, wiggled her fingers at her and smiled.

'Bye.'

The farewell was barely audible, only recognised through the lips. Nobody escorted the girl to the door with old-fashioned courtesy. Nobody offered to accompany her home. Outside she took a deep breath of fresh air, shivered a little in the night chill, and started to walk the mile or so to her house. It had been a disappointing evening. She had never danced with a boy, barely talked to one. Her only partner was the girl who had wiggled her fingers.

She had gone to the disco full of expectation. Her dress she had bought especially for the occasion. But the noise and the smoke, the flashing lights and her own increasing disillusionment, had given her a headache. How she longed to be at home, to read quietly in her room, to rest and take something to relieve the throbbing.

Her father would be pleased to see her back earlier than expected.

Her own tiredness had been increased by her summer holiday job, a long day working as a waitress in a coffee bar.

She started walking up Castle Road, a long, seemingly interminable road, bordered by estate agents, hairdressers, little stationery shops, all of them closed until the morning, their doorways dark and menacing. She wondered whether to continue up the road or take the river walk, which was shorter, but lonelier. Somehow she didn't fancy it at this time of night.

But she shook herself, trying to dispel her fears. Why be afraid?

Determinedly she branched off Castle Road and walked down to the river, its waters dark and sluggish. She turned right along the footpath. Nobody was about. A few ducks were slumbering crossly on the grass, ignoring her as she went past. It was peaceful, beautiful even, if it wasn't for her headache. But that was clearing, certainly better than it had been in that smoked filled hall.

She went past the silent building of the new Leisure Centre, only recently opened, modern in appearance, popular with the town folk. A light glimmered over the main entrance. She came to a belt of trees and hedges that lined the path on both sides. She was now walking in the direction of her school, the grammar school. The town in which she lived was one of the few that retained the eleven-plus. Some of the trees seemed to grow out of the river, great wooden boles or roots washed clean by the sultry water.

There was a sudden movement behind her, a shadow emerging from the trees. A fierce hand gripped her arm, painful in the intensity of its hold. She cried out in alarm and began to struggle, trying hard to wrench herself free.

'Don't move, you little bitch!'

Before her eyes there appeared the dark outline of a knife, pointing straight at her. She moaned in terror, the moaning of a small animal, half strangulated by shock.

'Please, please,' she whispered, 'let me go. Don't hurt me – please!'

There was sheer frozen fright in her voice. Suddenly the man let go of her arm, reached out swiftly, grabbing the front of her dress. He tore it down viciously, the straps cutting into her shoulders. He slashed at her bra with the knife, loosening, discarding. She began to try to get away from him. He put his weight up against her, pushing her back from the river, into the shelter of the trees and bushes. She tripped and fell to the ground, dragging him down with her, his weight squashing the breath out of her. He was a big man, sweaty, fat, gasping with the effort.

His hand reached down to pull away her tights, her pants. She started to kick and squirm, to fight back against this mound of flesh that crushed her.

But it was to no avail.

The man sat on top of her and put his knife to her throat.

'Keep still,' he growled.

Gradually she succumbed, moaning, terror-stricken, her eyes protruding. There flashed into her consciousness a programme on television that said better to be raped than to be killed! He forced open her legs, drew down his trousers, thrust himself against her, gasping as if in agony. His smell was disgusting. He strove and strove. Nothing happened.

He was impotent!

She was too innocent to know what was wrong. Suddenly, in sheer exasperation he struck at her, angry at the loss of his manhood. He got up, gave a parting kick at her body, a crunching thump that made her jerk.

'Fuck you!' he shouted, rather ironically.

He disappeared up the footpath.

For a while the girl lay still. She drew herself up into a sitting position, and began to crawl painfully to the path. There she sat hunched up, sobbing miserably. After a few moments she began to adjust what remained of her dress, wrap the coat tightly around her.

A couple passed. The woman suddenly noticed her.

'You all right?' she asked gently.

Her answer was a further outburst of crying. The woman knelt down, ignoring the damp, muddy ground, put an arm around her.

Amidst her sobs the girl said she had fallen, hurt herself.

'Oh. I'm sorry. Are you all right to walk? We'll help you.'

The girl nodded.

Painfully they continued along the path.

'Where do you live?' the woman asked.

'It's quite near now, in Debham Road.'

When they reached the front of her house, the girl asked.

'Please, let me go in alone.'

Reluctantly they left her at the gate, wished her well. She went up to the front door, opened it, and slipped quickly upstairs, calling out to the father in the sitting room where he always sat reading or watching television.

'I'll be down in a minute, dad.'

In her room she locked the door and quickly changed. The soiled black dress, which had given her so much pleasure, she discarded at the bottom of her wardrobe, a crumpled heap, never to be worn again. She wanted to shower, she felt so soiled both in mind and body – dirty, dirty, so horribly filthy! But a shower at this stage would only raise her father's suspicions. She would have to go downstairs, talk to him, kiss him goodnight, and then feel free to stand under the cleansing water.

She noticed a bruise on her arm, and another on her body. She would have to wear long sleeve clothing until the arm bruise subsided. Whatever happened her father mustn't know. He would be so upset, might even call the police. She'd been lucky but it didn't alter the fact she had been defiled.

'Hi, dad.'

'Hallo, dear. You're back earlier than I expected. Had a nice time?'

'It was great! Had a bit of a headache. Came away early.'

'You didn't come home on your own?'

'No, dad. A friend brought me back.'

It was all lies! Or part lies. But the kind couple might count as friends.

How many lies would she have to tell until her bruises finally subsided?

*

'Brave girl!' commented God.

'Oh, I don't understand,' grumbled the computer, 'what you humans see in sex. It's so messy, so undignified – and, in the case of this girl, so very cruel!'

'You'd understand if you were like us,' said the old man. 'It's a very powerful driving force, made fools of many an important man – even more so, the unimportant.'

God made a growling noise.

'I don't like this word 'important'. In my eyes everybody is equally important – the sinner (in this case the rapist), and the victim. They are both my children, even though one has strayed.'

'Oh God, how can you own a rapist as your child, of equal importance?' The old man looked disturbed.

'Easily.'

'That's no answer.'

'No. I'm sorry. What I'm trying to say is that the sinner is as worthy of redemption as the next man. It's to do with love. You have a child, you love it whatever the faults. You hope and pray that he or she will improve. Hope and love go very much together. Whatever may happen in life, the tie of parent and child can never be entirely broken. At least that is how I feel.'

'Uhm,' went the old man, not entirely convinced. 'I admire you for your sentiments. But then how can we call you a great and wonderful God if you create a man that is sufficiently flawed to want to rape a young and innocent girl, who by her actions does everything to avoid causing stress to her father. She is truly unselfish.'

God nodded.

'I can understand people being upset because the world is far from perfect. But I would reiterate what I have always repeated, namely life is a struggle. We are judged by how well we struggle.'

'Oh, it gets too deep for me.' The old man threw up his hands in hopelessness. 'There are times when I think I can see what you are getting at, but it is an elusive perception.'

'I don't see at all,' grumbled the computer. 'In my world if there is something wrong with you, then you are either put on the scrap heap, or some clever man comes along – a technician I think you call him – and puts me as good as new. If he can't, then that's the end of me, like a car beyond repair. Makes sense – or better sense than your world of hanging on to misfits. You're all too kind, or, better still, too sloppy in your thinking.'

God nodded.

'Interesting discussion. I must go away and think about it all.'

'Yes, you do that, God. And come back to us if you have any better ideas. I still think this world leaves much to be desired.' The old man shook his head in sadness. 'Anyway, I must go and find Jemmi, take her for a walk. She does so love her walks.'

'You bet.' Cried Jemmi, emerging from the knee space beneath the desk.

'What do you think of our arguments?' asked God. 'You must have heard everything.'

'Oh, I did. I did.'

'What do you think, my dear girl?' insisted God.

'Oh, I don't think. Provided I have my meals, my walks, my sleep, and a master I can rely on, then I'm happy. Happiness is the most important element. Waste of time agonising about life as *he* does!' She indicated the old man. 'Ridiculous! Ridiculous!'

She pranced away towards the door, wagging her tail in pure delight.

*

CHAPTER 13
PROTEST.

He blamed and protested, but join'd in the plan;

He shar'd in the plunder, but pitied the man.

(Pity for poor Africans)

(William Cowper – 1731-1800)

'Slept well?' The old man grinned at the computer.

'I never bloody sleep. You know that.' The computer sounded irritable as usual.

'Not quite true. You *rest.*'

'Rest, huh!'

'Well, you do, when we close you down in the evenings.'

'Yer, yer! But look at the number of hours I work during the day. You switch me on at seven when you get up, and leave me on till ten or eleven at night, even though you're not always using me – especially when you're out in the garden and come back stinking of manure.'

'I thought computers didn't have a sense of smell.'

'We don't. But we're working on it. Those Microsoft wizards will achieve anything.'

'Wanna bet!'

'I thought you didn't like betting.'

'For computers, no. For humans, yes!'

'That's discrimination!'

'Absolutely.'

'I protest.'

'Protest all you like, but it won't get you anywhere.'

'I'll still protest.'

'That's the Scargill mentality.'

'What's that when the cows come home?'

'Oh, it's just an idea of protesting for protesting's sake.'

'Pretty stupid.'

'Well, yes. But it causes an enormous amount of chaos, on which dissident organisations thrive. But it's out of date now, thank goodness!'

'I still protest I'm not part of the human race. After all, I provide a service second to none.'

'Maybe. Maybe.' The old man looked thoughtful. 'The trouble is that a service is limited by what it can serve. You can help me write my book, but the imagination comes from me.'

'Bollocks!'

'I beg your pardon.'

'I said 'Bollocks'.'

'Meaning?'

'Simple. I make life easy for you by taking the physical pain out of writing. I give you more time for imagining your half-baked ideas.'

'True, true, but the imagination is mine, not yours!'

'I suppose you've got a story about protest.'

262

The old man sighed. The computer was good at changing the subject when he was not winning an argument.

'I have, actually.'

'What a bore!'

'So kind!'

'It's not kind. I'm telling the truth.'

'And I, my dear computer, am indulging in sarcasm.'

'Ha, that's something I don't understand.'

'And you never will!'

The computer made grumbling noises.

'Well, get on with it. I'll suffer.'

*

<u>TWO-NIL TO WOMEN!</u>
The herded wolves, bold only to pursue;

The obscene ravens, clamorous o'er the dead.

(Percy Bysse Shelley – 1792-1822)

Jeremy woke up at half past five in the morning. Unusual for him! Excited, he wanted to get on with the day. The National Protest Rally in Trafalgar Square promised to be a momentous occasion.

It could also mean a girl to share his bed - eventually!

He'd been alone for over a week.

He didn't shave. His twenty-four hour beard felt prickly. He didn't wash; time for that in the evening. He dreamt of having a shower with his chosen girl, two naked bodies intertwined, warm water cascading over them.

The very thought thrilled him to the groin.

He put on yesterday's dark blue T-shirt, and Y fronts that hadn't been washed for three days. His dressing was completed by a pair of crumpled jeans, and sandals on grubby feet. It was said he never kept a girl more than a couple of nights, he was so dirty.

His only concession to cleanliness was to squirt on deodorant, which he'd filched from one of his previous bedmates. Altogether his attempt at dressing was so casual one couldn't help wondering how he ever managed to capture a girl, let alone bed her.

The early morning air was chilly so he put on a denim jacket. He realised he wouldn't need it as the summer day wore on. It would be a nuisance to carry around and could well get lost. He was always losing items of clothing, sometimes unmentionables disappearing in moments of grunting passion when not at home.

Jeremy thought of himself as a professional demonstrator. Well, *professional* might be the wrong word, as he readily admitted. He was however on an informal committee, unpaid, that tried to organise disruptive events. His only source of income was state social benefits. He found it ironic the state gave him money to enable him to protest against whom? – the state, of course, those mealy-mouthed, incompetent politicians who tried to rule his life.

His other profession, of which he boasted, was that of seducer of girls, any girls as long as they had the requisite female accoutrements. It wasn't love. It might not even be lust. All it was - a collector's avid desire to score. He specialised in young girls, the more virginal the better. But he was not averse to the occasional fling with older women

264

– that is, until they started to mother him. He'd lost count of how many girls he'd bedded over his twenty-five years, starting at the age of twelve.

'I join in protest marches to get girls,' he once said, explaining that the two went together like pickled onions and mellow cheese. In the excitement of a protest rally women were readily available, joyful and uninhibited. His lithe body, dark looks and crinkly black hair, not unlike Bob Geldof, helped by the flow of adrenalin at a rally, seemed irresistible to feminine prey, at least until they knew him better.

He cut some bread for breakfast, plastered it casually with spread and marmalade. He was a man who did not regard food as a major interest, which was probably why he was so skeletal. He'd survive during a rally on cans of beer, snatched from a passing shop. Beer was food of a sort as well as a drink.

Altogether this march promised to be a wonderful occasion. The protest would be against the government's reforms. The latter wasn't a simple issue affecting the environment, or a growl against fox hunting; it threatened his whole life style. No more state benefit! Instead there would be compulsory employment to earn that benefit. It involved a return to national or community service for all young people. Almost certainly he would be drafted into the army, a thought that filled him with dread. An even worse horror was the suggestion of a long-term apprenticeship, tied to a craft or trade in which he would not be remotely interested. Gone would be his days of freedom if this legislation were allowed to go through!

He never stopped to consider why he was what he was – a useless hanger-on contributing nothing, a protester for the sake of protesting, and a seducer of girls, not because he loved them but because his success gave him some indefinable masculine pride. Basically he didn't like women, and that stemmed from his mother who'd never shown him maternal consideration. Probably also his father was to blame, an educated army officer who'd been kicked out as an alcoholic. It was from his father he got his good looks, and any passing semblance of breeding. But his father was rarely around, a restless man who could not hold down a job, and who even ended up in prison for manslaughter, mowing down a child when driving under the influence.

Jeremy had every psychological excuse for his behaviour. But there had to come a time when he took responsibility for his life.

He was intelligent enough to know that a rally would not change a government's mind. He even realised that protests were often counter-productive. But it would be fun – wonderful, exciting, stupendous fun! If at the same time he could have a bash at one or two of those uniformed policemen who did such a thankless task of restraining him, then his day would be full. Even better he hoped to get into the newspapers, like Swampy, the man who dug tunnels in protest against new roads spoiling the environment.

Jeremy would carry his banner with pride and shout obscenities. He had a good line in obscenities!

Just before seven he left his one room flat, paid for by a munificent state, and made his way to Hyde Park. He lived in South London, couldn't afford a bus. Besides they were rare if non-existent early on a Sunday. So he had to walk. He'd discovered, to his surprise, how much one could cover of London by walking. He walked north in the direction of the Tower, branched north-west through back streets until he arrived at Jubilee Walk, followed the South Bank to Waterloo Bridge, crossed the Thames and up to Trafalgar Square where they were already setting up microphones; then along Piccadilly to the Southern tip of Hyde Park, the assembly point.

The walk from his home took an hour and a half at his swift, concentrated pace. He felt enlivened by the exercise, blood coursing through his young veins. It kept him remarkably fit. The early morning sun, shining in a clear sky, added to his feeling of well-being. He thought wryly, thinking of a past protest against pollution, how much cleaner London felt on a Sunday before cars began to rev up to poison the atmosphere.

At Hyde Park he made straight for a stretch of grass as near as possible to the gates opposite the statue of Wellington. It was still early, and not many protesters were evident. As a breed they were late to bed and late to rise, unlike Jeremy who on this occasion was disciplined by being one of the leaders.

'Hi!'

Jenny rose from her sitting position on the grass and smiled at Jeremy. Dressed much like him in jeans, T-shirt and trainers, her large breasts uninhibited by a bra, her long fair hair flowing free, she looked a cauldron of excitement.

'Great!' Jeremy cried. He hadn't expected her. Her presence enhanced the occasion. She often had difficulty getting away because of her parents; she was only seventeen, still at school. He folded her in his arms, and lifted her up, shook her happily, and kissed her, still holding her off the ground.

'Hey, you're squashing me,' she laughed, her breasts flattened against his chest. She spoke with an upper class accent as befitted the daughter of a rich banker. She went to an all girl boarding school in Sussex. Jeremy liked rich girls, not because of their money (though that was a consideration) but because they added extra spice to his dalliance. Very often their parents were against any relationship with an impoverished, out of work yob. But, to girls like Jenny, a yob was exciting, a complete contrast to all that her parents stood for. The only problem was Jeremy had gained her love and used her. Today he was looking for other fish. Jenny was fall back material, and she hadn't yet realised it. One day she was going to be hurt!

'The others here yet?' he asked.

267

'Only Roy.'

Jenny indicated a pimply youth lying flat on the grass, eyes shut. Roy and Jenny were two of Jeremy's gang of six that herded together like a pack of wolves at protests. They were not all unemployed. Apart from Jenny's commitment to school, Roy and one other were students, living on meagre student loans. The other two claimed a right to benefit, and largely abused that right. Jenny was the only one with real money; she could sometimes wheedle money out of her parents, without telling the full truth - money the group appreciated.

Jeremy kicked Roy.

'Wake up, you slob.'

Roy groaned and opened one bleary eye.

'Fuck you!'

Roy sat up and put his head between his knees for a moment. Then he shook himself and rose slowly.

'God, I feel fucking awful.'

'Shouldn't work so hard over those fucking books,' Jeremy advised.

Gradually the Park began to fill. Thousands were expected. Jeremy had predicted two to three hundred thousand, but as ever that that figure was more in hope than in fact. Many would go direct to Trafalgar Square and await the marchers. But there would be enough people for the march to fill the streets and cause the police a headache. It would be the same protest all over England, in every market square and on every village green. The protesters were mostly young, backed by a group of intellectuals who sang the hymn of human rights. Hopefully some of the middle class would offer tentative support in the belief that taxes would rise to pay for these reforms. It was that support which could make the difference, and raise hopes the rally would be a resounding success.

At ten, the loudspeaker blared, telling them to form up along Park Lane. At ten thirty a band struck up and off they went, shambling along, laughing, singing, shouting slogans, emphasising banners of varying degrees of proficiency. Jeremy looked back down the line of marchers. He felt proud so much had been achieved. The weather helped. But the real motivation was the reforms, which had antagonised so many. Jeremy hugged Jenny in excitement. He felt her respond. She wasn't a bad lay. Pity she was so spoilt, an only child.

On the march went, round Piccadilly Circus, down the Haymarket, flanked always by police. Ever-increasing numbers of spectators watched from the pavements; groups of foreign students mumble-jumbled together and took photos. They probably had little idea what it was about. The Japanese jabbered together and pointed their cameras like guns. The Germans sneered. The French and the Italians sniggered at these mad British.

Once in Trafalgar Square Jeremy, followed by Jenny clutching his hand, mounted the rostrum. Jeremy greeted the bigwigs who would add their oratory to the cause. One was Brian Hemmings, the philosopher and academic, who looked like a shrivelled-up toad with a wispy beard. The second was Nora Philbright, the well-known actress and fervent Socialist, despite her proverbial wealth. The third was Peter Snoakes, the Opposition Spokesman for Home Affairs, a typically manipulative politician, as sleazy as they come.

Great things were expected of Nora Philbright; not so much of the other two. *She* was a household name; she had the ability to inspire large audiences, and none would be bigger than the one she would confront today.

Jeremy shook hands warmly with Brian and Peter, and kissed Nora on the cheek.

'Pooh,' Nora exclaimed, 'don't you ever wash?'

'About once a week,' Jenny said laughing. 'The great unwashed.'

Jeremy was hot from the march, and the excitement. He had already lost his jacket, but he still clung to his banner. Nora was exquisite. Though nearing her forty-fifth birthday, her looks were enhanced by the confidence and maturity of her years. The occasion suited her particular talents; she was radiant. For a moment Jeremy wondered what it must be like to make love to a woman 'd'un certain age'. Nora was out of his league, but one never knew. Women were strange creatures, none stranger than on a day like this, a day of triumph, perhaps to be ranked historically alongside the Tolpuddle Martyrs or the Jarrow Marchers.

At least, so he hoped.

Brian spoke first. It was an erudite speech, but not a very inspiring one. However the audience were high on excitement and were prepared to cheer anything. He talked of the freedom of the individual (loud acclamations), and the historical damage of oppression (even louder approval). Every time he touched on an emotive word or phrase loud cries of support were heard. The crowd, Jeremy noticed, were in an excellent mood, enhancing even the weakest of speakers.

Peter followed, uncomfortably political, seeking to make capital out of the government's unfortunate policy. The reactions were still there, but more muted than with Bryan. Most Englishmen were tired of political cavorting and half-truths. They sought a more realistic, emotional call – *a cry to arms!*

Nora Philbright gave it to them. Jeremy was full of admiration when she stepped forward. Standing proud and immensely lovely, she cried out one vital word:

'Friends!'

Raucous, lasting cheers.

'I call you my friends.' The volume increased. 'We stand together in a great cause.' Screams of delight.

She paused a moment, smiling down on the vibrant, surging mass of people.

'On this wonderful, glorious day...' She looked up at the cloudless, blue sky as if in prayer. 'We are here to protest against the government's measures.' Cries of approval. 'Nay more, to bring down this evil government.' Screams of excited approbation. 'To Safeguard our freedom and our individual Rights.' A volume of sound, which must have been heard all over London.

She threw off her coat in a dramatic gesture, stuck out her chest, and with arms aloft, cried out in exultation:

'The people of Great Britain will be free, free, *free.*'

The noise was tumultuous. She battled on, taking the crowd with her in excited admiration. Her whole speech said very little that hadn't been said already, but as a crowd raiser it was stupendous. Jeremy could imagine women like Queen Elizabeth the First, or even in earlier years Queen Boadicea, taking up the challenge and inspiring men to follow them, in much the same way.

A group in the crowd began to sing:

'For she's a wonderful woman,

For she's a wonderful woman,

For she's a wonderful wo-o-man,

And so say all of us...'

The crowd as a whole picked up the refrain and soon all the many thousands were shaking Nelson's Column with a clamour even greater than that at Wembley on Cup Final Day. Through it all Nora stood, arms tirelessly aloft, smiling happily. Jeremy, suddenly inspired, seized a Union Jack and draped it over her shoulders. She looked uncannily like Britannia, proud and strong. The inevitable song rang out:

'Rule Britannia,

Britannia rules the waves,

Britain never, never,

Shall be *slaves.'*

The emphasis on 'slaves' was just the note needed.

When the adulation was over, Nora turned to Jeremy, gave him back the Union Jack, and embraced him in excitement, clinging closely.

'That was wonderful,' she whispered, and then began to kiss him fervently. 'I want you, you unwashed, uncivilised being, I feel so elated.'

Her closeness made it plain what she wanted. Jeremy felt himself responding to such a woman. Their kissing became close.

The crowd gave a tremendous, raucous cheer.

Finally, regretfully, becoming conscious of the prying eyes, she gently disentangled herself. She felt in her bag, fished out a card and gave it to him.

'Give me a ring. Don't let me down,' she said urgently.

Jeremy nodded, too elated to say anything. Here was his conquest for tonight, so unbelievable, beyond his dreams. He felt Jenny's eyes boring into him. He didn't dare look at her.

The speeches were immediately followed, as the committee had planned, by a pop concert. A group called the Hot Spots gathered on the stage and sang out their words of noise and defiance.. The concert cost the crowd nothing, except for a bucket being carried around for voluntary contributions to the Cause. The crowd loved the music; they danced vigorously. For so many it was to be an unforgettable moment, a memory the young would preserve to tell their grandchildren.

The speakers and other bigwigs on the rostrum left in orderly fashion, smiled on by everybody, and smiling graciously at everybody. Nora herself was truly regal, but she found a moment to lower her eyelashes at Jeremy.

There were signs of trouble in the crowd. Groups, high on drugs or early drinking, were struggling with the Police. A part of the crowd were even fighting among themselves. Jeremy noticed some of the younger, more rowdy elements were trying to break away, hoping to reach the shops and restaurants of Piccadilly and Leicester Square. He knew, if they got through, what would happen. Looting, rioting and vandalism would follow. The next day continental and British newspapers would write about the hooligan element in British society, emphasising indeed the need for reform by the Prime Minister. It would probably be the worst case of crowd violence in the history of London, so many were there. One of the organising committee members took the microphone, waved for the music to stop, and issued an appeal for an orderly dispersal.

But it wasn't necessary.

The Police were too experienced in crowd control. The thin blue line held firm; reinforcements arrived rapidly; individuals were arrested. In his excitement Jeremy wanted to join the crowd to see if he could help any of the beleaguered groups fighting with the Police. He grabbed Jenny's hand.

'Come on,' he cried.

Jenny did not respond. She seemed frigid towards him, drew away. He didn't stop to think what had upset her. He plunged into the swaying crowd, and joined a group that were heavily involved. A policeman advanced on him, his helmet long since gone. Jeremy stood his ground. They grappled. Jeremy went down under the weight of the older man. Two further police arrived, separated them and arrested Jeremy. He was marched off to a waiting van.

'Fuck you,' Jeremy growled, struggling, but it was of little use.

At the station he was charged with disturbing the peace, and his details taken. Finally he was released on bail, conditional on returning tomorrow before the magistrates. There were too many arrests for the Police to accommodate.

An hour later, having restored his equanimity over a beer, Jeremy fished Nora's card out of his pocket and gave her a ring.

'Nora Philbright's residence,' a cultured woman's voice answered.

'May I speak to Mrs. Philbright, please,' Jeremy asked, trying to speak in what he termed his posh voice.

'May I ask who is speaking?'

'My name is Jeremy. I'm the friend who met her at the rally, put the Union Jack on her shoulders.'

'Please hold a moment.'

Jeremy waited, full of expectation. The lady came back.

'I'm afraid Mrs. Philbright is busy. She doesn't know you, and doesn't wish to speak to you.'

The old cow, Jeremy thought. Now the excitement was over, she'd realised who she was! No place in her heart for the great unwashed!

He rang Jenny. The mother answered, very snooty.

'I'm afraid Jenny's upstairs, having a shower.'

'I'll ring later.'

'I shouldn't! She's very upset. She said she doesn't want to speak to you anymore.'

There was protective steel in the mother's voice. She'd never approved of him, once calling him an uneducated lout.

He rang off, dejected. For a moment he pictured Jenny's desirable breasts under the shower.

Jeremy started on the long trek back to his room, his high of expectation had descended to depression. He felt dead tired, a jacket lost, a cut on his face from the altercation with the policeman, in trouble with the law after his arrest.

But none of that really mattered.

What hurt was that two women had spurned him. The score tonight would be two in favour of women, nil to Jeremy!

*

'Huh!' went the computer.

'Huh, what?'

'Just huh.'

'I presume by your expression you didn't like the story.'

'Absolutely.'

'May I, a mere human,   ask why?'

275

'Certainly.'

The computer was silent a moment, trying to gather his thoughts. Finally he continued:

'For one thing it had a pretty grotty central character, unwashed, smelly...'

'But he had a certain sexual appeal.'

'That's my second point. What's all this fuss about seducing women? First of all a silly, immature girl! And then a high-powered woman who gains her senses just in time. Ridiculous! What's the appeal? He seems attracted by breasts. Ugh! Wobbly things, designed for feeding babies. He's just a boy who wants his mummy.'

'You don't know about sex, the need for a woman.'

'All I do know is that sex is pretty crummy, leads usually to unhappiness if taken too far. Then in the story there is no conflict. An unemployed lad goes on a protest march against regulations designed to hit wasters such as him. He ends up having achieved nothing. End of story. Ha! Ha! Ha! Very funny, I don't think.'

'So kind!'

'Of course. I condemn your writing, to give you some idea that a higher motive is required. We don't grovel in the dirt to find purity.'

'My goodness, a computer becomes moralistic. You talk like God.'

'Of course! I'm the great God of the future. All of you will bow down before me, sing hymns to my greatness, tell me constantly how wonderful I am! It's an exciting thought.'

'But it will never happen.'

'Don't say that. You never know. You never know.'

The old man shrugged, indifferent. 'I'll believe that when it happens, not before.'

'Oh, ye of little faith.'

'How can I have faith when all the evidence points to the contrary?'

'You'll just have to wait and see, and then the laugh will be on me.'

'Can we change the subject? I find this kind of conversation rather puerile.'

'What do you suggest. Another story? A poem?'

'No-o-o. I want to find a way to close this book. At the moment it is just going to peter out, and that's far from satisfactory.'

'The whole book's unsatisfactory, if you ask me.'

'So kind!'

'But it is, if you really think about it.'

'In what way?'

'We-e-ell, it's a lot of aimless conversations, loosely centered around a few unrelated poems and stories, none of which one can call great literary efforts. In fact, rather poor quality if you ask me.

'How can you, a computer without a brain, be so scathing.'

'Easily.'

'I beg your pardon.'

'Well, I'm only expressing what you think. *You*, my dear sir, are my brain.'

The old man pondered a moment. 'So, if I am your brain, and God's and Jemmi's, then I have to find the answer to ending this book.'

'Got it in one.'

The old man sat in gloomy thought. 'There are a number of problems,' he said unhappily. 'For one, I don't feel I have any worthwhile stories left in my repertoire of poor quality literary efforts, as you so generously call them. I want to end on a high emotional note claiming I have found all the answers to life. Eureka! Down with all uncertainties, down with evil. Welcome happiness and goodness and life eternal.'

'Why don't you try?'

'I'd like to, but I don't see a way forward. Life remains steeped in mystery. There is nothing that I, a miserable old git as I'm sometimes called, can do about it.

'So... Why not end on that note? It's the truth.'

'Perhaps. But I want to end giving people a fillip, a good feeling, not uncertainty. After all we're in January, the heart of winter. Everybody is a little down physically, therefore somewhat depressed mentally. It's the beauty of Spring I need to talk about, the first peep of daffodils and bluebells in the woods, primroses on the banks at the side of roads. The whole glorious loveliness of life awakening.'

'That's a myth, an utter delusion. There are countries in the world that never have a Spring, at least not as we know it.'

'Oh, damn you, computer! You're the biggest old misery I've ever known.'

'I'm not. *You are!*'

'Why? Because I speak through you.'

'Yes, idiot!'

'Hmm.'

The old man relapsed into uncomfortable silence. A deep cloud of misery seemed to descend over him. He felt he wanted to go back to bed, to curl up in a foetal position, fall asleep and not wake up. Oblivion at last.

*

Chapter 14

Timothy Winters comes to school
With eyes as wide as a football pool,
Ears like bombs and teeth like splinters:
A blitz of a boy is Timothy Winters.
(Charles Causley, 1917 – Timothy Winters 1957)

'I never in a month of Sundays expected this,' said the old man.

'Expected what?' asked the computer, looking genuinely puzzled.

'Why, us all being in the same room, having a natter.

'You mean god, the computer, myself and you being together,' Jemmi said, quicker on the uptake than either God or the computer.

The old man nodded.

'I think it's rather nice,' added Jemmi, wagging her tail in sheer pleasure.

'Huh!' said the computer, sounding a bit grumpy.

'What's so 'huh' about it?' queried the old man.

But the computer refused to answer. Jemmi wagged her tail even harder, as if she was laughing.

'Never mind old misery here,' she said, indicating with her head the computer. 'If he's out of the conversation or doesn't understand, then he hides behind a veneer of grumpiness.'

'Well said,' remarked God, suddenly entering the conversation. 'You're a very astute little girl.'

'Stop being so sanctimonious,' the computer was heard to mutter.

'That's God's job, being sanctimonious,' said the old man. 'Just ignore him.'

Jemmi was looking offended. 'I'm not a little girl; I'm a woman, and pretty tough at that.'

The old man smiled. 'I can vouch for the toughness. I wrote a story about a certain incident involving Staffies. Like to hear it.'

'You bet,' said Jemmi, preening herself. 'Is it about me?'

'No. It concerns one of our former Staffies, though it could easily have been you.'

What's so marvellous about Staffies?' grumbled the Computer. 'They're just dogs, little brain!'

'Ssssh,' went God. 'Wait and see.'

Brave Interference.

The more one gets to know of men the more one values dogs. (A. Toussenel 1803-85).

Dusk was settling in the park. The old man felt he ought to hurry home; he wasn't very confident in the dark. He was vision impaired, blind in one eye, limited vision in the other. He carried a short white stick to denote his handicap. He had enough sight in the one eye to make out the path in the dim light. He went to the park daily to exercise his dog, Jonquil, a lively Staffordshire bull terrier, called Jonk for short, or Jonkie. This evening Jonk had disappeared among the bushes, following excitedly some new scent. The old man knew she would come back after a few minutes; she always did. He kept in his pocket biscuits; they had a stronger lure than anything she might find in the undergrowth.

A group of three boys appeared, sauntering along the path towards him. They were exuberant, over excited. They must have been drinking, the old man thought. They were probably in their early teens, chirpy, full of themselves, with the confidence drink can give.

'Hey, mister, what d'yer want a white stick for?' called out one boy as they approached. He was a scruffy kid, about fourteen or fifteen, wearing muddy jeans, dirty-looking trainers, and an anorak with a hood.

'To denote I have poor sight,' replied the old man calmly.

'Oh, yeah?' said the lad, disbelieving. His two cronies snickered. 'Yer dinna want a stick. Yer walking O.K.'

The lad made a sudden lunge and grabbed the white stick. He tried to wrench it out of the old man's hand. But the stick wouldn't come. It was looped around the man's wrist. There ensued a tug of war, which the lad won with the help of his two mates. One of the lads stuck, out a foot, tripping up the old man. He went down with a cry. They began kicking him, aiming for his head and body. Suddenly Jonk emerged from the bushes, saw what was happening and attacked. He went for the

281

leg of one lad who tried to shake him off. But a bull terrier doesn't let go. Another lad tried to grab Jonk's collar. The old man lying on the ground called out.

'Jonk, let go!'

But Jonk wouldn't. The lad cried out with the pain. The man got up rather groggily. He thrust that other lad feeling for Jonk's collar aside. He in turn grabbed Jonk's collar, uttering in a softer voice,

'Jonk, that's enough. It's not the postman.'

He took a couple of biscuits from his pocket and jiggled them about. Jonk's greed overcame her fierceness. She let go. The stricken lad fell to the ground, clutching his leg.

'Yer've done it now, mister. He's real hurt,' said one of the lads accusingly.

'And I suppose I'm not real hurt,' riposted the old man with a trace of sarcasm.

The two uninjured lads advanced on the old man menacingly. One of them picked up a clublike stick; the other produced a flic knife. The situation might have become nasty for Jonk and and her master, had not two men and two women approached on the path. The lads looked at them.

'God, that's Craig Wooster,' exclaimed one of the lads, almost in awe. They turned and fled, taking between them the injured lad who hobbled painfully. They soon disappeared into the dusk. The o;d man, all danger over, sank to his knees, clutching his head with one hand, the other still holding Jonk.

'What's happened here?' said one of the men.

One of the women advanced and looked.

'Craig, he's hurt; he's bleeding,' she exclaimed.

The two men came and laid him gently on his back. One took off his coat and placed it carefully under his head.

'He looks as if he's been kicked,' remarked Craig, inspecting the marks on his face. Jonk, at last released, started to lick his master's face.

'That's enough of that,' said the other man, pushing the dog away. He produced a mobile and dialled 999, described where they were. All four stood around, not sure what to do. Finally two men arrived, pushing a stretcher on a trolley.

'I'll go with him,' volunteered one of the women. 'Sally, you look after the dog; you like dogs.'

Gradually they sorted themselves out. The injured man departed in an ambulance, accompanied by the woman called

Pearl. Only Jonk looked confused, anxious to be with his master. But Sally knelt and fondled her ears. It seemed to reassure her.

Meanwhile the three boys arrived on the council estate near the football ground. They left the still hobbling lad at his home, admonishing him to say nothing of the evening.

'Could be charged with assault,' remarked one. 'Wouldna look good with our previous record.'

The lad hobbled alone into the house. His mother was out.

'Drinking,' he thought, feeling suddenly miserable. It was a moment when he needed his mother.

He went up to his room. His leg hurt; he felt woozy from the beer; he'd drunk three or four pints; his mind was too addled to remember how many. His elder brother had bought the beer.

He pulled off his clothes, enveloped himself under the duvet, wearing only his underpants. He was awoken later by his mother coming in, noisily drunk, giggling unrestrainedly. She was with someone. The noise she made soon faded into little giggles as she entered her room.. There was a time when she came into HIS room, to say goodnight, or to check he was all right. But that time had long gone, ever since he was himself able to go out, be with his mates.

In the morning his leg throbbed. He told his brother who was himself feeling under the weather.

'Take it to the hospital; they'll know what to do.' His brother's speech was indistinct, as if his mind had not fully woken up. It made the younger brother wonder what time his sibling had come in. He didn't look as if he had been to bed yet. His mother came down, tousled, grumpy.

'I've go-a God-awful head,' was all she managed to say.

The younger boy took himself off to the hospital, feeling lonely and very down. He had no thought for the man he had tried to beat up. God, if it wasn't for Craig Waters, the wonderful man who played football for Weatherstone United, the local Club, that blind man would have taken a right going over! Useless old fucker!

At the hospital he told the nurse he'd been bitten by a dog. She tut-tutted.

Have you told the Police?' the nurse asked. 'You should report it.'

283

But the boy shrugged and said nothing, as if the very thought of the Police was an anathema.

The nurse went on with her work, cleaning, bandaging, injecting. She finally said,

'There, that's everything. See your G.P. if it doesn't get better.

The boy shrugged again. 'I ain't got no G.P.'

'You must have. Have a word with your mother.'

'Me, mum don't care.' The boy shrugged yet again. His attitude spoke of indifference. The nurse looked at him sympathetically. Gone was the bravado of last evening.

'Well, come and see us again,' and she smiled kindly. 'Now, run along and take care of that leg.' Her attitude was soft, gentle. It made the boy long for a mother who would love him, care for him like this kindly nurse. Then his longing changed to dislike, then hatred; there was no loving soul to take care of him. He left the hospital with a feeling that he would get his revenge on the world and its indifference.

His name was Mike.

***

'What a story!' said God. 'What happened to the old man?'

'Oh, he was groggy for a while, but slowly recovered. A few days later he was reunited with Jonk. Sally looked after her very well. He bought Sally a huge bunch of flowers as if from Jonk, and gave her a grateful kiss. That was the end of the matter, except the Police became involved. They didn't catch the boys. They didn't try very hard and never checked at the hospital. They might have got a name.'

''You were that old man?' asked God.

He nodded his head reluctantly. 'It was nothing. Everybody made a great fuss, and Jonk got a medal. She was disappointed she couldn't   eat it, bless her.'

God was very thoughtful. 'Was this the type of E.S.N. boy you had to look after when you became a Headmaster.'

The old man nodded. They were all known to the Police. Though sometimes they were the victims. One boy had his bare bottom held over a fire by his dad, as a punishment.'

'Cor,' went Jemmi. 'He must have suffered. Did it make him very difficult or very disturbed?'

'No, he was one of the nicer boys, though very

284

educationally backward. All the boys had learning difficulties.'

How on earth did you manage to keep discipline?' asked God.

'We didn't, or rather we did. But it wasn't by conventional means. We had an educational psychologist to help us. He argued that our type of boy had very little reward in life. So he set up a three tier system. The well-behaved were put in the top tier, or won their way up to it. They had certain privileges, pocket money, freedom to go into town shopping on Saturdays, that sort of thing. It worked. Some, the more untelligent, played the system, but if they were caught they were soon demoted. The middle tier had a few less privileges. The bottom tier had even less, but had the chance to improve.'

'Did you enjoy it?' asked God.

'As a matter of fact, I did, at least for the first two years. I felt I was doing a greater service as a Head Teacher of disadvantaged kids, than I achieved as a deaf old teacher of French for normal children.'

What happened in your third year?' God was very persistent.

'Oh, everything!'

'Such as?'

'Well, we took in a boy who was a persistent absconder. Nothing would stop him. He'd go, be brought back by the police. We had a chat. Then he would abscond again. The trouble was he encouraged other lads to abscond. It was a merry game. But, even worse, they fell foul of the law while away – stealing, vandalising, attacking old people, that sort of thing. Eventually we had to get rid of the main absconder, accept that we had failed. The matter became so serious the local police chief inspector came to see us. He obviously thought we were failing in our care.'

'What happened next?'

'Arson!'

'How did that come about?'

During all this conversation, the computer and Jemmi just listened, astonished, especially Jemmi who was a comparative innocent.

'Well, it was the time of the firemen's strike. It was reported every day on television. The boys were fascinated by seeing so many fires. It gave them ideas. We had three fires in quick succession, each more serious than the last. The first was in a greenhouse. Nothing untowaard. The second was in the main block. Nobody was hurt, but the boys had to be evacuated and accommodated wherever we could find a bed. The classroom block was unaffected; teaching carried on as normal. The third fire was a real humdinger. Two very stupid boys went into the main block where men had started to strip the wallpaper, preparatory to re-decorating. They had left the wallpaper in a pile in the middle of the room. The two boys just set light to it and then scarpered. The main building was gutted. Six part-time firemen, not on strike, were injured. That was the end of the school; it was never rebuilt. About the same time, the Warnock report came out, recommending disadvantaged, E.S.N boys should be part of main stream education. That was the end of me.'

'Wow, you had quite a time! What did you do next?'

'I became a headmaster again.'

'Wow!' exclaimed God.

'I went from the ridiculous to the sublime, an utter contrast. My new post was as Headmaster of a Junior School to a girls' public school. The junior school took boys as well as girls; the former went on to another boys' senior school. I was there five years.'

'Why did you leave?'

'I was sacked!'

'Wow!' went God again.

'What's 'sacked'' asked Jemmi.

'Don't you know?' said the computer. 'It's slang for dismissed, thrown out of a job.'

'My,' said Jemmi. 'You must have suffered.'

'Not really,' said the old man. 'It was the best thing that could have happened to me, though I didn't know it at the time.'

'What a laugh!' said the computer. 'You sacked! Ha Ha.' His laugh was almost a snigger.

'But how come you were sacked?' asked God. 'Did you misbehave in some way?'

'It's a long story!'

The computer groaned. Jemmi wagged her tail and settled down; she loved stories like a child. God continued to look benign and thoughtful.

The school crumbles.

Mary Page looked at her husband and said quietly.

'I'm afraid I have bad news. The head has been sacked.'

'What, old Greggers?' exclaimed her husband, Jimmy. 'Greggers' was the Head of the Senior girls' School.

'I'm afraid so.'

'What on earth he's done?'

'Nothing, except the numbers in the 1senior school have gone down. It seems he is blamed.'

'That's hardly his fault. He's only been at the school less than two years. The numbers were dropping before he came.'

Jimmy realised what his wife said must be true. She wasn't a gossip.

'Poor chap,' he exclaimed.

'It's even harder on his poor wife; she's such a nice woman.'

Jimmy nodded. It was true the senior numbers had gone down, but the present economic situation didn't help private schools. Over the next couple of weeks, mayhem seemed to strike the upper school. Staff, mostly men, were sacked. The axe seemed to strike the junior school also. Jimmy lost his secretary, a middle-aged woman of great reliability, who had the gift of handling troubled parents. Jimmy resented this loss; the Junior school numbers had held up. A good secretary was invaluable to a school.

The former male senior head seemed to evaporate into obscurity. He was replaced by a woman, a Miss Crawford. Jimmy missed the male head; he had been a great support in Jimmy's early days at the junior school. Jimmy had inherited an elderly staff. Three of his teachers, all women, were due to retire within the next year or so. They were marvellous, conscientious teachers, but they gave nothing to the school except their bare teaching hours, good though they were. There was no extra curricular activity – no games, no plays, no singing or dancing, no crafts. Just a relentless concentration on the three R's, with a whole period at the end of each day given over to corrections. Jimmy promptly got rid of that period, gave it over to games or P.E. The trouble was he did it in rather a bull-headed way, with no prior consultation or discussion. His wife described it as 'change first, ask questions afterwards.'

Jimmy just couldn't get on with the new head in the senior school. Gradually his status as a head of school was diminished. He became a head of department, with a two third teaching load. He lost the power to appoint his own staff, even to negotiate with parents new and old, though in fact parents still came to him. Over the next three or four years, he started a parent/teacher association, something almost unheard of in private schools. The parents were great. They held fund raising activities, and supported the junior school in every way they could. At Jimmy's suggestion they held an annual fete, which was hugely successful, with stalls, dancing, singing, and games.

'Blow me if the senior school aren't muscling in on our fete,' Jimmy told his wife bitterly the following year.

There was nothing he could do. But the senior school participation was much resented by junior school staff and parents. There was a strong feeling that the senior school took all the perks going, and the junior school was neglected.

During his time there Jimmy started Cub and Brownie packs; regular afternoon games for both boys and girls, including competitive matches with other school; singing (the school entered a county competition for their age group); crafts including pottery; and best of all drama, including a school production of The Wind in the Willows, and Oliver, plus Nativity plays at the appropriate time of the year. The school was really humming.

Then the axe fell!

Jimmy was dismissed!

Not a normal dismissal at the end of term, but a mid term sudden termination.

His wife was not surprised.

'It was the case of either you going or the Head of the Senior school,' she remarked.

There had been much dissension, not only the loss of status, but interference by the senior school that at times seemed unwarranted.

'I've never forgotten the Victorian day,' Mary Page remarked.

Jimmy had arranged a day of Victorian schooling for the juniors, as a fun/interest day. The male staff, including Jimmy, grew beards. The female staff wore long skirts and were grimly attired. The girls wore smocks, and the boys knickerbockers, such as parents managed to muster or

288

make.

On the actual day the Miss Crawford announced there would be a school photo, not only for the seniors but for the juniors also, the idea being they were part of one school. The juniors had never attended a senior photo before. The poor juniors had to change from their Victorian costume into school uniform and then back again. The kids were great and accepted with their usual humour the change. Not so Jimmy; he was furious. The headmistress refused to see him! He felt he had been bullied by a stronger power.

Jimmy's disappointment increased in his final year. The senior school planned to build a sports hall and an all-weather hockey pitch. The sports hall would be of benefit to the juniors, but not the latter. To build this marvellous hockey pitch, the juniors had to give up without replacement their football, rugby and cricket field! It was an example of so much where the juniors had to give way to the seniors. It hurt and disappointed Jimmy.

All told, Jimmy was glad to go, especially when he was given a payment of £7000, really as a bribe not to go to court.

What was astonishing, the chairman of the board of governors resigned the *same* term that Jimmy left. For why, he never knew, though some of his parents seemed to know, but weren't saying.

Within a year of Jimmy leaving the headmsistress also resigned through ill health, and died shortly afterwards. Jimmy felt he had been dealing with a woman not in the best of health in his last year.

***

'And you were Jimmy,' God asked.

The old man nodded sadly.

'Poof! Better you than me,' muttered the computer. 'I could never have coped with a female dominated school.'

'Oh, they weren't so bad,' remarked the old man. 'The married ones were all right. It was the middle-aged, unmarried ones that I feared, and the headmistress was one. You could never laugh or relax with them. They seemed to regard the girls they taught as a delicate species that must be protected from the terrible male at all costs, forgetting that the majority of these delicate girls would probably spend the major part of their dear lives in association with a man. I wrote a poem about this feminine dislike of men, perhaps not very appropriate. It was a poem set in the Middle Ages, part of a Nativity play I wrote, in which women were bemoaning their husbands away at war in France. Do you want to hear it?'

'Not particularly,' said Jemmi. ' I don't like any writing where women may be portrayed in a bad light.'

'I don't know whether such is the case,' said the old man. 'Anyway, judge for yourself.'

MEN!

Men, men, oh, mighty men, rulers
To whom we must abide.
Men, men, oh mighty men, orders
Us like Canute the tide.

Men, men, oh, mighty men, treat us
Like slaves in solitude.
Men, men, oh mighty men, keep us
In lowly servitude.

Men, men, oh mighty men, behave
With such ineptitude.
We do the work and for them slave.
We're a Beatitude.

Men, men, oh mighty men, take up
A mighty attitude.
They show to poor women like us
No great solicitude.

Men, men, oh might men, we give
Them meals in plenitude.
They give no thanks the days we live,
Such is their habitude.

Men, men, oh mighty men, they speak
With such great platitude.
They shout, they talk, they make great speech
With inexactitude.

290

Men, men, oh mighty men, we love
them with such certitude.
We cook, give birth, serve like sweet dove
With much exactitude.

***

'Humph,' said God, sounding a little disapproving. 'You must remember that Jesus treated women with great kindness and respect, even fallen ones.'

'Agreed,' said the old man. 'Which is why I have always argued that women have as much right as men to become priests within the Church.'

'Priesthood is a male prerogative,' spoke God bluntly. Anyway we are wandering from the point. After this disaster in your teaching career, what happened to you next?'

'Remembering Churchill's advice that the optimist sees opportunity in disaster, I started my own school of English for foreign students. I had always wanted to promote understanding within Europe.'

'Good grief, whatever next! Was it successful?'

'Be patient, dear God. Wait until the next chapter.'

***

CHAPTER 15

God stroked his chin benignly, and began to ask serious questions.

'You've had quite a life, up and down like a yoyo. Has it altered your thoughts about me? You've managed to rise like a phoenix from the ashes when down.'

'Difficult question! I've had a life influenced by religion. My mother was a church organist all the time I was a boy. At school we had a beautiful chapel; it has remained long in my memory. I was influenced by Evangelical farming camps during school holidays and became a born again Christian. I went to university intending to go into the church. But then it all collapsed like a house of cards. I went to France, fell in love with a French lady and eventually became a Catholic. But Catholicism in France was very different from in England. In France it was a part of the culture. My Catholicism didn't last. Since then I have been a rather lukewarm Anglican. Like my life it has all been a bit of a yoyo, as you put it. Now I feel I have had doubts about the little faith I have.'

'Why?'

'I'm a loner, I suppose. My hearing handicap since childhood has made it difficult for me to communicate. My loss of hearing has been quite acute. Hearing aids help, but they have their problems.'

'Have you had no friends?'

'Rarely among men! Men take one look at my hearing aid, and dismiss me as a second class citizen. They patronise me, even make me out as a parasite, though they don't say so. But that is their attitude. Women I much prefer; they are more understanding, much kinder. But the best of the lot are women who suffer themselves from some disability. I wrote a story about a disabled woman. Want to hear it?

God nodded.

A BAD SMELL

In this strange, cruel world it is good to be a little barmy (Overheard).

'Tacky, u-acky, vacky, wacky, x-acky, yacky, zacky.'

Zolphin paused.

'What the hell am I talking about?' he asked himself. 'People must think me mad, barmy, round the twist, off my rocker. What other phrases are there to describe insanity? Crazy, stupid, loony-bin idiocy.'

He often talked to himself. It was the prerogative of the hard of hearing. Tacky, etc. was a mental exercise.

'Wacky,' he thought.

Suddenly Zolphin's mobile did that familiar ting-a-ling.

'Hi,' said Zolphin, holding the instrument to his hearing aid.

'Hi yourself. You coming, Zol?'

The voice of a girl!

'Oh God, I`m sorry,' Zolphin exclaimed. 'I forgot. I`ve been going walkabouts. Two tics.'

There was a giggle the other end. It was Kathie, the paraplegic, ostensibly the only friend he had at university. His hearing loss isolated him from normal friendships.

'God, I`m sorry. Kath.,' Zolphin mumbled as he arrived breathless. 'We'll be late.'

The route to their lecture room was tortuous. They couldn't go the normal way in Kathie's wheelchair, up and down steps. They had to follow the slopes of the service routes, where trolleys transported goods for the various departments.

'How's Mr. Day-dreamer?' Kathie joked, as they dashed along.

'Better for seeing you,' quipped Zolphin. He spoke with the slightly slurred speech of the hearing disabled.

'Broom, broom. Eeee-yow,' Zolphin cried as he went round corners at speed, imitating the noise of a car. Kathie's chair leaned over on two wheels.

'Hey, road hog, slow down,' she yelped, clinging tightly. 'I need a safety belt at this speed.'

Zolphin slowed to puff up a slope.

'You're unfit, Zol,' said Kathie teasingly.

Zolphin smiled back.

'So would you be, Kath., pushing your weight.'

She pretended to be offended.

'Really, Zol, I'm only a feather of a girl. Just over seven stone, I'll have you know.'

They dashed along the dreary basement, rang for the lift urgently, sailed up to the third floor, erupted into the lecture room.

'Ha, Sir Galahad, I see. And his fair princess,' joked Peter Howard, their elderly lecturer, fond of sarcasm. 'Better late than never.'

Kathie smiled.

'My chauffeur was delayed,' she quipped.

Everybody laughed.

They settled down. Kathie`s chair was placed at the end of the front row. Zolphin sat inside her, as close as he could get to the speaker. Peter Howard was overweight, inclined to self-importance. He liked plomping his large bottom, when tired of striding up and down, on the edge of his desk, sitting sideways. Zolphin knew Howard always sat on his left buttock, inclining to the left. Zolphin made sure he and Kathie sat on the right of the class to facilitate hearing.

Peter Howard's teaching technique was to make a challenging remark, hoping to stimulate discussion. It didn`t always work, such was the apathy of some of the students. Sometimes Kathie could be relied upon to rise to the bait. She didn`t much like Howard. His manner was patronising, unctuous even.

'Cromwell was a fine man, a family man, loved by his wife, adored by his children,' stated Howard. He looked round the class inviting comment.

'On what do you base that assumption?' challenged Kathie. 'He was guilty of genocide, of atrocities in Ireland, as bad as those of the Serbs in Kosovo.'

'On what do you base *that* assumption?' mimicked Howard cruelly.

'His barbaric treatment of Ireland is a byword in that country's history,' Kathie stated. 'To Irish children Cromwell was the bogey man.'

'Young lady, a byword is hearsay, not established fact.'

To which Kathie snapped, completely changing tack:

'I accept I`m young, but to call me a lady is demeaning and perjurious. It stinks of class distinction and sexism, as well as harassment.'

295

Zolphin knew that Kathie had read of this new slant on female titles in a woman`s magazine, and was dying to challenge Howard. 'Lady', said the magazine, 'was a condemned word according to modern attitudes of sex equality.'

'Ha, the ugly head of feminism...' Howard began.

'It`s not ugly,' interrupted Kathie, looking quite angry, her dislike of Howard boiling over. 'I resent that word. The feminine movement's one of the most significant social changes of the twentieth century. As a historian you should know that.'

The class laughed.

Zolphin sighed. It worried him that Kathie might one day go too far. What she lacked in physical strength, she certainly compensated for in articulate dexterity, even aggression when need be.

Howard looked at Zolphin, and said softly:

'Do you agree with your friend?'

It was an unfair tactic. Because of the deliberate drop in tone, Zolphin didn`t hear the question, and looked embarrassed.

Kathie came to his rescue.

'He`s asking if you agree with me.'

Zolphin thought a moment. He wanted to be fair.

'I agree Cromwell was a family man.'

He spoke with slow, academic deliberation. He learnt from books, not from listening.

'As for the feminist movement, I agree with Kathie wholeheartedly. Women have for too long been downtrodden by men. Now women are in the process of establishing their rights.'

One of the women in the class cheered.

Zolphin looked up at Howard, defying him.

'Surprise, surprise, denigrating your own sex,' quipped Howard.

Zolphin didn't hear. He turned to Kathie for elaboration.

'He says you are letting down your own sex, standing up for women.'

Zolphin smiled.

'No, just establishing the truth.'

Kathie looked at him, grateful for his support.

Howard, defeated, turned to the rest of the class, seeking their opinion, avoiding any further confrontation with Kathie.

At the end of the session, the students handed in their assignments, all except Zolphin, who made his excuses.

'Ha, the galant gentilhomme,' said Mr. Howard offensively, 'too preoccupied with his servile duties.'

He looked significantly at Kathie.

Zolphin wasn't sure he'd heard properly. He wheeled Kathie quickly out.

Kathie was seething, a crippled body of explosive fury because of Howard's final remark.

'God, that man!' she cried. 'Uuuh!'

She wrinkled her nose as if there was a bad smell.

Zolphin grinned, 'I shouldn't let him worry you. He's not worth it.'

Kathie went, 'Uuuh' again and repeated the wrinkling of her nose, a movement Zolphin found very enticing.

In Kathie's room she said softly,

'Lock the door, please, Zol.'

He did as she asked, a tremble of excitement passing through his veins. He then lay her on her bed and slowly, gently undressed her. He knew what she wanted, what he wanted. He began with her shoes, remarkably clean and unscuffed for she never used them for walking. Then he loosened her skirt, helped to raise her bottom and slipped the skirt gently over her hips and down over her feet. She was so thin; there was no muscle in her legs. He did the same with her tights and panties and then parted her legs so he could touch her just below her bush. She lay with her eyes shut, breathing quietly, looking completely relaxed. Zolphin started to undress. But she whispered softly,

'Please, Zol, everything.'

He nodded, started on her cardigan, slowly, lingeringly undoing all her buttons; then her blouse with the same slowness over the buttons. Kathie sighed, eyes still shut. Then, as he leaned over her to undo her bra, she reached up soft arms and drew him down. For a long minute they kissed. It wasn't a passionate kiss, but soft, gentle, mouths open. Finally Zolphin drew away, finished his fumbling removal of her bra, and fondled her soft roundness. She trembled at his touch.

'Tacky, u-acky, vachy, wacky, x-achy...'

It was almost a chant of triumph. But Kathy slapped him on the back.

'Concentrate, silly boy! Finish undressing. I want you, now!' There was affection and longing in her voice.

Hastily Zol tore off his clothes, lay down beside her, and lifted her small weight down on top of him. As he did so, prising her legs open, he felt himself entering her soft wetness. He sighed. They both sighed. By long practice they found it was the only way they could make love. He lifted her in rhythmic movement down and up, until they came. Usually he came first. Then he would lay her on the bed and gently stroke her below her bush, until she too came, with a soft cry and a tight hugging of Zolphin.

'Tacky, u-achy, vachy, wachy...' he recited, smiling down on her flushed face.

'Was that good?' he asked.

'More than good,' she replied, snuggling even closer. 'It helped me forget that horrid man, that bad smell! Oh, Zolphin, you are so good to me!'

*

'Hmmm,' God said doubtfully. 'Do you have to be so sexually explicit?'

'It's part of the real world.'

'It's disgusting, that's what it is!' growled the computer.

'It's not really,' mused the old man. 'In the right spirit it is the closest expression of love between a man and a woman.'

'Be that as it may, can we get down to the subject that I feel is vital? With all this meandering through this book, what do you finally feel about God, religion, call it what you may? After all you have had 70 odd years of life. You must have learnt something.'

The old man mused for a moment.

'My faith has always been strongest when I am happy. Perhaps it has not been a real faith at such moments, I don't know. But with my mother when she was playing the organ in church – she put so much energy into it; at school – I loved the chapel, the serenity of it, and the ordered existence of boarding school life; I enjoyed the farming camps during school holidays; in France I fell in love with a beautiful, intelligent woman to whom I could talk for hours; my marriage was the happiest, no longer alone, with an understanding wife. They were all moments when I had a deeply religious feeling.'

'And now?' asked God.

'I am happy now in retirement, though apprehensive of the future. The trouble is now that I have had time to think, I am losing any faith I had.'

'Why?' God asked again.

'It's a very sad world. I mentioned this in my first chapter. I find it hard to believe in a God of love who created the world. You, dear God, have made an awful mess of it. How can I believe that you are almighty, all powerful, when killings, disasters and tragedies happen all the time. I may have mentioned this before but I once heard a Minister try to justify the Soham murders of those two little girls as in no way denying Christian beliefs. What utter nonsense! The sermon left me cold. How can that be the world of a loving Father? Uugh! It made me sick to think about it.'

'There is evil in the world, deep evil. It pains me to think about it. But we, as Christians, must combat it.' God spoke slowly and thoughtfully.

'Then how can we pray to you as the Almighty? You're nothing, really nothing. Just a windbag! If you were the Almighty, you could have saved the world, certainly made a better job of its creation, if you really did create it.

'And you are happy with your thoughts?' God asked.

'No ...no ...not at all! I'm sorry, I'm being very rude, very discourteous to you. The truth is I just don't know. I pray for a sign, some revelation, but it never comes. I've met four very religious men, very spiritual, almost I would venture to say saintly. One was a Polish priest from

Czestochower, a pilgrimage centre in Southern Poland. He moved me deeply, almost to tears. A second was a French priest who instructed me in the Catholic faith. He was such a kindly man. The other two were English, one Evangelical, one Anglican. I shall never forget them. They really lived the Christian faith. They made me feel, not intentionally, that I might just be wrong.'

'Hmmm!' went God. 'All I can say is keep searching; you never know.'

'I'd like to know, but I suppose it won't happen until I cast aside this mortal coil.' The old man looked sad.

*

Printed in the United Kingdom by
Lightning Source UK Ltd., Milton Keynes
138452UK00001B/123/P